The Morell Compass

The Morell Compass

Connor Melvin

Copyright © 2024 Connor Melvin

All rights reserved

No part of this publication may be reproduced, distributed, or transmitted in any form or by any means, including photocopying, recording, or other electronic or mechanical methods, without the prior written permission of the author.

The story, all names, characters, and incidents portrayed in this production are fictitious. Any resemblance to real persons, living or dead, is purely coincidental.

The moral right of Connor Melvin to be identified as the author has been asserted by him in accordance with the Copyright, Designs and Patents Act 1988.

ISBN 9798326849687

Cover design by Creative Paramita

For Hannah

Drugs treat you like the best friend you never had. A warm smile, a firm handshake, a promise of bliss and oblivion.
They keep both ends of that promise.
Right down to your last smile.

1

Shoes on the Tube

October, 2040. London.

No one really smiled in the 'Monday crush'. Maddie thought about the term as she steadied her legs and threw out an arm to prevent her face from being pressed against the closing doors. Commuters found their spot and settled, accepting the situation as the underground train hummed and carried them off through the darkness.

After a few bends in the track, Maddie concluded that 'Monday Crush' would be a good name for the cocktail she would make herself that evening. In the suffocating space, she could already taste the pineapple tang through the cool, crushed ice, the bitterness of vodka or rum, tempered with the sweetness of some other fruit juice. Whatever it was, it would be delicious. Needed, especially after today.

She forced her headphones from her handbag, fighting for every inch before slipping in the soothing sounds of anything that drowned out the screech and grind of the underground rattler. State-of-the-art electric trains or not, the brakes and rails had still rusted and scratched. And yet she knew that without her earphones, the deafening silence of the awkward London commute somehow prevailed. Technology bounds on, but some things never change. Even the Victorians had referred to the packed carriages as 'padded cells'. Now they carry up to two billion passengers a year. Fluorescent metal worms crawling endlessly beneath the earth.

Most onboard were likely making a forty-minute commute to a job they weren't particularly fond of. That was where Detective Constable Maddie Evelyn liked to think she was different. She wondered if the middle-aged banker with the bulging gut would give her more room if he knew about the badge nestled in her jacket. Probably not.

How did she know he was a banker? The clues were plenty, but the real giveaway for Maddie, was the shoes. She scanned the multicoloured forest of footwear. To kill the time, she liked to guess what type of person someone was, or at least what job they had, just from their shoes and lower leg. A form of playful profiling. Something to help keep her in tune. Odd as it was, she had developed quite the knack for it.

Forward and to the right, a small pair of leather brogues, duck-toed. Too small to be a man. Slightly scuffed. Could be a boy, but unlikely given the black tights. Her intuition said teacher. A glance up to the lanyard peering between the zips of a raincoat confirmed the same. Maddie stifled a grin as she waited for her stop. The only smile in the Monday crush.

She shuffled off the train and waded through the choking, stale air. The escalator guided her up toward the cool winter sky above St James's Park station. Bright advertising holograms flickered on the central reservation between the ascending and descending escalators. Most commuters were pre-occupied by their augmented reality headsets. Glasses that allowed you to see the world while projecting information onto part of a lens. The time, date, a tv show, a news feed or social media. Scrollable with a simple movement of the eye and linked directly to a phone. Most kept one lens free for walking and the other dedicated entirely to a virtual world, only half paying attention to the real one. Many in the crowd were happier living with one foot outside reality.

Maddie wasn't obliged to wear her police-issued glasses until she was officially on duty. Unlike a personal set, they came with built-in restrictions, only allowing the use of apps required for the job, restricted internet searching and a news feed.

Maddie made the short walk to the squat stone and glass rectangle of New Scotland Yard. She stopped at a coffee van outside to grab a triple shot caramel latte, donned her glasses, then took the stairs up to the third floor. The office was simmering away gently. Not the chaotic warzone that emerged after ten, merely the calm before the storm.

As she dropped her bag and coat onto her desk, she was met with the clearing of a throat. Christina Richards, or as Maddie had known her for five years, Chrissie. A striking woman. Not overweight, but tall, size eight shoes, and broader shoulders than many women would be comfortable with. She threw them back nonetheless and made quite the entrance into any room.

'Oof, get me one of those,' she said, eyeing the coffee.

'Sorry, can barely afford this one on my salary,' Maddie said with a wink.

Chrissie didn't laugh, as she usually did. A forced smile followed.

'Can I speak to you in my office?' she asked, turning away from Maddie's desk.

Maddie nodded and followed.

The minimalist office of the chief superintendent was soulless. Not Chrissie's choosing. Her actual house was lavish, eccentric, wall-to-wall antique and homemade furniture. One thing it wasn't: boring. But the office was not to be changed from the easy-clean grey vinyl flooring and cheap regulation furniture, and that included the boss's office. Maddie hated it, but not as much as Chrissie.

'Minimalism is a sorry excuse for a lack of talent,' she would say.

Maddie approved of the small art deco clock next to a picture of her family. A mild rebellion.

'Sit down if you like.'

Maddie took the chair. 'Sure.'

Chrissie Richards considered the officer in front of her for a moment. The culmination of a long thought process finally landed on a decision. 'Maddie, you're vastly more intelligent than this place gives you credit for.'

'Finally, some bloody recognition,' blurted Maddie, milking the exaggeration.

Chrissie met the smile, but there was something serious in her deep brown eyes.

'There's an opportunity coming up. A good one. But I don't think you'll see it that way.'

Maddie forced herself to pause a few seconds before biting. 'What?'

'Well, you'd be promoted to a DS.'

'I'm liking the sound of it so far. What's the snag?'

Chrissie gazed out the window over the morning buzz of the capital. The usual technicolour lines of self-driving cars and buses clogged the road. 'It's not here.' She raised a finger to silence the inevitable protest. 'And before I say anything, it's only for three months...'

Maddie leaned forward. 'Where?'

'Newcastle.'

'Newcastle? Are you taking the...?' The words snapped from Maddie's lips. They landed without impact on the rock-steady face of her superior. A face that had stared down far worse threats.

Maddie had known her long enough and well enough to curse without consequence. She was more like a second mother than a boss. She allowed her nose to crinkle with rage and stabbed her tongue into the inside of her cheek to prevent thoughts from becoming unfiltered words. That wasn't an option. There was a line she couldn't cross.

The chief superintendent went on. 'As I've said, you'll be a DS, that part's permanent. Which means more pay, obviously, and a new...well, different car.'

Maddie sat silently for a moment as she considered everything she knew about Newcastle. Pretty much nothing came to mind. The Angel of the North? In the end, all she could muster was: 'Why me?' She rubbed her temple at the mere thought of packing for an entirely new city.

'Because you're the best we have. Never late, always professional, cross the T's and dot the I's on every case, and that's before I even get to your conviction rates and references.' Something of a proud smile cracked the corner of Chrissie's mouth.

'Sooo...then why get rid of me? There must be a position here?'

'The official reason is that this is part of an experiment, of sorts. What the hell did they call it?' Chrissie closed her eyes and squeezed the bridge of her nose, massaging the memory back to life. '*An inter-regional exchange of experience*,' she recited. 'In other words, every force is sending one of their detectives to another force. They learn from us, we learn from them.'

Maddie said nothing. She felt her heart rate increase at the realisation of a growing thought: this was an order, not a request.

'It's only for three months. And to be honest, you don't have a choice. I've already signed you up.'

There it was.

'What!' Maddie now felt almost entirely like a girl whingeing to her mother.

Chrissie sat on the edge of the table. 'You're bored.' Maddie moved to speak, but Chrissie waved her long hand. 'Don't, shh. Just listen. I know you better than anyone here. You're bored, and you're stuck in a rut. You're too good to do the dog work. You've been banging on for a promotion and rightly so. You asked,' she motioned with her hand, 'and Newcastle has opened a door. Besides, I need someone I know won't let us down or embarrass us. An exemplary representative of the London Metropolitan Police.'

Chrissie gave in to temptation, took Maddie's coffee and swilled down the last gulp.

'Fine. Newcastle should be a breeze anyway compared to here,' she said through gritted teeth.

Chrissie raised her eyebrows and moved to say something, but stopped, dabbing her lipstick with a tissue.

Maddie frowned. 'What?'

'It might not be as easy as you think.'

'It's not exactly London, how hard can it be?'

'The North-East of England has one of the highest drug abuse rates in the country. The organised crime groups are well funded and exceptionally well run. You know who I'm talking about. But that isn't the only problem.' She withdrew a file from her desk drawer and slapped it down onto the table.

'You're DI. Adam Morell. He's...unorthodox, apparently.'

'Good unorthodox?'

Chrissie snorted. 'I've never actually met him myself. It's just what I've heard, but it wouldn't be fair to colour your view. Give the lad a chance and all that.'

'Famous last words.' Maddie said. She swiped the file, dropped the cup into the bin, and walked out.

'So, I'll take that as a yes?' called Chrissie.

'Yes, but you owe me a fancy coffee when I get back, like three months' worth.'

2

All the Drugs They Found

October, 2040. Newcastle.

The whole thing crashed through his mind in crystal clear high-definition. The acrid metallic fumes from the bullets that strangled the nose, the fluorescent lights, the intense white glare when one exploded and the searing pain it sent through eyes accustomed to the gloom. The flashes of muzzles, the warm red spray that met the cheek, the screams, the scrambling. When it was over, they found two dozen bags of LSD at the bottom of the oven, and an attic room stacked with weed plants and magic liberty cap mushrooms. Then came the hard stuff taped to the underside of a sofa: five kilos of cocaine, one of ketamine, four of heroin. In the basement, four washed out paint tubs re-filled with glue, and a swollen rucksack bursting with benzodiazepines. Not discounting some beer in the fridge, that was all the drugs they found.

Detective Inspector Adam Morell massaged his temple, pushed the fractured memory aside, and laid down his pint glass. Beer foam spilled and mixed with condensation before running to the base, soaking the newspaper in a bleeding circle. Adam watched as the liquid encroached across the headline.

'Six Dead as Police Seize Largest Drug Cache in Two Years.'

He took another swig, tearing the sodden page as he lifted the glass, and squinting at the clock over the rim: 10 a.m., a quiet time...prime time. No one to ask questions in the peaceful early hours. Actual printed newspapers were hard to find, and he begrudged paying through the nose at ten quid a pop. But he rationalised the price as the cost of keeping his sanity if he had to spend any more time staring at screens or holograms, or wearing shitty augmented reality glasses.

The Silver Lining pub sat on Westgate Road, right in the centre of Newcastle. Most of its soul had been ripped out and tossed into a skip by the company that bought the chain ten years earlier. Echoes and shadows of character survived the renovation. The original bar countertop, polished smooth by a century of leaning elbows, the grandfather clock, some fading horse racing pictures, and for now, the aging regulars perched on the barstools.

Adam came here because the regular guys liked peace and quiet, and because of that, the chain owners at least had the sense not to include holograms, projectors, augmented reality, folding screens or anything more advanced than a 2018 flat screen that kicked out the sports channel at a low volume. If nothing else, they knew their clientele and what they wanted. Adam supposed that was the silver lining of The Silver Lining.

He was not a regular, not at this place anyway, nor did he sit at the bar. He couldn't afford to be recognised. The cold grey light of day made poor ground. The room went deep and the lights low. A long, dark, quiet room. The regulars were, of course, alcoholics on the back foot, smiling through daily pain as they put the world to rights over the rim of a glass that would slowly take them out of it. They knew that The Silver Lining was occasionally used as a sort of sanctuary for the desperate, especially in the winter. And Adam knew that as long as he didn't visit too often, no questions would be asked.

Adam nestled himself within a booth surrounded by high wooden stalls inlaid with stained glass windows. Just him and his augmented reality glasses. The prescription lenses accounted for the slight stigmatism in his right eye. He had taken them off as soon as he entered the bar and tucked them in their charging case. Any excuse to take them off. No work calls, no texts, no news alerts or bullshit advertising pop-ups. Just silence. It was police procedure to wear them at all times while on duty to 'optimise' performance. Clearly a policy thought up by some idiotic, politics-driven number cruncher, thought Adam. Someone who had never been an actual police officer, let alone a narcotics detective. Never been someone who needed a clear head and, most importantly, time to think.

The memory clawed. It scratched and tapped somewhere on the window of his mind. The glasses had recorded it, of course. But he needed to think. He absentmindedly picked at the frayed edges of the wet newspaper.

There had been one more thing. The kid. Charlie. Fourteen or fifteen? The report said: 'Fifteen, male, deceased.' But despite the endless files of data and hard facts, there were things the glasses could not compute. The smell of him, for one, the aspect of fear that lingered in his eyes long after the light had gone out, or the chill of the tainted air, still and cold after the carnage of thrashing around for help that never came. Adam flicked away the small pieces of sodden newspaper that had gathered under his nails and took a breath. The coroner's report said the cause of death was overdose. Adam had seen enough overdoses in seven years to know what they looked like. This particular one was strange. Strange enough to send him to a dark pub at ten in the morning on a Tuesday. Somewhere, he could turn everything off without being eyed with suspicion.

Somewhere above his head, the eyes of a Durham Light Infantry unit from World War Two stared down at him from a dusty photograph. He scanned the proud sepia faces through a film of dust. Before joining the force, DI Adam Morell had been Lieutenant Morell, a pharmacist in the British Army. Most people don't even know pharmacists exist in the army. They do, and the job comes with many responsibilities, not least making sure enough of the right drugs are in the warzone at the right time. There's nothing scarier than an empty morphine cabinet. Then there were the ward rounds for the wounded but stable soldiers. Some were easy. Ten a penny cases that blended into one. Pain relief, antibiotics, fluids and rest. Visits from the nurse, dietician and physio would see them right. Others were more complex. Nightmares without answers that stuck firmly in his mind. A bleed on the brain where the shrapnel had glanced off the skull, and a risk of clotting due to the blown off leg. So the question is, do they give blood thinners to prevent the clot but risk a brain haemorrhage, or leave it, hopefully stopping the bleed on the brain and risk the clot in the leg which could break off at any time and trigger a stroke?

'Lieutenant Morell, thoughts?' said the on-duty doctor, wiping at the sweat and indecision on his face.

Sometimes, there were people who just needed moving around, blood to be mopped up, grunt work. Adam had seen death in its many forms, heard its screams and stifled them the best he could. But there was only so long he could bounce around an army base dishing out prescriptions. The force was a viable option, and what better division than narcotics? Seven happy years later, and here he was.

Adam twirled his glass as it caught the light. One pint was never enough to drown thoughts like these. Not for Adam. The urge had been growing in his mind. The itch that he would inevitably scratch, gnawing at him until he gave in. What was the point in resisting? He popped the lid of a silver flip lighter adorned with a poppy. The ignition system was customised so that one flick of the spark wheel opened up the eyelet. The lighter fluid and fuse had long burned away, leaving room to store seven or eight hidden pills. He tipped one out and eyed it in the gloom. One white pill, morphine, straight from the poppy. Thirty minutes later and he could feel the calm finally sink into his nerves. Soothing, numbing. That was the goal, the relief, slightly numb yet functional.

He lifted the augmented glasses from their case and sighed. He clicked the touch screen and propped them up against the case as they projected images against the old-fashioned wall paper.

The initial loading screen, then the profile login. Adam showed the camera his face, and the projector loaded his home screen profile — 'Welcome, Adam Morell. Role: detective chief inspector. Height: 6 ft, 1 inch. Date of Birth: 27th August, 2005.' The text scrolled down in a matter of seconds beside Adam's profile picture. He glared at it for a moment. An old memory of the day it was taken, the flash that captured his beaming optimistic face. A face that had no idea what it was letting itself in for.

There was a glow in those eyes that had since worn, where optimism had been partly replaced with realism. Some things were the same. The thin stubble, and hair cut short back and sides, left long enough to be styled on top. Hair kept thick and plentiful by lucky genes. He was still wearing the same leather jacket over a plain white T-shirt, jeans (black or blue) and boots sturdy enough to kick in doors.

Adam swiped away the image, manipulating the hologram with his fingers. He cycled through files within files, dated and recorded meticulously in his own system, pulling out one he had idealistically entitled 'Not Quite Cold'. Within that, the most recent document was listed *Charlie Lang, Sept 2040*, among three others. He flicked the holographic file and all four documents spilled out onto the wall in miniature before him. Moving them around, he lined them up. Four faces with four cases, three closed, officially. Death by drug overdose, simple. Funerals followed with respectable services and the world barely noticed. Overdoses weren't uncommon. But four this close together, on the same estate. Adam had wrestled with this in his mind. And he reached the same conclusion as always. Gut feeling gripped his hand and forced it to drag the profiles back into the file Not Quite Cold, where they belonged. He didn't know what it was, but the kid's death was suspicious.

Something drew his eye to the aged clock. The hands read quarter past ten. In fifteen minutes, he had been told to pick up the new recruit. Someone from London.

3

The Girl in the Mini

January, 2037. Newcastle.

Adam met Clara in unusual circumstances. He had barely been on the job for two years and recently promoted to detective constable. DC Morell. He liked the sound of it and paced out of the station with a spring in his step and a new set of keys in his fist.

The undercover BMW X1 was parked right outside the door. Pristine, black, only one-year-old. As far as undercovers go, this one was a ghost. The deep grill hid the LED lights well and tinted windows concealed most of the gear on the dashboard.

Adam was under the supervision of Chief Superintendent John Pearce, a stocky fifty-year-old guy displaying the first signs of old age in the thin patch of grey above his ears. He smiled as Adam gave the pedal a jerk and showed the tyres eighty-five miles an hour on the dual carriage way, before sliding down onto the motorway. The 80kWh battery pack meant the car could do zero to sixty in a heartbeat. Adam allowed the car to spread its wings down the outside lane. Three tradesmen huddled into the cabin of a muddied white van gave them the finger as the BMW drifted by with ease. Pearce chuckled with his deep guttural growl, a tone of voice that could only be achieved by bathing your vocal cords in thirty plus years of cigarette smoke.

'Right, that's enough of that,' said Pearce, pointing to the next exit. 'This is me.'

Adam slowed the car and glided across to the left lane before swinging up the slip road, feathering the brakes and sticking to the speed limit. He knew Gosforth well. Upmarket without being extortionate, a good place to live and one that reflected the salary of a DI.

No more than two or three roundabouts and a traffic light later, a flash of racing green ambushed Adam's peripheral vision. That was all he glimpsed before the airbag wiped out his consciousness. When the cars stopped skidding, the road had claimed its fair share of the tyre tread. Thick black lines that recorded the incident.

Adam had taken the brunt of the blow. He felt Pearce's hand on his shoulder and the distant calls of concern somewhere far away. Adam squinted and waited until his eyes focused before glancing across to Pearce. He was the source of the sound, and although Adam could hear him talking, it was as though his voice was trapped behind a sheet of thick glass. A few seconds later, his ears stopped ringing, and the sounds morphed into something decipherable and close to normal.

'Adam. Can you hear me, son?' said Pearce. He was calm, a good sign that Adam registered immediately. Not that something like this would phase someone like Pearce, but it suggested that he wasn't seriously injured.

Adam nodded and squeezed his neck, scrunched his toes. Nothing untoward, nothing a stiff drink wouldn't fix. He felt his heart rate drop and the cold tension beginning to evaporate.

'I'm fine. I'm fine. What the fuck did we hit?' Adam said.

'*We* didn't hit anything. It was *her*.'

Adam followed Pearce's stubby finger to the green Mini Cooper, complete with white racing stripes. The tyre tread showed where it had spun several times before halting across both lanes, facing the undercover car. The windscreen was cracked, the front left bumper crumpled, and the axle snapped entirely. There was no sign of movement, just a head of distorted blonde hair sat in the driver's seat.

Adam hopped out of the car. Something immediately twinged and he bent double as a shooting pain ran up his back.

'Alright?' called Pearce. Adam steadied himself, waved it away and moved over to the Mini. The window was smashed on the passenger side, and through it, he could see the shaken figure of a woman. Hazel eyes frozen in shock, manicured nails, and mousy brown eyebrows that betrayed her dyed blonde hair. She was head to toe in gym gear, and the lack of sweat and kit bag on the back seat suggested she was on the way to a workout.

'Late for spin class?' said Adam through gritted teeth. The notes of impatience hung in the air as he used every ounce of willpower to control his anger.

The woman was still gripping the steering wheel, but the initial shock in her eyes faded into something softer and she smiled. She laughed, out of relief more than anything. Relief that the man she had just hit was alive, and even well enough to check on her.

'DC Morell,' said Adam, flashing his shiny new badge. His stone face and blunt delivery had the desired effect of lowering her tone.

'Oh, god!' The woman found panic again. 'My luck to hit a bloody...' She slapped the wheel and turned away to hide the tears forming. It was then that Adam saw the blood on the back of her head and forgot his frustration.

'Looks like you've hit your head,' he said.

The woman glared at herself in the rear-view mirror, confused, irritated with herself.

'No, I haven't,' she snapped, examining the pristine skin of her face.

'No, it's on the back,' said Adam.

Her fingers dived somewhere into her curled hair and emerged wet and red. Nothing to get worked up about, but enough to shake someone up. The hospital was a definite.

'Stay here. I'll just be a minute. Try not to move.'

Adam trudged over to Pearce, who was already calling in help through his augmented glasses. Adam noted the damage to the driver's side of the BMW. Not much better than the Mini. The crumple zones of the body work had lived up to their name. Spectacular steel and carbon fibre chaos, the grill shattered, and the wheel buckled.

'How is she?' asked Pearce, covering the mic on his glasses.

'Hit her head, but it's not too bad,' Adam said.

'Ambulance is on its way.'

'Ah, I'm sure we can take–'

'For both of you,' Pearce said sternly, turning away and continuing his conversation with headquarters.

Two police cars showed up in as many minutes. Adam stood beside the woman in the car and watched as uniformed officers cleared the road and directed traffic. He wrapped his coat around her and felt her shiver in the winter chill as the fading daylight quickly burned a red sunset into the sky. She thanked him and gave another smile. But it was her eyes that trapped him. Something about them meant he was caught staring long enough for her to look away with a nervous grin.

The ambulance pulled up behind the tow truck a few minutes later. The screaming siren seemed to reach inside his head and squeeze his brain. He winced and turned away until it stopped. Then a searing in his back shot through his nerves as a chaser.

'You're the one that needs looking after,' said the woman. Adam smirked as his mind came back into focus. She was right.

Five minutes later and they were both in the back of the ambulance. A minute after that, he felt her delicate hand squeeze his. They spent the night together in an A&E waiting room, nursed by painkillers and episodes of quiz show re-runs, and the next night together at her place. A year after the accident, almost to the day, they tied the knot in the same winter chill.

4

Dreams of Finer Things

October, 2040. Newcastle.

The evening still held the light. A clear sky framed a cluster of clouds hovering over the vast expanse of the Town Moor greenbelt, north of the city of Newcastle. An area typically host to runners, strollers, e-bikes and due to an ancient law, cattle. The evening wore on, and the dying sun poured an orange, pink and gold treacle sunset over the whipped cream clouds.

Dylan Bright shuffled off the main path of the moor, where green meadow suddenly gave way to the city, and into The Leazes, his usual pub.

He clocked a group of students occupying the corner on some kind of society night out. Judging by the polo shirts, chinos, shorts and the odd visor hat, it was pub golf — a bar crawl themed like a round of golf, so they wouldn't be staying too long.

Lucky, thought Dylan. The Leazes had a darker side. Of the remaining ten men and two women nursing drinks, almost all of them belonged to some part of the criminal underworld. No big hitters, but part of the scene.

The owner and barman knew the names of each of them, and roughly how involved they were. Although they tried to know as little as possible, it's difficult not to overhear in a quiet pub. The students in the corner provided some light relief, and their noisy chatter and occasional cheers as someone downed a shot was enough to mask the usual hushed murmurs and talk that could leak out any kind of conspiracy or horror. The dishevelled barman on duty finished loading another tray of their drinks onto a battered, second-hand robot waiter. An early model without a screen, the thing was essentially a glorified tray on questionable wheels, made more of patched DIY repairs than original parts. Dylan edged aside to let the robot approach the commotion in the corner, raising the tray to its masters. Junk or not, it did the job, and the barman appreciated not having to force a smile or bounce back a joke with the students.

Did the police know about The Leazes? Of course they did. An eye was usually kept on the place. Rarely from the inside. Strangers were asked questions unless they were obviously a bunch of students. But it wasn't worth the visit for the police. And there was not enough evidence to warrant a raid or arrests. Besides, nothing was kept there as far as Dylan knew. You might find some people carrying drugs or weapons, but you might not. And kicking the hornet's nest only migrates them somewhere else. At least here, they knew where to look for certain people.

Dylan gave a thumbs up to a middle-aged man sat nursing a cheap scotch in the corner as he tipped a mock glass to his mouth and pointed a finger at a beer pump. The middle-aged man returned the thumbs up and mouthed, 'Lager'. Dylan exchanged a few words of courtesy with the barman and ordered the cheapest pints on tap.

The murmuring drone continued. It was likely the students saw him as a rough bloke but probably harmless, given how skinny he was. The shot of heroin he had pumped into a vein of his right forearm twenty minutes before meant that, for now, he was calm, and whilst slightly drowsy, he was as functional as he ever could be, able to carry two pints with rock steady precision. The same shot of heroin would have killed a non-user, one of the students, for instance, but Dylan had built up a tolerance.

'Stevie, lad,' said Dylan, placing down the glasses.

'Alright, mate? This is the life, isn't it!' Stevie grinned, revealing three distinct gaps of absent teeth. Those that remained were yellowed. A disgusting smile, but a genuine one, accompanied by a twinkle in the eye. Not often they had enough left over for a few pints in a pub. Usually one, once a month or so. More so for Stevie Wilks. A permanently buzzed, full-blown alcoholic, but he did well out of the street. It was a running joke that Stevie was technically not homeless since he had his own clapped-out Citroën, the fuel cell now running with the battery power of a TV remote. Uninsured, no MOT, but a car. Stevie rubbed a thick, worn hand through his short, thin hair, so sparse it merely resembled a shadow. He wore an old navy blue fleece, a pair of blue jeans and battered trainers.

Dylan was in a tracksuit; his brown patchy beard still held the colour of youth. He, too, could not hide the smile that came with a real pint. They clinked glasses and took a generous swig. Dylan relished the cool liquid washing his dry throat accustomed to cigarette smoke and thin soup. It was almost medicinal. Over-the-counter medication that fed the soul.

They caught up on the small things and sat quietly for a few moments. Then the conversation quickly turned to dreams of finer things. A discussion heard by the walls of every pub and bar in the world. Despite the desperate circumstances, Dylan found that dreams were as abundant in the user community as they were in the highest circles, perhaps more so.

'Do you remember Bobby Anderson?' said Stevie. 'You're probably too young. Little feller, always wore a flat cap. Good footballer, hell of a free kick taker in his day, Bob.'

Dylan pretended to think hard. 'Doesn't ring a bell.'

'Anyway, apparently he found twenty grand. Found it!' Stevie's pint sloshed dangerously close to the rim of the glass as he waved his hand.

'Fuck off. Where?'

'In a holdall at a bus station. Just left there, middle of the night.'

'Sounds like drug money.'

'Too right it does. Anyway, Bobby gets it home, stashes it away until he can figure out what to do with it. Then, the next week, his wife finds it and hands the fucker in to the police. Gave Bobby an earful.'

'You're joking?'

'Nah. And the worst part is, she gave her name and everything, and the blokes who were after it worked for Marshall.'

'Fuck.' Dylan shook his head slowly.

'Yeah, so as you'd expect, they paid Bobby a visit and he spent the last three weeks in hospital.'

'Just shows you, dunnit?'

'Yeah, don't get caught.'

They laughed. Stevie went on — it wasn't often he was listened to by a younger man. It almost made him feel like a father regaling stories of life wisdom to a son. 'Twenty grand, though. Not a fortune, but I tell you what I'd be sorted with that me. Get clean, pay off a few of me debts, rent a little flat of me own and take the odd little job here or there. Don't need much me. Decent TV and a few cans.'

The students erupted with another song as slick-haired toff stood and downed his pint.

'Nice one, Jonno mate,' said one of their friends. The slick-haired Jonno reeked of private school. Dylan didn't have anything against private schools in principle. He even wished he had gone to one. But he also knew that if he'd had the same chances, the same pathway, he would be absolutely trouncing Jonno in the game of life.

'Politics,' Dylan muttered to Stevie.

'What's that?'

'That's the degree that idiot will be doing. Future Tory back bencher, that's what you're looking at there. Or Labour, he won't be bothered as long as the pay cheque and lifestyle role in.' He scowled.

'How do you know he won't be a front bencher?' asked Stevie with a grin.

"Cause then he'd have been at somewhere like Oxbridge. Obviously not got the brains for it, but he'll have the connections, don't you doubt it.' Dylan spoke in a mock posh accent: 'Thanks to mummy and daddy.'

Stevie chuckled.

'Give over, and get that chip off your shoulder, lad. Thought you were getting clean, anyway?'

'I am.' Dylan thought about the irony of being lectured by a man who regularly started each morning with a pint of supermarket brand vodka. A pure-bred alcoholic.

'Piss off. Can't kid a kidder. I know a fresh hit when I see one.'

Dylan shrugged. 'Yeah well, I'm...I'm getting there. Need to ween myself off, don't I?'

'Rather be a back bencher than a dead man in a gutter,' said Stevie with a wink.

'Well, I'll drink to that,' said Dylan, raising a glass.

Stevie leaned in. 'Seriously though, listen. I'm an old fart who's lucky to even make it this far, to be honest. Hell will freeze over with me in it before I get clean, but you're still young. I've seen it done. Not easy mind, but it can happen.'

The students began to stand and gather, shuffling out the door and leaving behind a litany of empty shot and pint glasses. Dylan swilled down the last of his pint. Savouring the nectar as though it might be his last.

'Well, that's me off,' he said. 'No point staying in a pub when I've got no money. Good to see you mate, stay safe.' He rose from his seat with a groan.

'Aye, you as well, kidder. Look after yerself.' They gave each other a warm handshake. Handshakes from Stevie were the closest thing to a fatherly hug Dylan ever really had.

He stepped out into the gloom, the sunset glow now well and truly on its death bed on the horizon. He watched as the gaggle of merry students sauntered down towards the city, towards the next pub and a hopeful future.

For him, it was a chilly walk through Leazes Park and onward further into the city. Somewhere in the middle of the park, among the trees half stripped of their leaves, the world went black.

5

The Secret Cave

Adam thought back to 5 a.m., when he had strolled into the office in blissful silence and slipped his augmented glasses over his eyes. The heads-up display flashed into action. He could see the dimly lit police station office with his left eye and the overlayed text on his right lens as he cycled through profiles.

He called the augmented reality voice assistant Luna, after his ex-girlfriend's cat. An annoying black and ginger thing, with an insatiable craving for attention. Unusual for a cat, but no less irritating. The glasses were exactly the same, there in the morning when he woke up, following him round the rest of the day. What he saw, they recorded.

Unable to sleep, he left Clara without waking her. The electric car was silent enough, and he waited until the bonnet was facing down the street before flicking on the headlights.

Clara worked as a statistical analyst for the tax man — His Majesty's Revenue and Customs (HMRC), based at Pilgrim's Quarter in the city centre. She had explained the details of her job several times, but Adam always got lost when she started using words like 'linear regression'. She was good with numbers and helped HMRC keep theirs right. That's all he needed to know. And unlike Adam, she worked nine to five like clockwork. Not a minute more. She wouldn't need to be up for another two hours.

In the police station, most of the motion sensor lights had turned themselves off within one minute. This was partly to save energy, but also because augmented glasses were easier to see in low light, so that's how the drugs squad office was generally kept. Only one strip of LED lights above Adam illuminated his desk as he occasionally waved his arm to find his coffee and scan his notes.

A twelve-foot whiteboard at the far end of the room loomed and dominated the space like a roadside billboard. Plastered across it, an array of targets, key criminal players, victims. A collage of open cases, loose ends and unsolved puzzles. A jigsaw with only half the pieces, roughly scattered and yet connected by one common denominator: drugs. At the centre of the web sat the looming figure of Luke Marshall. Unlike many of the photos, his was not a police mugshot. Rather, a hulking figure stepping out of a black four-wheel drive, taken from a distance. It was clear that the suit was custom made for his gargantuan frame, cut and tapered to highlight muscle while allowing for easy movement. He carried himself with the cold certainty of a drug dealer of his level. A drug lord. Heavy aviator sunglasses stretched around a powerful head. The remainder of his face rested easy, confident, and curled into a wry smile.

The big fish. The giant squid with tentacles that touched every part of the city and beyond. In some way, Charlie Lang's death would almost certainly stretch all the way up the chain to the king sitting on the throne, as did many deaths. But they would amount to tenuous whispers where Marshall was concerned, rumours in the wind, ultimately inadmissible in court. He was highly intelligent, there was no doubt about it. Cunning, feared and audacious enough to carry the pressure of his position as easily as the silk handkerchief in his top pocket. Adam shrugged at the thought and turned to the matter at hand.

'Alastair Coyne,' Adam said. Luna immediately pulled up the profile mugshot of a dishevelled white male sporting tattered dreadlocks, a yellow Hawaiian shirt, and smiling like an idiot.

Many drug squad officers had informants. It was messed up, but that was the way the game was played. The war on drugs had forced the blunt instrument that was policing into desperate measures. Dealers at various levels willing to drip feed minor nuggets of information in exchange for not being arrested. Adam had Alastair 'Magic' Coyne. And Adam knew Magic was not as stupid as he looked.

The screen fed through his file.

Alastair Coyne, first arrested in 2023 for possession with intent to distribute. Sentence revoked due...

The text ran off the small screen. Just another reason to hate Luna.

'Print,' said Adam, glancing across to the white machine in the corner. He ripped the glasses off and tossed them on the desk before he could hear Luna's soulless voice reply, *Printing document.* He half hoped they would break. That usually meant two days Luna-free while IT fixed them or assigned his profile to a new set.

The printer lit up and the mechanics glided, sliding sheets of paper this way and that. He collected the hot documents and tapped them into an even pile before punching a staple through the corner. He would get stick for using the printer. Karen breathing down his neck. He always did. Bad for the planet, and the usual bollocks about being a paperless, digital police force. But Adam didn't give a damn about a few trees, or Karen. Magic was part of the puzzle forming in his head. For good measure, he went into the printer's recent history and deleted the last entry. Save the headache.

He read through the profile twice and then shredded it. He always did this before visiting an informant. A quick refresh on the main parts of their life. Little notes here and there that always helped. Details were everything. Girlfriends' names, birthdays, anything to make them feel remembered. Adam found nothing more effective at making someone feel valued than remembering details about their life.

The bitter notes of burnt coffee drifted from the kitchenette beside the shredder. Adam watched as steaming black and white dribbles fell out of the decades old coffee machine into a paper cup. Karen could be relied on to change the milk, that much she was good for.

Returning to his desk, Adam sipped the cup until he felt the caffeine tingle in his brain. He spun around slowly in his worn office chair, as he glared at the mish mash of ten desks and workstations sprawled out across the room, each one decked to reflect their owners' likes and personas. Some were scattered and disorganised, others like Adam's were organised with military neatness.

Through the door to the main station, he could hear the shuffling of feet, shifting of chairs and clanking of cups as some officers arrived. Uniforms. Most of them known to Adam by face alone. The door of the drugs squad office remained locked. A mystery, even glamourous to the uniformed officers who could not enter without permission, that was seldom granted. Information in this room could expose dozens of undercover officers. One wrong set of wandering eyes in here would see a gun or blade pointing at the face of an innocent officer. The windows had even been blocked-up to add extra security, earning the office the tongue-in-cheek nickname of 'the secret cave'.

On top of this, the drugs squad also had the luxury of wearing plain clothes. To the rest of the station, they were like VIPs at a nightclub, bouncing in, wearing whatever they liked and locking the door to their secret world behind them. Adam didn't care much for showing off. There were other units doing equally important work, and he had as much respect for uniformed officers as he did for anyone in the room, more in some cases. He simply liked the relative lack of regimented order that was found in uniform. A world that over the years had become so wrapped up in red tape, you couldn't wipe your arse without filling in a form. His jeans and open leather jacket were less constricting than a stab vest, and so were the rules. The drugs squad offered a certain independence.

The clock ticked on towards eight, and the light above the door lit up green as the facial recognition camera whispered to the automatic lock. One by one, figures sauntered into the room, yawning, straight to the coffee machine, triggering a trail of lights on overhead. Gradually, the room became brighter.

Pearce was first, his short, square bumblebee-like bulk hovering through the desks. He gave the usual gruff 'Mornin'' and shuffled into his office. He wasn't a morning person. A minute later, his head popped out and asked Adam to join him.

The square, secluded office of John Pearce was a perfect reflection of the man. Squat, ordered, and rough. He had one foot in retirement and echoes of a distant generation, even beyond his own, were plain to see. He still preferred to work mostly with paper, printing off enough to vex Karen virtually every day, only she knew he would have her moved to a different department in a heartbeat if there were any complaints. A few piles were stacked here and there, and the office was made considerably smaller by the filing cabinets, now almost non-existent elsewhere in the station. The desk hosted an ancient early 2020s computer and keyboard. He even had an ashtray on the window ledge with a few stubby ends crumpled by his own stubby fingers.

'Take a seat, son,' said Pearce, gesturing to a chair on the opposite side of his desk. He sometimes called Adam that when no one was around. Usually when he was concerned or when he wanted something. A headache was imminent, that was a guarantee, but Pearce was nothing but fair. When Adam scratched his back, the favour was always returned. Pearce lit a cigarette and cracked the thin high-level window. Adam noted the smoke gliding over the smoke detector that hung slightly loose where Pearce had disconnected it.

'There's a newbie startin' this morning,' Pearce said.

'Who? Are they from uniform?'

Pearce pulled a file out of a drawer and slid it to Adam. A standard police profile. Every officer had one, although he wasn't used to seeing it in print.

'Her name's Maddie,' said Pearce. 'She's been sent up from the London Met.'

'London? Why?' Adam said, not looking up from the file.

Pearce grunted. 'Some bollocks about learning from other forces. Too much money to piss away on management consultants that lot. Couldn't run a bath. But from what I hear from Danny Sellars...do you remember him? Used to work in CID.'

Adam nodded. 'Vaguely.'

'Well, he's in the London Met now, and he reckons they didn't have enough space for her. Over recruitment.' He tutted. 'She's on a probationary course as a DS. Three months only. *You* will have to sign her off and she'll know it.'

'Does this extra responsibility come with an extra few quid, then?' Adam said with a knowing grin.

'She can do some of your paper work, that's all your gettin', and you'll be grateful.'

'Thought so.'

Pearce leaned over and stubbed out his cigarette, wafting away the smoke towards the window. 'Hey, you never know she might be alright. She *might* even be helpful if you give her a chance.' He smiled, as Adam sighed, got up from the seat and left his superior's office feeling like a kid with extra homework.

The sanctuary of the Silver Lining was sorely needed.

6

Adam and Eve

Adam placed his empty pint glasses on the bar of The Silver Lining and waited until he had left before putting the glasses back on. They wouldn't go down kindly with the regulars. As he stepped from the antique wood of the past into the present, he squinted through the lenses at the sunlight. Luna lit up in front of him, displaying his location and the time. The reminder on his calendar told him he was due at the station in ten minutes. Plenty time. He flicked his eyes to clear the screen and snorted at the memory of some kids who couldn't read the analogue clock the last time he was at Central Station. Staring at it like some cryptic puzzle. Phones and glasses out of juice, they gave up on analogue and found a digital cousin on the departure board.

Five minutes later, those same great Victorian iron hands read half past ten as Adam stood beneath it on the platform. The holographic screen read 'Delayed 2 mins' beside the 8 a.m., from Kings Cross – Platform 4. He rested on the cold steel benches between a student and an elderly couple. His weight was enough to rattle the bench, although not enough for anyone to stop staring at their phone.

Central Station was still housed in its impressive Victorian shell, with high stone archways and flowing ceiling that leapt across all eleven platforms. Thick, ornate iron pillars were dotted here and there amongst the modern coffee kiosks and shops. In the thick entrance walls to the left, there was a fast-food burger place, an old railway station lounge pub and the entrance to the metro, Newcastle's underground train system.

A chill was beginning to bite through the station when the sluggish metal snake slithered in beside platform 4. A true Newcastle welcome. The snake emptied its belly of passengers, collected bottom up from the length of England.

Adam tapped his glasses and said, 'Maddie Evelyn, profile.' The file read: '5 foot 8 inches, DOB: 10/05/2013'. Beside the text, an image appeared over the left lens, showing a young woman. The serious face required of a profile photo was always a poor indicator of character. Only a few rungs above a criminal mug shot. But the image did reveal tidy black hair, brown-eyes that hinted at confidence and intelligence, all within a pretty face. At least, Adam thought so. She wouldn't be difficult to spot.

After a minute, Adam saw her wrestling two large suitcases across the platform as the crowd thinned.

'You must be DS Evelyn?' he said, trying to sound cheerful as he approached.

The woman looked up, throwing a handful of stray hair behind her ear. A frustrated frown quickly turned into a polite smile,

'Oh,' she said. Adam felt himself being scanned and assessed. Even his shoes. 'It's you. Didn't expect a personal escort.'

He shrugged. 'I can leave if you like?'

She grinned.

Adam stifled his surprise. It wasn't often people picked up on his dry humour so quickly. He usually delivered it with a dead serious face that caught people off guard. 'Welcome to Newcastle.'

He took one of her suitcases and they made their way to the car.

'So, where to, the station or digs?' asked Adam.

'Station,' she said, surveying the main platforms. Adam saw her eye linger on one of the coffee kiosks. 'I'm in with the recruits for a few weeks until my flat becomes available, so I'll avoid it as much as possible, thanks.'

'Fair enough.' Adam could feel himself forcing the cheerful façade. He decided to drop it down a few gears. Something closer to himself. After all, she would be working with him. He flashed his badge and the ticket attendant waved them through the barrier. Adam flicked his keys at the gunmetal grey electric Audi and loaded the cases.

Maddie froze and grabbed the door handle as Adam manually reversed out of the space and edged towards the barriers faster than any self-driving car would allow.

'What the hell! Why are you driving?'

'What? Ah, yeah, I don't trust self-driving cars. If I'm going to crash, it'll be my own fault, thanks. At least I'll have a chance to do something about it,' he said, pulling the car forward and onto Neville Street.

Her eyes widened as she instinctively gripped her seat belt a little tighter. 'You know, statistically self-drivers crash far less than human driven cars,' said Maddie, looking at him.

His eyes remained on the road, but he could sense DS Eveyln's body tense at every corner. 'Well, statistically, I've only ever been in one car crash and they hit me.'

'Why don't you trust them?'

Adam pretended not to hear and changed the subject. That was a conversation for another day, maybe.

'Why the move, then?' asked Adam.

She made a *pfft* noise without thinking. Then, realising, Maddie cleared her throat.

'Oh, well, it's a promotion, obviously. But I fancied a change, you know? And Newcastle seemed like a good opportunity.'

Adam just about stopped himself from snorting. Maddie picked up on the rebuff.

'I've read your file,' she said as they pulled up behind a backlog of buses fighting for road space with cyclists.

He raised his eyebrows as he glanced at her. 'Have you now? And?'

'Quite impressive. Although if it was a football match, I'd say you're prone to getting yellow cards with the occasional red.'

He chuckled. 'Football fan, are you? What team?'

'Arsenal.'

'I won't hold it against you. But I can't speak for the rest of the team.'

She turned to look out the car window, falling silent as she concentrated the way a nervous passenger does. Her thigh tensing intermittently as she squeezed invisible brakes at her feet, adjusting her seat belt, and stifling the urge to comment here and there.

Adam was relieved to be spared too much small talk. He'd forgotten about his unusual driving habits. Only emergency service vehicles had been allowed to routinely override the self-driving feature since 2037, and he took advantage of the loophole even when he was off duty.

He wondered for a moment about the woman next to him. His previous partners had never really clicked. No coming around on Sundays for a BBQ in the summer or a nickname for their kids. The last one didn't stay long. Definitely not three months.

***

At noon, Adam leaned against the doorframe of the meeting room, watching the new recruit wait for her introduction to the department. He had brought her the short distance from the train station to the drugs squad office, offered her a coffee and left her with Pearce for a quick personal introduction before she was ushered into the meeting room. Two lines of four chairs were filled. At the front, Pearce stood next to the fresh face. In the past three decades, the police had decided to attract a newer breed of police officers, primarily hiring university graduates and fast tracking them into higher positions. Adam was one of them technically, although he liked to think his time in the army made him a bit of an exception, because he didn't come straight from university. That and his entire youth spent dancing with life on a council estate rather than some suburban middle-class safe haven. But the newbie was different. Adam now clocked it in her eyes and the subtleties of her dress. Knock off handbag, cheap trousers, trimmed nails. An effort to look presentable.

'Right, listen. Morning. The eagle eyed amongst you will have spotted our newest member.' Pearce glanced around the room and extended his arm to his left, where Maddie stood, shoulders back and a half smile on her face. 'DC Maddie Evelyn comes highly recommended from our friend in the South, Chief Super Richards.'

'Oof, hope you brought your big coat,' blurted a figure in the front row. DC Paul Gardner was a skinny little runt with a flat nose from a largely unsuccessful boxing career. In Adam's book, he was harmless, and a decent cop. Every class needs a clown.

Maddie Evelyn laughed off the quip and Pearce went on.

'Morell,' he said quickly, searching his morning brain and peering down his nose at the next thing on a crumpled list. 'Morell, as you know, she'll be with you.'

DC Gardner chuckled to himself.

'Something funny, Paul?' asked Pearce.

Paul turned to look at Adam and held his hands up. 'I've got to say it,' he said, turning to Maddie. 'Your name's Evelyn?'

'Erm...yeah,' said Maddie.

'So...' he waited for a response from the audience that didn't come. Adam clocked it a mile off. 'It's Adam and Eve!'

Paul clapped his hands as scattered chuckles and stifled smiles filled the room. Adam grinned at Maddie, who knew as he did that it would stick. Cops love a nickname.

Adam gave Paul the middle finger. Pearce coughed and told the room to shut it. Despite his short stature, he commanded respect and felt that probably came because he was willing to have a bit of a laugh, but they also knew he could be a tough, sharp-tongued hard face when he needed to be. He tied up the meeting with a few minor points and they filed out of the meeting room back to the office.

'Show Maddie to her desk please Adam and get her started,' said Pearce, trotting off to the toilet for the second time in two hours as middle age rasped on his prostate, doing its best to push retirement along.

'Follow me, we're over here,' said Adam, leading the way. He motioned to the desk wedged between his and the wall. 'Been empty for months. Anyone's guess what's in the drawers.' He raised an eyebrow.

'Should do fine,' said Maddie, looking at the drab wall and battered desk. She pulled out her augmented glasses and laptop.

Adam slumped into his chair and took out a pencil and paper from his drawer. Numbers were scattered across it as he pulled out the calculator on his phone.

'What are you working out?' asked Maddie.

'Breaking down some deals done recently by a bunch of screb kids that look like trouble in Morpeth. That's a town north of Newcastle,' he added, sensing the next question. 'I want to get an idea of how serious they are.'

She leaned over.

'It's about twelve grand,' she said. Almost without thinking.

Adam raised an eyebrow, finished tapping the last few numbers into the calculator. It spat out £11,780.

'Looks like I won't be needing this anymore then,' he said, swiping away the calculator from his phone. Maddie grinned.

'I thought a pharmacist would be good at maths.'

'Wow, you really did read up on me then?'

She shrugged. 'I need to know who I'm working with.'

'Rightly so. You probably know a lot more about me than I do about you. Didn't even know you existed a few hours ago.'

Adam's phone buzzed.

'Time to go,' he said. 'Unless you want to spend the whole day reading in here?'

Maddie eyed the list of case files and introduction emails on standard operating procedures sat in her inbox.

'I still haven't done the paperwork. Will it take long? Where are we going?' she said.

'To meet a contact,' he replied, putting his jacket on.

'An informant?'

'Yup. On Green Meadows estate.'

'Should be cute,' she said.

'Oh, I see, can't be anything compared to London, eh?' he said with a playful smile.

'Well, can it?'

'I can honestly say with a hand on my heart that I couldn't give a shit. But I'll let you decide.'

7

Magic

Most people called him the Magic Coyne. Only two people called him Alastair, his own mother, and DI Adam Morell.

Adam rolled his car into middle-class suburbia. Heaton, east Newcastle. He parked three streets away from where they needed to be and walked the rest. Even here people bought and used drugs. Even here the curtain twitchers could talk.

'Doesn't look that bad,' said Maddie, glancing around.

Adam laughed. 'This isn't his digs, it's his mother's.'

Maddie frowned. 'What? Why are we here then?'

Adam opened a white picket gate and closed it quietly behind them. He approached the door of a neat little bungalow and rasped the knocker. A white perm pressed itself through the laced kitchen curtains.

'He's not here,' barked an elderly woman.

'Just need a minute,' said Adam calmly.

The door edged open and jarred on the chain. A round, haggard face stared through the darkness. She spoke quietly but with a sharp authority.

'I told you...ah, it's you.' She scowled at Adam, shooting a look of poisoned suspicion at Maddie. She knew what he was, and how her son sat firmly in Adam's pocket. Adam shrugged at the thought. That was the path Magic had chosen, and he could do a lot worse than having Adam as his handler.

'He's staying here,' said the woman, scribbling furiously on a post-it note and shoving it into Adam's hand.

Adam read the address. 41 Stainmore Street, Green Meadows. He smiled and winked. 'Cheers Linda,' he said without looking back.

The door slammed and he could feel her eyes on him through the window. She would call Magic within seconds. That was the agreed process.

Maddie felt uneasy as they stepped back into the car and set off. She rubbed her mouth and wondered if DI Morell had in fact got away with more than his fair share of yellow cards. There was no way contacting an informant through their mother was legal, let alone safe. What was it Chrissie had described him as? Unorthodox.

Green Meadows was a council estate on the outskirts of Newcastle. Row upon row of terraced housing. Not the six-bedroom types found in Jesmond, built for Victorian industrialists. These were two up, two down, plain and simple. At one time, they were the houses of miners, shipbuilders, working folk. People who had enough pride and self-respect to take care of where they lived. Even if you only had a small backyard, that didn't mean you shouldn't sweep and tidy.

Now half the people who lived in Green Meadows couldn't spell dole. Half of them. The other half were just unfortunate in where they were born. Good people, often single parents, working several dead-end jobs while trying to keep their kids away from the wrong crowds, because the wrong crowds were close at hand.

The address was 41 Stainmore Street, as well as 43, 45 and 47. From the outside, a row of shitty houses. On the inside, Adam knew you could walk through holes smashed through the walls between each one. They kept a sofa outside in the front garden. It wasn't unusual in Green Meadows to see a bit of discarded tat in the garden. The difference was *this* sofa got collected and redelivered once a month. It was possibly the least subtle drug trafficking Adam had ever seen. But it was mostly weed, and he could live with that. He knew where they were, could easily keep tabs on them and so he left them alone, provided Magic kept his side.

'Standard dodgy council estate,' said Maddie, flicking a piece of dust from her sleeve as the run-down houses passed through her indifferent eyes. 'Ours are usually tower blocks or complexes, but the hallmarks are the same. Weather's a lot better though,' she added, puffing out her cheeks and gazing at the gun metal grey sky.

'They not tell you about the weather in the North East?'

'They told me, but this is something else.'

Adam peered at the sky as though only noticing the clouds for the first time. 'Yep. Bad weather, good people...on the whole. Feel free to turn the heater up on your side, southerner.'

Maddie rolled her eyes. A few moments later, as Adam checked over his shoulder, she flicked the heater up a notch.

Adam drove past the houses slowly enough to make out the figure hovering by the upstairs window of number 43. He didn't stop. They drove on three streets. On the corner of the first street, Maddie spotted a man, well built, wearing a dark blue hoodie, trackie bottoms and bright red expensive trainers. For a second, she noticed something behind the thick beard. A familiar note somewhere in the face that stared the car down as it passed slowly. And something in the way he held himself. She shook the thought as the car swept around two more streets and parked up where the council estate ended beside some rundown garages and a razor wire fence that concealed the train track.

'Climb into the back,' said Adam.

Maddie felt a chill on her neck. Waiting for a chinwag with a known drug dealer, potentially carrying a knife or gun.

In five minutes, he appeared, ironically, as if by magic. Maddie jumped slightly as the car door was ripped open and he slumped into the front passenger seat, hooded, checking the wing mirror for any signs he was being followed. The life of a drug dealer is married to paranoia. Just part of the deal. And if anyone saw him climbing into a police car, especially an undercover one, he was a dead man.

'Your mam said hi, Alastair,' Adam said, flashing a grin.

'Fuck off,' snapped Magic. His eyes were bloodshot and wild. Classic drug dealer. They come in all shapes and sizes, but they had one thing in common: a vile temper. An inevitable consequence of chronic paranoia. A curse unifying them all the way up the chain.

'The windows are blacked out, you can take the hoodie down,' Adam said calmly.

Magic ripped down his hoodie, spilling his dread locks over his shoulders. Underneath his hoodie, Adam could see his signature Hawaiian shirt. He had hundreds of them, apparently. One for each day of the year. Today's was blue, with flamingos littered across the whole thing.

It was then that he spotted Maddie and swung around.

'Who the fuck is this? This a fucking set up?' he placed one hand on the handle, ready to click open the door and leg it.

Adam spoke calmly.

'Oi, she's with me. She's new.'

Magic clenched a fist. 'How do I know I can trust her? We have a fucking deal, man.'

Adam leaned in and spoke with the quiet authority of someone holding every single card.

'Calm down. You'll trust her, otherwise I'll turn on the blue lights and drop you back off at that shit hole you call a house.'

Magic shifted uneasily. His nostrils flared, his brow remained furrowed, but his shoulders sagged slightly. Some improvement, at least.

'Do you know a kid called Charlie Lang? Lived in Green Meadows. Apparently, he buys gear round here, so there's a good chance you do.'

Magic sucked his teeth. 'Yeah, rings a bell, might've sold him some stuff now and then.'

'Open the glove box.'

Magic hesitated, then flicked down the plastic flap. The small light in the glove box illuminated a brown envelope. He took it and spilled the contents onto his lap: photos Luna had taken during the raid. The dead eyes of an emaciated fifteen-year-old boy stared back at him.

Magic perused the images. 'How did this happen?' he grunted, as though he was just browsing a newspaper.

'The lad was found with a few stones of crack. And word is you've been branching out.'

Adam let the silence sink in. Magic was smart enough to know not to argue.

He shrugged. 'Yeah, I've sold a few stones here and there, but it's still mostly weed.'

'How much did you sell Charlie?'

'One or two.'

'The Coroner's report confirmed an overdose...'

Magic scoffed.

'What's funny?'

'No chance he overdosed on that shite. It's only like fifteen percent purity, man. Most of it's just baking powder. In fact, here.'

Magic fumbled in his coat pocket and pulled out a small torn off piece of a plastic carrier back tied with an elastic band.

'Check it for yourself.'

Adam peeled away the band and opened it up. There in his palm was a stone of crack. He folded it back into the plastic.

'I will,' Adam said. He threw it back to Maddie, taking the chance to assess how she was holding up. She was clearly still nervous, barely catching the package in time, but doing a good job of hiding it.

Magic nodded and moved to open the door, but Adam gripped his shoulder hard and pulled back. Magic sighed and Adam could see his cheeks tense where his teeth were grinding hard, fighting his anger.

'One more thing. The lad went missing for two days before he was found dead. It's not the first time this has happened on this estate. Know anything?'

Magic shook his head.

'Nope.'

Adam read his eyes. That was where the truth lay. Seven years of looking into the eyes of low-life career criminals and liars taught him how to get a read on someone. Micro expressions that could not be hidden behind even the most experienced poker face. Magic was telling the truth. His pot was also dangerously close to boiling over, so Adam decided to drop the leash.

'Right. Off you fuck then. Oh, and stop selling that shit.' He pointed to the stone of crack. 'That's not part of our little arrangement. Which, let's not forget, is the only thing keeping you and your shit shirts out of prison.'

Magic stifled a comment. His hands shook as he flicked the photos into the footwell. He slammed the door, pulled his hood back up, and slipped back into the grey mists of the afternoon.

8

Blood, Bone and Brains

The hallway stank of ammonia. Dylan tried to ignore the puddle of piss in the corner as they stepped into the lift. It wasn't difficult. Not while adrenaline surged into overdrive, and frantic thoughts waged a war for attention in his mind. Palms sweating, a fresh ice-cold bead formed at the top of his spine.

PJ stood behind him wearing a face that gave nothing away. A young, vicious face that gave zero fucks. Dylan knew it, and PJ knew that he knew it. Try anything and you're dead.

Dylan shuffled slightly, glancing in the cracked mirror that covered the top half of the wall at the back of the lift. He watched PJ click a button with his left hand, and then rest it across his right, where a handgun nestled comfortably against his leg.

Dylan was an addict without any money. He knew that was not a good combination. Five thousand pounds was owed. A drop in the bucket for these guys. Less than a drop, really. He fought the tremors and twitches bestowed on him by years of abuse of his nervous system. Crack did that, and so did heroin. In an attempt to look somewhat presentable, he flicked his short, unwashed hair forward, zipped up his tracksuit top and tried to dust off a stain on the sleeve. The brown smudge wasn't going anywhere. Dylan gave up, and forced himself to think about his options. Scavenging the dustbins of his mind for scraps of hope. He knew people, knew the estates. He *could* be useful. Work it off, run messages, even do some dealing. Whatever was needed.

The elevator halted, the door pinged and scraped open onto the top floor of a block of high-rise flats in Gateshead, just across the River Tyne from Newcastle.

Dylan had only heard rumours about this place. Rumours he now hoped were exaggerated with every fibre of his emaciated being. Based on identical tower blocks in the area, he knew for a fact that every other floor of the building contained three flats. But the rumour was the top floor of this particular block contained only one.

The corridor was a million miles from the graffiti and piss puddles of the ground floor. A clean, fragrant air washed into the lift. Thick, pristine red carpet, painted walls, sleek chrome spotlights, and ornate panelling interspersed with paintings. Dylan felt the surreal room start to tick off the rumours one by one. To the naive eye, the journey from Hell to Heaven was merely a twenty-second elevator in Gateshead. Dylan knew the truth. He was as close to Hell as a murderer at the gallows.

PJ knocked firmly on the nearest door. It swung open and Dylan was pushed through into a slick, modern apartment. The shadow that had opened the door sauntered back down the hallway without even looking back at Dylan, a small fish in the pond. Heated tiles and white walls led to a brand-new kitchen.

'Shoes off,' PJ grunted. 'Fuck knows where you've been.'

Dylan raised an eyebrow, only to receive a snarl from PJ. He did his best to appear submissive and shuffled off his battered bubble heel trainers, leaving him in his sweating socks, with one hole where a toe peered through. It was the first time he had ever felt the warmth of heated tiles. In fact, it was the first time he'd felt any real warmth for weeks. And yet, the reality of his situation grabbed him by the collar once again as a distant, muffled scream reached his ears, and the heated tiles of Hell somehow felt colder than cathedral stone.

PJ jabbed the handgun into his back and nodded down the hallway. Dylan took slow breaths, as fear gripped his lungs in a vice and began the slow squeeze of panic. He kept his head down and simply walked where he was pushed, fighting to keep his footing. They moved into a living room adorned with expensive and garish art, a wall of back-lit shelving housing a bar of spirits and wine, lavish furniture, and a brand new one-hundred-inch TV projector. Dylan saw it as proof that you couldn't buy taste, and that was coming from a man who thought very little of himself.

Another heavy that Dylan didn't recognise stood beside a closed door. When they approached, the screaming became the only focus of his mind, and another rumour, perhaps the worst, was ticked off the list. For a moment, he wondered if the flat must be soundproofed. Although he wouldn't be surprised if they owned the floor below as well, just in case. The heavy gave a surprisingly gentle, almost civilised knock that brought a muffle to the cries, then silence.

The door edged open and Dylan froze. Everything in him wanted to run, but that would only secure his fate.

Instead of a continuation of the modern apartment, this room was dark. If the apartment had a soul, it was in this room, cold and festering, its true nature hidden behind the façade of plush living. Every wall was lined with black plastic taped at the seams with duct tape. Only a single bulb offered light.

The handgun found the back of his head, and Dylan forced his knees to bend as he was pushed into the room. His heart rate soared, and the heady dizziness that comes with pure terror threatened his balance when he saw the figure tied to a chair. A bag over his head and a screwdriver protruding from his thigh. Blood poured, pooled and meandered with a fold in the plastic towards a massive leather shoe. The shoe stepped over the incoming stream. Dylan, visibly shaking, forced his head up to the owner of the shoe who, mercifully, had his giant back to Dylan. Tight shirt, crew cut, sleeves rolled up over bulging muscle.

PJ cleared his throat.

The man turned and stared straight through Dylan. A malicious, almost evil stare. Then followed the smile to match.

'Dylan Whetherly,' said the man in a faint geordie accent, diluted by years living God knows where. 'Or should I say Dylan Bright?' He spoke relatively quietly. Not the booming voice anyone would expect from such a figure. But then, Dylan knew that men with real power had nothing to prove. His throat went desert dry.

The big man scrunched his fingers, marked red with a mixture of fresh and dried blood concealing light bruises.

Dylan's eyes flicked momentarily back to the shape in the chair, unmoving as the blood flowed from his leg like a tap. He guided his eyes back to the chest of Luke Marshall. Not many on the street knew Dylan's real name, and what that really meant. Even less knew what Luke had done to his brother. The thought of it made the nightmare almost unbearable. But very little passed the ears of the man before him now.

'Mr Marshall,' said Dylan, forcing the words past the concrete forming in his throat. He maintained eye contact for long enough to show respect before turning his gaze down quickly enough to allow Luke Marshall the dominance he was accustomed to. Dylan knew more than he wanted to about the man before him. Certainly, more than he would admit. In a strange way he was one in a million. Just being in the same room as him was hard to convey to anyone. Everyone asked. Some things just have to be experienced to be truly understood. The atmosphere of every room was worse for his presence. Heavier, suffocating. Compared to most serious criminals, he was just...more, thought Dylan, considering the figure before him as though he was an unnatural mistake.

A mysterious imposter in this world, like a computer virus or a genetic glitch. International gangsters of his calibre and standing aren't supposed to be this involved, dirtying his hands at the coalface of the criminal underworld, dangling himself right under the noses of the police. He didn't need to be here, he wanted to be. To some he was a role model. Rags to riches, so it went. If he can do it, so can I. But in a room like this, there was a sense of awe that could not be taught. The air was filled with unbearable tension that he himself breathed in with verve. In a room like this, the true colours of Luke Marshall came pouring out of someone's leg in a thick red stream.

'I'm told you owe me five grand. Where is it?' said Luke, wiping his hands on a fresh white towel.

'It's...I haven't got it on me. Got jumped by some tossers in Leazes Park.' Dylan was able to say this with confidence, because it was the truth. He felt Luke searching him with his eyes. The warmth of the flat seeped out of him. The stare was everything. Even if Luke Marshall were a normal size man with no real money or power, the stare would be enough to petrify. The colour of his eyes was highly unusual, gunmetal grey, but from the pupils, strains of yellow stretched outward slightly, so that the overall impression was a surreal blend of silver and gold.

Dylan could feel his daily rattle coming on, as it did when he went too long without a fix.

Luke finally nodded.

'Jumped by who?' he asked.

'No idea. I'd just sank some pints, was halfway through the park when they hit me, then next thing I knew I was out cold and woke up in the bushes.'

What Dylan had not said, because he knew Luke wouldn't believe him, was that it was two days before he woke up. Two days out cold in the park. Even for the most hardcore users, that was extreme.

Luke walked slowly, stopping within inches of Dylan, towering over him. A wall of sheer muscle, well fed, toned, healthy, stacked against a withered, starved mid-twenties addict with the cardiovascular system of a 75-year-old. Luke's head was almost twice the size of his own. His face was stony, unreadable, and then he smiled, enjoying the fear of the man before him.

'One chance, son. Five grand, one week, otherwise...'

Dylan nodded at the unspoken threat. The figure in the chair stirred, conscious again. There was gentle sobbing, interspersed with the cries for help that faded into gasps for air.

Luke flicked his eyes at PJ, who stepped forward and pulled the trigger of his gun in one fluid, practiced motion. Blood, bone and brains slapped onto the plastic, and the room fell silent.

Dylan forced himself to turn and walk out the door, longing for the smell of piss on the ground floor.

9

Death in Black and White

Crack cocaine has many names. Blow, smack, snow, toot and ironically for the kid...charlie.

The small rock that Adam held in his hand had undergone a global journey. A journey he had studied a thousand times. Initially at university, then again as a detective. Pharmacists don't need to know minute details of illegal drugs. Their business is with prescriptions. Proven licenced products manufactured under tight safety and quality regulations. But Adam had always found the darker side of the coin interesting, long before the thought of entering the police was even a green shoot poking through his mind.

He knew that this stone, like all of them, began life as a bunch of coca leaves in South America. Probably in sunny Columbia. The leaves were picked, dried and mixed with solvents like ether to allow the good stuff to precipitate out, before being heated and pressed into cocaine. This is then stripped of its hydrochloride through liquid extraction chemistry, leaving the basic form: crack cocaine. So named for the cracking sound it makes when smoked. Eventually it would be sold in bulk, and trafficked across the world by a complex international network of corruption and deception.

One day, it would pass into the hands of a high-ranking UK dealer. Someone high enough and wise enough to never actually be in the same room as the product. It would be broken down into smaller packs and cut with baking powder to decrease purity and maximise profit, before filtering down to the low-end dealers on the streets of Britain. Sifting into the unwashed hands of people like Magic. Weight for weight, crack and heroin cost more than gold itself. Alongside heroin, this stuff fuelled the criminal world. Well over half of all prison sentences were tied to drug crime in the UK. And the money from drugs was the fuel behind almost all organised crime. Collectively, all other crime, including robbery, prostitution, and scams, didn't even come close to the river of cash that flowed in the form illicit drugs.

Adam sniffed the stone of crack. The stuff stank like burnt rubber. The high would last about twenty minutes when smoked. In biochemical terms, smoking a flammable drug as opposed to swallowing it means delivering a devastating surge to the brain receptors. Drug concentrations soar sky-high in a matter of seconds. But what goes up must come down, and the higher and faster the hit, the sharper and more severe the withdrawal. Ever since humans have taken drugs, the brain has been at the mercy of this age-old recipe for addiction.

Three days after sending the stone to the lab, the result came in. Magic was telling the truth. Only ten percent purity. Barely even crack. This fact alone made Adam sit up with interest. He pulled the coroner's report. Overdose had been confirmed with initial testing on the day of the crime with automatic sampling, and he had read the report twice when it initially came through. With purity this low, anaphylaxis would have made more sense. Maybe Charlie had an allergic reaction to a small dose, a freak one in a thousand explanation for the situation. Instead, the report stated overdose as the cause of death in plain black and white. It was possible the kid had bought from another dealer willing to sell higher grade gear, but it was unlikely. He bought from Magic, and no one else. Sometimes, word from the street had a strange way of being reliable, without any way of proving it. If he was buying elsewhere, people would know. The grapevine would be vibrating with whispers and clues.

The coroner had followed procedures. A drug overdose always triggered a pathological investigation. The pathologist had requested a tox study from the toxicologist and the whole thing is pieced together. Blood, urine, and hair samples. A battery of analytical tests conducted with the latest in chemical spectroscopy. This kind of equipment delivered unquestionable accuracy in record breaking time. Breakthroughs in the late 2020s mean that only a few drops of blood were required, rather than the ten millilitres needed before. Getting that much blood from an ageing corpse was a classic problem, but it was a problem of the past, mopped up by the progression of technology.

In the cold light of day, the case seemed closed. Ironclad. It was the word of the street versus hard scientific fact.

Adam removed the augmented glasses and squeezed the tension from the bridge of his nose. The light above flicked into life, nearly blinding him in the gloom of the drugs squad office He flicked out his wrist and glanced at his watch — 5.15 p.m. For once, he would finish on time.

Since the meeting with Magic, Maddie had spent her time reading through and signing dozens of standard operating procedure documents. She dropped in questions here and there as Adam read through the evidence he'd gathered. He'd knocked down a few more doors of dealers and users in the area and they all confirmed Magic's position — the crack was poor quality. Each time he returned, Adam gave her a full update. Her quick questions and subtle telltale signs in her voice suggested she was itching to join him, but didn't want to show it.

'Isn't it against procedure to knock down doors on your own?' she asked curiously, hiding a sly smile.

'You tell me. You're the one knee deep in the rule book.' He pulled out his lighter and flicked the lid, striking the spark wheel as he replayed that morning's activity. It had become an unconscious habit developed over years to play with the lighter. The pills concealed within didn't make a sound thanks to a ball of cotton wool stuffed in the bottom.

'That needs a refill,' said Maddie, 'the lights not catching.'

'Yeah, it's just a fidget thing, really. I don't smoke.'

Adam thought back to this morning's door knock. An associate of Magic they called Yakuza Dave. He was about as Japanese as a haggis, but he lost his little finger on a building site, covered himself in tattoos and was occasionally known to wear a kimono when the mood took him. Despite his claim of having links to the yakuza, anyone with the faintest flicker of a brain cell knew that was bollocks. But he was more dangerous than Magic. Prone to whipping out a flick knife in a heartbeat and forcing his way into homeless groups, hooking them with cheap deals until they were caught in his web. When he wasn't dealing, he was usually doped up to the eyeballs himself, so there was no knowing what version of Dave would be waiting for him after an early morning knock. Adam had knocked his door down more than once looking for information, but came up with nothing worthwhile. This time was no different.

Maddie's curiosity really peaked when he told her about his theory. About the file that was 'Not quite cold'. He didn't trust her. Not yet. He didn't trust anyone. Bent coppers were real and often it's ones you least expect. New cop, new town. The war on drugs had made it so. The harsher the restrictions on drugs, the more violent the criminals become, and the more money they make. The more money they make, the more bribes they make. Everyone has a price. It only takes one wrong move and a criminal can own you. Many of them were clever, very clever, and shrewd at finding those who might be tempted by forbidden fruit. Who more likely to be tempted by forbidden fruit than Eve? She would need to earn his trust. And so, he withheld the details of his theory, only outlining the main aspect. They were coming back as overdoses, but something didn't quite add up.

'Sooo, the coroners state overdose, right? End of?'

Adam simply grunted and shrugged. He took the opportunity to slam Luna back into her charging case. Maddie saw her chance to ask a question without seeming too keen.

'Are you off then?'

'I think so,' said Adam, almost in disbelief himself.

'So, are you closing that case?'

Adam flicked the lighter lid closed. 'As you say, it's hard to argue with the tox report. I've got sweet nothing, and nobody out there is giving any signs of anything else.'

'Shame. I was looking forward to getting stuck in.'

Adam laughed. 'Sorry to disappoint, chin up. Tomorrow's another day. I'm sure some lady or gentleman of the street will oblige you with a crime to work on.'

'Anything to get me off these SOPs. Not many left now, though. I think I'll just stay and finish them tonight.' She sighed, puffing out her cheeks and blowing her black hair into a mess at the fringe.

'No one waiting for you at home then?' said Adam, slinging his battered leather gym bag over one shoulder. Maddie looked away for a second, shrugged and returned her gaze to Adam.

'Jake didn't want to make the move. We're trying long distance.'

'North too cold for him?' grunted Pearce, who was swinging through with a chocolate bar from the vending machine. A smile cracked somewhere in the folds of his face.

'Something like that. Said he wouldn't go past Peterborough even if it was good weather.'

'But he would go to Peterborough?' wondered Pearce through a mouthful of chocolate. 'Strange. My brother got married there. Thought it was a shithole. Bloody Londoners, think there's nothing beyond the M25 some of 'em.'

Adam grinned at Maddie. She knew they were winding her up. Prodding for friendly weak points. Maddie shielded herself with the graceful smile of someone receiving new office stick for the first time. She knew that to snap was exactly what they wanted. The fishing bob to go under the surface, hook, line and sinker.

Gardner had walked in behind Pearce and flopped a bag on his football-themed desk across the aisle. The motion sensor flicked a spotlight on him as he spoke in a cockney accent.

'He must prefer the knife crime and human trafficking in sunny London, eh Eve?'

Maddie rolled her eyes. She thought about attempting a geordie accent and then thought again. She enjoyed doing different accents. It was a bit of a party piece and not without its uses in policing, but that one would need to be practiced before she fell over it in public.

Instead, she shot back with a wink, 'Yeah, yeah, well, when I see the sun here, I'll let you know.'

Adam noticed she remained calm, genuinely unflustered. And for that, Gardner and Pearce left her alone.

'Right, see you tomorrow then,' said Adam. He picked up a pair of sunglasses and slid them on in front of Maddie. 'Hey, you never know.'

She gave him the finger.

Twenty minutes later, Adam nudged the lock to the front door of his house and gently clicked it open into the hallway. He was used to doing it quietly, arriving home after ten and hoping he didn't wake Clara. But at this time, she was nursing a glass of wine in the living room and watching some kind of science documentary.

Her eyes lit up as Adam edged his frame into the light of the TV.

'Well, well,' she said, 'this is a nice surprise. You should have texted! I could have put the kettle on.'

'Not when you're having that, you won't! I'll grab a beer.'

'Adam Morell, home on time and having a drink with his wife as soon as he walks through the door,' she said playfully. 'Have you not got any work?'

Adam shook his head.

'Nope. Just closed a case.' He leaned over the blue sofa and kissed her head, breathing in the light scent of her peach shampoo.

'Catch the bad guys?' She reached her spare hand up and rubbed his cheek before he stood back up to get a beer from the kitchen.

The image of Charlie flashed through his mind. He forced it into a box as he forced a smile.

'Not exactly, just a bit of closure,' he said, plucking a magnetic bottle opener from the fridge door and levering off the cap.

As the evening wore on, one drink became four, with a take away somewhere in the middle. Adam felt his mind slowly switching off, and his worries melted into the laughter, conversation and booze.

It wasn't until 3 a.m., that he woke. Clara slept next to him in bed. Adam stood up, stepping on her underwear, and sauntered into the bathroom.

Even as his own tired face stared back at him through the cabinet mirror, the image of Charlie was bright and vivid in the silence of the small hours. The report said overdose, but Adam's gut said otherwise. Booze and takeaways can only numb a nagging feeling for a few hours. A feeling he knew would never go away. He was accustomed to it, a thorn in his mind, something not quite right. It would eat away at him until he figured it out, or at the very least left no stone unturned.

10

Wallet, Phone, Keys, Gun

The inky black Land Rover was almost invisible in the midnight fog. A shadow within shadows. By day it prowled through the city, well known to folk of the street: the homeless, addicts, dealers, and some who were all three. To them, the car was a monster, a beast, unpredictable and something to be feared. They kept their eyes down as it passed by.

The police knew it, and the police left it alone. They knew there would be nothing incriminating in the belly of that beast. A crime without evidence, stalking the roads without a care.

Now it glided through the roads in the north of the city. It swung right and onto the gravel of a forecourt in front of a disused warehouse. The dipped headlights exploded into full beam, washing the expansive metal doors in a sickly blue and white LED glow. Five figures emerged from the car. Four walked with purpose to the building. One stayed with the engine running, leaning against the door, puffing on an e-cigarette.

PJ led the way to the warehouse, just pleased to be out of the car, stuck in the back between the two sets of muscle. He recognised them as doormen from different nightclubs. They had exchanged knowing nods, but nothing more. Both seemed uneasy being in the car, unsure about where they were going or why. They had said yes because Luke had asked, simple. Nightclub doormen offered a relatively steady supply of gangster muscle. Controlling the door of a nightclub was a common tactic of drug lords. Control the door and you control the drug supply, no need to own the actual club. That would demand taxes, leave a paper trail. Luke had taken these two guys under his wing a year ago. Never asking much, but when he called, they came.

PJ tugged his puffer jacket together, pinching the two halves of the icy metal zip as he considered the situation. Like everyone in Marshall's organisation, he never had the full picture. So, he began his process by considering what he knew. He knew the warehouse was essentially a crack den and that some low-level dealers operated in the area. He had been told that a van was due a few minutes after they arrived. A body? The thought lingered. Probably more than one, otherwise a car would do. So, there's probably a few people ready for the slaughter. He unconsciously felt his lower back for the shape of his gun — knowing it was there, never leaving the house without it. Wallet, keys, phone, gun.

PJ then considered what he didn't know, which was always a lot more. Luke was as spontaneous and unpredictable as he was organised. He planned his life months in advance and yet somehow PJ, one of his right-hand men, was a book with missing pages. He never fully understood his employer. The bastard could speak French, for crying out loud. How many British gangsters can do that? Spent half of his time reading, playing chess or watching football.

The guy was an encyclopaedia, a word PJ had learned himself by reading it from the spine resting on a coffee table as he waited for Luke to finish his breakfast one morning. He even occasionally ordered him to drive them to an art gallery. And even there, sometimes business was done. PJ usually strolled around watching the clock, but Luke was in his element, even correcting the tour guide a few times. The poor sod nearly said something back, but he took another look at Luke and thought again. And yet, despite his almost constant uncertainty, PJ knew that in the grand scheme of things, he *was* well informed. In an organisation that survived on secrecy and scattered information, where most seldom even clapped eyes on Luke, he was privy to a lot of information — and Luke demanded loyalty above anything else.

PJ lingered on the starless sky as he watched five aeroplanes drifting across an otherwise blank black canvas. In a way, the more you knew, the stronger the prison bars were. To leave the game was not an option. Regardless, putting this and the generous pay cheques aside, Luke's unusual behaviour for someone in their line of work was another hook that kept PJ hanging around. Luke was a genius and left PJ with no doubts that they would actually stay two or three steps ahead of other gangs and the police.

Despite all of this cycling through his mind for the millionth time, he took a long drag of the cigarette, flicked the ash, and accepted once again that he always knew less than he wanted to. But that still wouldn't stop the questions forming. Why were they there? Why this time? Who were they killing? Why? Where would the bodies go? Who would take them? What about the witnesses? This place was a nest of addict eyes at the end of the day.

Inside, gaunt, hungry shapes scuttled from the light like cockroaches as the iron doors were dragged wide open by the two heavies.

The men entered and stopped at the centre of the room, breath vaporising in the chilled night air.

The headlights revealed a litter of waste scattered here and there. Old mattresses, worn clothes, used needles, sandwich packets, empty beer cans and cigarette boxes. Splashes of colour in a concrete desert. At the centre of the room, three bodies lay in a relatively neat line. Someone had lain them out with some kind of respect. Hands by their sides. PJ felt the weight ease in his chest at not having to kill someone with this many eyeballs on him.

Then something made his blood freeze momentarily. Soft padded footfalls of a giant Doberman drifted by almost silently. He turned to see the driver had opened the boot to let it out. The driver shrugged at PJ and leaned back against the car. In fairness, if that thing wanted to be out, he wouldn't have said no either. How many had it killed? It stopped short of Luke and stood stock still. The name tag hung loosely behind its bulging neck: 'Cavall'. When Luke had first introduced the dog to him, he had said it was the name of King Arthur's dog like it was a well-known fact. But it had another name, one that Luke was probably familiar with but never discussed: 'Gun'. Luke didn't carry a gun. PJ thought that was partly confidence. It sends a message to any rivals: this guy is so powerful, so untouchable, he doesn't even need one. It was also partly because he always travelled with at least two guys who did carry, but mainly because of this...thing he called a pet.

Luke crouched and patted the hound without looking at it. His own vast shape concealed the figures from view as he examined the bodies. From that, the smell, and the state of the room, he derived the key information. Two women and a man, limp, lifeless and pale. Their clothes were charity shop cast offs at best. Probably the only outfits they owned. Two of them wore wedding rings. No obvious wounds. Conclusion: Overdose.

Three was unusual, thought PJ. Three dead users. Enough to warrant a police investigation. Probably why Luke had a personal interest. Ensure proper disposal and track covering. He knew they were nothing to him personally. Not even the faintest flicker of sympathy ran through his soul. They were one thing and one thing only: reliable buyers. A small but incremental part of what he would probably call the revenue stream.

'Get rid of them,' said Luke. His voice was cold and dismissive, like a king giving a command he knew would be followed without question. He stood. Cavall did the same.

PJ nodded to the pair of hired muscle in hulking black hoodies with nylon snoods pulled up over their noses.

They took the first two bodies, rolled them into plastic and fixed the crude wrapping with generous strips of duct tape. It was slow work, even when performed by practiced hands. Withered junkie frames were still heavy when dead.

Five minutes later, a small van crunched the gravel beyond the main door and pulled up beside the Land Rover. Body removal. Its headlights revealed a little more of the room. A shape shuffled out of the newly lit corner of the room into the darkness.

Luke lit a cigarette and gazed over the glowing stub into the gloom beyond. The back wall of the warehouse, bathed in shadow, where terrified figures lurked. Faint sounds betrayed their positions. He knew they had lain out the bodies, their friends, maybe even family. That explained why they were arranged neatly. He held his gaze and took another drag, blowing out in a large plume. A combination of smoke and breath in the chilled air.

The final body was rolled onto its side, ready for wrapping.

'Stop,' Luke muttered, the cigarette hanging in the corner of his mouth.

He crouched and motioned for the heavies to move aside. PJ held the body in place with a cast-iron grip, fed daily with a regime of protein shakes and free weights.

'Lift the sleeve up.'

PJ did as he was told, folding the edge of the T-shirt up to the shoulder.

A heavy bruise where the elbow crease met the upper arm, purple, black and sickly yellow, stuck through the middle with a thick needle mark. Junkies were covered in the marks of their life choices, but this was unusual.

PJ glanced at Luke for some kind of clue. Luke gave nothing away, his cold stare drifting away into space. He was deep within his own mind. Then, after a moment, he stood and crushed his cigarette under a thick leather shoe.

'Freeze them,' he said, and wandered back to the car. Gun followed without so much as a sniff, weaving soundlessly among the litter like just another shadow in the room. Before he reached the door, Luke addressed the hidden sounds lurking in the distant corners of the room. His voice boomed in the cavernous space and carried the tone of stating an absolute fact. 'Anyone says anything, I'll burn this place to the ground with all of you in it.'

PJ told the heavies to finish wrapping. No one spoke as they lifted the three bodies into the back of the van. Even the van driver only gave a sharp lift of the chin. This man was known to PJ, but where he took the bodies was known only to Luke and the van driver.

11

Technically Not Against the Rules

The call was answered after only two rings. That was unexpected.

At 7.30 a.m., Adam expected voicemail, hoped for it even. If the call wasn't answered, he could justify taking more time to think. But he also knew procrastinating was just delaying and denying the voice inside him.

The other reason he had not expected the phone to be answered was because he was calling from a withheld number, courtesy of a cheap burner.

'Who is it?' answered a surprisingly awake voice. 'If this is another bloody car warranty scam, then I swear to God...'

'Maddie, it's me,' Adam said quickly.

'Different time zone in Newcastle, is it? What time do you call this?' she said. Despite the comment, Adam thought he could hear the surprise and subtle intrigue behind it.

'Sorry, it's important.'

She sighed. 'Can this wait until I've had a shower?'

'Uh yeah, course.' Adam cut the phone off and the sound of a stifled 'see you lat-'.

Slipping the tiny handset into his jeans, he shuffled into the kitchen to make a coffee. Clara was already there, munching on some toast and scrolling through her phone, which was projecting an identical, larger holographic screen in the air. She swiped at the hologram with one hand and glanced at the passing news headlines. Adam couldn't tell if she was looking at him or the newsfeed.

'Who was that at this time?' she muttered through a mouthful of food.

'Just Maddie, the newbie. Work stuff,' he replied, prodding the screen on the coffee machine.

'Oh?' Her eyes adjusted slightly left. Now she was looking at him through the hologram. 'How is she settling in?'

'Well, I think. Still early days, though.'

Adam watched the last few drips of steaming black liquid fall into his cup and turned to leave.

'One sec,' said Clara, swallowing a mouthful of toast. On her right wrist was a smart tattoo of a red rose. Interactive tattoos still baffled Adam. But as usual, the trend rocketed when the right celeb got one. And eventually they became more affordable and the inevitable lines formed for the latest gimmick. The ability to lock and unlock your phone with the swipe of a tattoo. Now they tracked body temperature, steps, heart rate, hydration levels. You name it, the tattoos could do it. Clara caressed her own delicate red rose from the green stem up to the head of the flower. The petals shifted, and the red rose became a white rose. The holographic news feed closed. Clara stood up. 'What do you think, contacts or glasses with this outfit?' she asked, spinning around.

'Uh....' Adam lingered. 'You'd look great either way.' He winked and left her smiling.

'Good answer, but not actually helpful!'

He kissed her on the head and went upstairs to shower. As he got dressed ten minutes later, he heard the door close as Clara left for work. Off to spend her daily £10 at some coffee shop before her shift.

The burner phone rang twenty minutes later, and Adam could hear a quick slurp of coffee on the other side.

'Right, what can I do?' asked Maddie.

'I want your opinion on something.'

'Yeah, sure, where are you?'

'I'll text you the address. I've got a virtual crime scene I need to make sense of.'

There was a pause.

'That's a bit vague,' Maddie said. 'Anything else?'

'Not on here. I'll text you my address.'

'Alright, I'll see you in a bit then.'

Adam hung up the phone, took off the back, squeezed out the sim and snapped it. Then he dunked the phone in the washing-up bowl in the kitchen, held it under the dishwater for a moment and then dropped the whole lot in the bin.

With Clara out, Adam cleared the living room, pushing the sofas and coffee table against the wall. Then he went out the front door to his car parked on the drive. Checking first for any curtain twitchers, he lifted the false floor above the spare wheel compartment, pulled back a blanket and took out a long black case.

Returning to the house, he closed the living room curtains. No need for anyone to ask questions. Plenty of dog walkers with wandering eyes. Then he opened the case to reveal a set of four projectors and sensors built on top of telescopic adjustable stands. He placed one in each corner of the living room, then took out a small set of surround sound speakers, each no larger than a golf ball, and clipped them into place on the projector stands. He scanned the room and nodded to himself. It would have to do.

Fifteen minutes later, there was a knock at the door. Adam answered.

Maddie was dressed more fashionably than your average cop, certainly more so than the drug squad. Beige blazer with gold buttons rolled up to the elbow, white shirt and jeans tucked into ankle boots. Adam noticed he was still not yet wearing socks, only his usual set of black jeans and a white T-shirt.

'Thanks for coming this early,' he said, walking back to the living room.

'No worries,' she replied to a now empty hallway. She spoke quietly to herself in mock conversation, 'Good morning to you too.' She sighed, then followed, surveying the makeshift set-up. Adam watched her eyes scanning the place subtly.

He cleared his throat. 'Coffee?'

'Had one, thanks. This place has got a woman's touch,' she added, nodding to a picture of Adam and Clara on holiday in Greece.

'Improved it, I reckon. Just had a TV and one sofa in here before Clara moved in.'

She lifted her chin at the projectors. 'So, virtual crime scene set up in your own living room as opposed to the purpose-built room at the station? Can only mean you're not supposed to be doing this.' She raised an eyebrow and locked her hands together. 'Why? And before you try to bullshit me, don't bother.'

Adam took a deep breath. 'Because it's about Charlie Lang. And the case is all but closed. I'd rather avoid the questions from Pearce.' He impersonated Pearce's gravelled tones. '*Case list as long as your arm, so why are you lingering on this one?*'

Maddie sucked her teeth. 'Sooo, why do you need me?'

'Because I've seen this a dozen times now. I'm numb to it. I need fresh eyes, just to be sure. Plus, it's a lot more interesting than reading SOPs, I promise.'

Maddie considered her new partner for a moment. Technically, she wasn't breaking any rules, Adam was. She nodded and pushed a wry smile through her lips. Finally, something interesting. She took a seat.

Adam moved to the table and lifted two cases. 'Contacts or glasses?' he asked, nodding to the projectors.

'Glasses,' Maddie said, and took the larger case. He withdrew a set that looked similar to Luna, only larger, with a plastic seal that moulded to the head and blocked out peripheral light.

Adam snapped on his own set. Then he threw on a black padded jacket coated with sensors and handed an identical one to Maddie.

'New kit,' Adam said. 'Gives you some actual feeling recorded from the footage. Lucky for you, I didn't get shot. These things pack a punch.'

'New for you, maybe. We've had these things for months in the Met.' She eyed the jacket with familiarity and yet trepidation. You never knew what you would see in the virtual recreation.

'Course you have. Sounds like nice and fair distribution of resources as usual. Right,' Adam said, loading a laptop. 'What I'm about to show you is a raid on a crack den a few weeks ago. This is...where I found him.'

Maddie gave a nod that said she knew what was coming.

Adam pressed play.

12

A Moment Frozen in Time

The living room vanished. In its place, the exterior of a terraced house materialised. Overhead, the white ceiling melted, replaced with a bruised grey sky.

The footage had been downloaded from Luna. Adam's view of the siege, stood ready, leaning to the left of a flaking blue doorframe. Black jeans, black Kevlar bullet-proof vest, knee pads and helmet. Behind him, four armed police officers were stacked in a line donning full tactical equipment. Three on the other side and one waiting with the battering ram.

'Ready,' said a firm voice behind him. There was a swift double tap of a hand on the shoulder which passed seamlessly through the motion jacket. Almost too realistic, like a ghost of the past reaching out. Although Adam had lost count of how many times he had reviewed the footage, the equipment was so accurate it practically dropped you back in time. And with every reset, he felt his own heart racing as though it was the first.

Brushed red metal flickered into view as the enforcer battering ram shattered the lock. Adam felt the adrenaline surge up his spine, the light-headedness as blood rushed to the brain, the cold sweat and tense muscles as he moved in, weapon drawn. The fluorescent lights flashed across his eyes. He was grateful the equipment couldn't re-create the reek of the house, but the sights and sounds were almost enough to squeeze the memory back into his nose.

Two dealers appeared as the footage swung through the door frame, one who had been asleep seconds before, and the other cutting coke on the coffee table beside a handgun and half a glass of orange juice. Instinctively, he scrambled for the gun. Adam aimed and shot twice. The dealer fell limp and crumpled between the sofa and the table. The other immediately threw his hands in the air and hit the deck belly first, begging them not to shoot.

Thudding feet drummed the floorboards above, grew louder and ended as a double-barrelled shotgun exploded from the top of the stairs. A chunk of wall shattered beside Adam's head. He remembered the dust clutching his throat and the first-person camera stumbled as he had done at the time. He heard Maddie wince.

Officers had already burst in behind. Their large armoured frames were pouring through the door, filling the room in formation. Aiming quickly, calmly, as they were trained. A rattle of gunfire. Six shots fired off in one second. The shotgun shooter on the stairs fell and rag-dolled to the bottom.

Adam stood and moved forward, leading three officers into the kitchen. Clear.

'You four, upstairs,' he commanded.

The officer covering the stairs took point and climbed cautiously, stepping over the shotgun shooter. Three others stacked behind him, with Adam now at the back.

Four doors off a small landing, all closed. The officer on point opened the first door, flicked through a flash grenade, closed it and waited. The grenade exploded, screams and coughing followed. There was a scramble from within mingled with shouting as the officers barked for their surrender. Metal clanged to the ground. Thankfully, no more gunfire.

'Get down! Get on the floor now!'

Adam moved in to see them handcuffing two more gangsters, a knife and a machete beside them.

The remaining two officers swept the next two rooms, empty. Clear. They stacked up on the final one and burst through.

Two police issue submachine guns. Their reliable, quiet and deadly patter, peppered with the sporadic bass notes of a high calibre handgun. Then silence. The radio crackled.

'One officer down. Medic, first floor.'

A medical officer rushed by Adam. He saw his own hand pointing to the room.

'Flesh wound,' came the response a minute later through the headset. 'I'll keep pressure on until the house is cleared.'

Adam glanced through to see a dead young woman in pyjamas collapsed in a bath. Her own blood seeped down her arms over collapsed veins and yellow bruises, before draining away down the plughole. On the floor, the wounded officer held his upper arm, the medic applying a fresh absorbent dressing that slowly ran red.

'Stay with them,' said Adam. He remembered the sense of calm that washed over him then. The worst of it was done. At least, so he thought.

Back downstairs, one room left: the basement. The same process, stacked against the door, then an explosion of adrenaline and the tinny CHINK as a pin of a flash grenade was pulled. It rattled down the stairs into the pitch black and exploded, ushering in more cries of panic. Adam tried the grimy light switch at the top of the stairs. Nothing. Something crunched beneath his boot. Jagged glass shimmered in the low light that leaked from the living room and confirmed his suspicion: they'd smashed out the bulbs.

'Night vision,' he heard himself say. They flicked their augmented glasses and the footage immediately followed suit. Dousing the basement stairs in shades of green.

They moved down. No movement at first, just the dull hum of a washing machine. The bastards were hiding. Waiting. He knew that some terraced houses of a certain age had surprisingly large basements. And they could have knocked through into several more. His suspicions were confirmed as he reached the foot of the stairs and gazed at a room twice the size of the house above. A room good for two things only, storage and hiding. A twisted jungle of shelving units, disused furniture, and old junk piled high comprising of God-knows-what.

Something moved beside a set of shabby lockers. Adam bellowed. 'Out! Now! Police! I fucking see you beside the locker.'

Then the carnage erupted again. Adam tossed a stun grenade into the thick of jungle. Panicked voices threw back expletives, drowned out by the inevitable BANG. Immediately, flashes from gun nozzles temporarily washed the night vision in bright white light as three or four dealers fired blindly. They succeeded only in giving away their positions as the officers stayed in cover, waiting for the misplaced bullets to stop chattering. Blind firing was natural, expected. To the addled mind still reeling from the grenade, varying combinations of drugs and perhaps most potently, fear, it was the logical thing to do.

The next step was to move in low, take a breath, and aim. There would be no time to reload here. Adam trained his rifle and picked off the T-shirt beside the locker, staining it red. He advanced quickly and two stray bullets tore through the air where he had stood milliseconds before.

Even as he re-watched, the same cocktail of fear, relief, and determination swept through his mind as it had at that exact moment. The moment no training can prepare you for. The horrendous thought of Clara receiving the call, after all the times he'd assured her his job *wasn't actually that dangerous.*

Two officers joined him and took up positions while another halfway down the stairs sprayed the room with machine gun fire to keep their heads down. Adam swivelled beside a broken washing machine and pointed at another dealer, thin but fast, crouching low against the wall. This one rushed forward. Adam shot once in the leg and dropped him to the floor with the butt of the gun. If he'd surrendered, that would have been it, but the loose barrel came back towards Adam. He squeezed his own trigger and slotted a round in his head.

He heard Maddie shuffle at the sight of the mutilated face, but chose to leave her. She would still be watching.

Behind him, another officer put down the final shooter. One final sweep. That was when Adam saw the skinny figure of Charlie Lang.

Minutes later, the room was flooded with light from a mixture of glow sticks and standing portable LED units.

Adam paused the image and set the video to VR search mode. This meant that with a turn of the head, they could explore the crime scene as it was at any given moment. The whole room had been captured from the augmented glasses of all the officers present and merged to build an overall picture of the crime scene. Paired with the photos taken after the event, it made for a reliable staging. The closest anyone would get to the real thing. A moment frozen in time, crystallised by computer code.

'So,' said Maddie. Her voice was steady and serious. 'This is him?'

Adam pressed his lips together and nodded slowly. 'Charlie Lang. Fifteen. Dead before we even got there. The report is saying crack overdose.'

'So, what's the problem?'

'It was only ten percent purity,' Adam said. 'Just as Magic said, *and* the lab confirmed the same.'

'Yeah, but the tox report...' Maddie began.

'I know. But is it possible there's another explanation?'

Maddie crouched low. Adam saw her virtual figure examining Charlie's face, moving around, assessing the scene.

'Have you got the report?' she asked.

Adam removed his glasses. Stepping out of the shot up, dingy drug basement into the comfort of his own living room.

He pulled the report from his backpack and handed it to Maddie.

Maddie read it through thoroughly. Start to finish, twice. Her face gave away nothing. The longer she read it, the more Adam felt she wasn't going to come up with anything.

'Looks pretty much water tight to me,' she said at last, placing the file on the high gloss coffee table.

Adam considered her for a moment. 'I've stared at that twenty times. And there's only one minor thing I can see.'

Maddie grinned and checked the report again. Her face twisted as she reached the end.

'There's no norcocaine,' Adam said, deciding she wasn't going to get it.

She turned to him. 'What?'

'You know, norcocaine?'

Maddie nodded. She knew the body breaks all drugs down into other chemicals before being excreted. Norcocaine was one of the by-products of cocaine.

'Of course,' said Maddie, 'but that's only a *minor* metabolite at best. Usually just traces left, if anything.'

'Not in an overdose,' said Adam.

'Even in an overdose it's possible there isn't any. Depends on how long his body had to break it down. But you're right, it's unlikely there'd be none if he OD'd.'

He rubbed a finger over his top lip before speaking. 'Maybe I'm clutching at straws, but it's a bit odd.'

Maddie ran her hand through her hair. She hadn't given the norcocaine any consideration. It was just the dregs, the afterthought of cocaine. It felt like a long shot.

'Also, there's not that much cocaine in his blood,' he added. 'I'd say moderate levels at the most.'

'True, but OD victims can metabolise quite a lot of a drug before they actually die, so there's not always that much left in a blood or urine sample.'

'It just doesn't add up,' he grimaced. 'It can't be both. Either the coke's metabolised and we see some norcocaine, or we should see higher levels of unmetabolised coke.'

Maddie nodded slowly. She saw what Adam was driving at. But again she couldn't shake the feeling he was reaching.

'I can probably clean that footage up a bit,' she suggested, feeling the need to offer something.

She reached into her bag and pulled out a dongle. Sticking it into the laptop alongside the headset, she booted up the screen and downloaded the video into some editing software.

'Evidential imagery software,' she said to a watchful Adam. 'Not the newest toy in the chest obviously.' She paused. 'Or...judging from that look, maybe it is?'

'Would've brought it if I had it,' he said with a sarcastic smile. 'More equal distribution of resources?'

'Well, I'll do my best to make up for it,' she replied with a grin. 'Basically, this uses AI to fill in the blurry parts.'

She typed in a line of computer code and hit enter. A loading bar filled as the scene rendered. Then the screen flashed and the images of the basement were back, clearer and crisper than they had been before.

Adam reluctantly nodded his approval. 'Not bad that.'

'Yeah. Should be configured to your headset as well,' replied Maddie, slipping her own set back on. She felt a familiar pang of excitement. The same feeling that came when she impressed anyone hard to please. People like Chrisse, and now apparently her new DI. Adam followed suit, and they explored the crime scene again.

'I can turn the brightness up a bit,' Maddie said. 'Hold on.'

Adam waited in the virtual basement while Maddie returned to the land of reality and fiddled with the laptop. Suddenly, the basement grew brighter, as though someone had just turned up a dimmer switch on the world. It was like seeing the room in broad daylight.

Adam scanned the room with new eyes. 'This is brilliant.' The blood on the walls was more vivid. The grime and general state of the place was horrendous. It looked better in the dark. But light would allow him to examine the missing detail that haunted his mind.

Charlie looked much the same. Adam moved around him, crouching low. Then he spotted it. A large needle mark and bruise on his right arm where the sleeve was pulled back.

Adam had seen the bruise before, but it was cloudy. Here in the strange light, it was clear in black and blue surrounding an injection site, where the upper arm met the crease of the elbow.

'What do you think it is? Heroin?' said Maddie.

'Well there's nothing in the report about that.'

'Flu jab?'

'Not bloody likely,' Adam scoffed.

'What then?'

'Well, we've still got the body for a few days until they tie up the paper work before the funeral.'

Maddie sighed and lifted the glasses off. Adam peeled his own glasses off his face and stared at Maddie. 'Thanks for the help on this.' He smiled at her and she returned the smile for a second before looking down to her hands, then back up to his eyeline.

'Hey, no worries. I think I've just made it more complicated, to be honest. This is pretty heavy stuff.'

'Heavier than you were expecting outside of London?'

Maddie turned away to collect the dongle. Part of her had to admit, so far, there was more excitement than she'd bargained for. Another part of her didn't want to give him the satisfaction of knowing it. So, she turned an indifferent face back to Adam and simply shrugged.

'You're looking tired,' she said. 'Life isn't just drug busts and dealers. When's the last time you took her out?'

Maddie gazed up at a picture of Adam and Clara on holiday in Greece. Her red dress flapped in the wind, in stark contrast to the smooth white buildings and the sea beyond. Adam held her waist from behind and they smiled the smile of a couple deeply in love.

Adam didn't reply.

'Exactly. I'd put this lot away before she gets in as well.' She nodded to the projectors and microphones.

Adam showed Maddie to the door and waved her off. He knew she was right. His work life balance was a joke, and his inability to leave a puzzle alone only made it worse. He made a note to take Clara out. But the buzz of adrenaline simmered around the thought of a new lead.

Somewhere else, a whisper of a deeper thought was growing louder. The unwelcome daily reminder that 'medication' was needed. The cravings scraped ever faster at the neurons of his nervous system like a demented violinist. He found the flip lighter in his coat hanging in the hallway and promptly stopped the music.

13

The Brothers Bright

Eliot Bright ran a successful, legitimate business. The bakery on Grey Street boasted three generations of healthy profit. From its excellent seat in fashionable Grainger Town at the heart of Newcastle city centre, it fed those who didn't think twice about splurging seven pounds on a coffee, and the same for a pastry or slice of cake. This, plus a sister shop in the nearby town of Ponteland (and two delivery vans) saw the family making a good, clean living. The books were balanced, taxes paid in full, and the building lease promised one hundred good years ahead.

It was the perfect place for drug dealing and money laundering.

Dylan Bright shuffled out of a newsagents. Shot nerves, tremors, sweats, headache and a sickening churn of worry lingered on every step, turning the typically easy six-minute stroll via Blackett Street into a sluggish half hour hike. Having no luck or opportunity in China Town, he was now forced to play the last desperate card up his sleeve. If anything, it was the Joker.

The walk of a desperate junkie in search of an overdue fix is well concealed by those as practiced as Dylan. But the words of Luke Marshall weighed heavily on his mind and his gait, and nothing short of raw courage prevented him from melting down and spewing up in the middle of the street.

Dylan moved one foot in front of the other around Grey's Monument, through the throng of shoppers, and down onto the sun washed stone of Grey Street. Frequently voted Britain's finest street, it wasn't hard to see why. Grand eighteenth century stone architecture swelled high on both flanks. Elegant Corinthian pillars loomed proudly. Dylan paid it no attention whatsoever. In his mind he was crawling through mud, fighting on another hundred feet until he stopped outside a glass fronted shop with the relief of a man who had just summited Everest. The polished sign above the door read 'Bright and Sons' in curved navy blue script.

Dylan pushed the brass handle into a warm room, where well-to-do students, young professionals, and retired folk sat brunching, muddling through essays or enjoying a quiet coffee in the twenty-five seats that occupied the bakery.

Dylan glanced along the counter. The fragrance was unique. A scent that could be sold *en masse* if only it could be bottled, but this wasn't something you could recreate in a lab. A blend of six different flavours of fresh baked rye bread, cinnamon buns, croissants, raspberry swirls, forest berry gateau slices, brownies, fruit pies, muffins, sandwiches, all intermixed with the subtle hint of coffee and overplayed with soothing wordless café music. For many, it was heaven, but the whole experience caught in Dylan's throat and threatened to empty his stomach.

He waited in line until he caught the eye of a hulking figure looming by the coffee machine. Dylan knew his presence made Eliot uncomfortable, because it made the customers uncomfortable. Stood there like a freshly dug up corpse at a wedding party. Dirty tracksuit, sweating pale skin and slightly jaundiced eyes. Not to mention the more-than-noticeable reek of body odour that somehow permeated through the blissful sweet pastry.

Eliot smiled at the customer by the till and handed them a tray of coffee and two pains au chocolat.

'There you go, love, enjoy,' he said warmly.

The customer, a young student with brunette hair, thanked him and gave Dylan a wide berth as she drifted to a seat by the window. Eliot caught Dylan's eye and gave an almost imperceptible tilt of his head. Dylan sighed, nodded, and left.

He made the long journey down the street and around the corner to the back delivery entrance. Another arduous trek through the mud of neo-classical architecture. Eliot was waiting, smoking with his heavy frame against the brickwork. Fourteen years older than Dylan, just shy of forty. He sported a trimmed beard that seemed to somehow compliment his red cheeks and welcoming front. Eliot had an air of the jolly, hospitable innkeeper about him, and it was imperative that he maintained this impression. He himself was part of the image of the bakery. It made people feel at ease the way he served them a slice of chocolate sponge with a smile and a twinkle in his eye. Sometimes even with a handshake to the old regulars. Dishing out local gossip and lending an ear where it was wanted.

Now, at the delivery entrance by the bins, something closer to the real Eliot presented itself in the cold light of day. A heavy rugged face that had seen its fair share of pain, given and taken. Workman's hands ran to thick forearms built by labour rather than a gym. And the assured stance of someone who knows their place in the world. Inside, he never wore short-sleeved shirts to hide tattoos that Dylan knew were littered across most of his body. Now he stood with his sleeves rolled up, the dark ink popping from his skin.

'I've fucking told you not to come in the front door,' said Eliot. 'You put people off.' His eyes narrowed as Dylan moved from one foot to the other.

'Sorry. I know, I...listen...I need some cash, just a bit. I owe someone and I've tried everything.'

'Straight to the point, as usual. How much?'

Dylan scratched his head awkwardly. 'Five.'

Eliot ran his tongue across his bottom lip and gritted his teeth. Dylan watched his brother battle with his anger.

'Marshall?' said Eliot.

Dylan stared at the floor and nodded.

Eliot sighed, pulled out his wallet and unceremoniously plucked out a large stack. He flicked it out between his giant fingers.

Dylan did his best to take it gracefully. Not too fast, but quick enough to avoid unwanted questions.

'Th- thanks so much, mate. You've got no idea how much I appreciate this.'

Eliot watched Dylan's trembling hands try to guide the notes into his pocket like a helicopter pilot struggling to land in a storm. He stared at him from under his bushy eyebrows and sighed. Whatever he felt about Dylan, shame, disappointment, frustration, there was also the unbreakable loyalty only felt by siblings, and in Eliot's case, it almost always gave way to pity.

'This can't keep happening.'

'I know.' Dylan waited. The beggar had no right to lead negotiations. There was a long pause.

'Do you need a slice of something stronger?' asked Eliot finally.

Dylan did what he could to hide the tears welling in his eyes. To a junkie, a free hit was a lottery win. Enough even to make a grown man cry.

Eliot sighed. 'C'mon then,' he said, turning and ducking under the old low door frame built in a time when men were a foot shorter.

Dylan emerged into a large tidy kitchen lit with warm spotlights. The room was steeped in the hot air of the industrial oven serving the main bakery. A few members of staff were working away in plain white aprons decorated with the flourished Bright and Sons logo. Boxes were stacked and labelled in neat lines. Seven identical American-style fridges adorned the far wall.

Dylan knew that most of the room contained ingredients for the bakery.

Eliot told the two employees to help out on the counter. When they disappeared through the door, he moved to the furthest of the chunky American fridges. A note stuck to the front said 'Out of Order. Do Not Use.' A wall of heavy boxes marked 'Do not touch' surrounded its feet. Eliot slid them aside and tugged the door open. And then, with great difficulty, heaved his bulk in and through the other side.

Dylan followed. His slight frame slipped easily through a four-foot white tunnel into another room.

'Close the door behind you,' said Eliot, motioning back to the fridge.

Dylan pulled the thick door shut against the seal, blocking himself in. Then he clicked the false back into place so that if it was opened from the kitchen, it would appear to be a regular empty fridge. The small room was lit by a single bulb and housed only a thin set of steep, spiralled steps winding down into the darkness. Eliot led the way, and Dylan followed with a jittering hand on the cold cast-iron handrail.

The windowless room he emerged into was a swollen underground space about half the size of a football pitch. Near the foot of the stairs, a set of computers and tables took up only a small portion of the room. The vast majority was dedicated to stacked shelves housing a cannabis and a magic mushroom farm. Two aisles of each, fed with the equipment and conditions they needed. Lighting and warmth for the weed, precise moisture and darkness for the liberty cap mushrooms. Pipes and cables fed water and electricity. Each row of plants and mushrooms concealed with translucent plastic poly tunnels. Elsewhere, boxes and shelves were organised and labelled. The order and precise placement of the kitchen upstairs spilled down into the cellar.

There was a fine line between baking and chemistry. For the Brights, the line was understood well enough for them to manipulate it.

An air vent hummed directly above the tables by the stairs, gently extracting a concoction of invisible molecules. A stick-thin figure in a baggy hoodie hovered by the equipment. Keen, electric blue eyes briefly flickered in Dylan's direction before returning to the delicate liquid in the glass. He began carefully unscrewing a flask and pipetting precise droplets into the brewing mixture.

'Dylan,' the figure breathed quietly, so as to not disrupt the droplets. He had black, wet brushed back hair. Strands flopped forward over his face where he leaned.

Dylan acknowledged his second brother. 'Tony.'

Eliot rummaged through boxes by the wall. Tony Bright looked his younger sibling up and down before turning to a laptop and typing in a few digits.

Dylan saw himself as relatively smart in some ways. He was certainly street smart, but he was not classically smart compared to Tony or Eliot. He found solace in the fact that very few people were. A master's in chemistry from Cambridge University, summa cum laude, and a PhD in organic chemistry and biochemistry. Enough said. He noticed another computer open to the dark web, the illegal browser of the internet, where sales of drugs (and worse) were listed like commodities of any other online store, complete with ratings, reviews, and prices. Tony had been uploading some of his own product images: weed brownies. That's how business was done.

'Nice to have the family together,' said Tony, now in his usual sarcastic tone, 'until you get shitted up again. You know it's a lot easier to sell the gear if you don't stick it inside yourself.'

Dylan said nothing. Usually, he would have a little dig at his brother's agoraphobia. The man who never left the basement. But his rattle was burning, and it took everything he had not to crumble to the floor. He couldn't, not while his brothers were here, and not while he was so close to a hit.

Eliot tossed a wrapped slice of something cold and dry into Dylan's lap. Dylan resisted his primal urge to tear up the cling film with his teeth and dive into the gear. Slowly, he unpeeled the wrapper as though he were an old man opening a cheese sandwich on a park bench. The taste of chocolate almost drowned out the taste of the marijuana and cocaine. But it was there, subtle notes, unbelievably so, acquiescing to Eliot's painstaking recipe. Not the exact hit he needed, but enough to take the edge off when it kicked in. Space cakes were developed in Amsterdam in the 1950s. But the Bright brothers had taken them to an art form. Edibles were their speciality, and with Tony the chemist, and Eliot the chef, hand-in-hand, they made something distinct.

'Where've you been anyway?' muttered Tony.

Dylan shuffled. Involuntary thoughts flashed through his mind; the freakish gold and silver eyes of Luke Marshall, the room coated in black plastic.

'I don't know. Got jumped in the park, woke up two days later.' Dylan rubbed his nose and took another generous bite of the cake.

Tony raised an eyebrow. 'Two days?'

Eliot stopped and gazed across the table, concerned. 'Know who did it?'.

Dylan shrugged. 'Some crack head. Piss head. Who knows? Had nothing on me worth stealing, anyway.'

Eliot had rolled two cigarettes and proceeded to roll a third. Then he stood and handed all three to Dylan.

Dylan hesitated and shoved them into his jacket pocket with a nod of gratitude.

Dylan caught Tony's surprised eye again.

'You not want that now?' asked Tony.

'No, nah I'm alright,' he lied. I'll wait until later.'. Everything he had was being used to stop his hands shaking and mind racing.

They said nothing. Watching him with the look of pity and hopelessness that stood behind every encounter. The look reserved for a relative on life support. Like they knew his time on earth was limited, as was the life of most addicts.

Dylan ignored it, adding it to the mountain of other pains that plagued his existence. 'Right, well, thanks again. You're a life saver.' He smiled weakly and moved to the stairs but bumped into the hand rail and winced.

'Somethin' wrong?' asked Eliot.

'No, it's nothing, just aching.'

'Let me see,' said Eliot. Dylan moved, but Eliot grabbed him. 'Show me.'

Dylan sighed, then removed his track suit top to reveal a large needle mark directly into a vein.

Eliot's mouth dropped. 'What the fuck is that?' The cloudy blend of ink black, purple and yellow gave the bruise the semblance of a sinister sky. Around the edge, burst red capillaries jutted out at every angle like the broken legs of a dead spider.

Dylan said nothing.

Tony rolled his eyes.

'You're gonna kill yourself,' Eliot spat coldly.

A pause. A single tear poured from Dylan's eye as his body gave way. He stumbled and caught the table.

Tony moved to speak, but Eliot waved him away.

'Who did it?' asked Eliot quietly.

Dylan sniffed. 'I don't fucking know. All I know is it wasn't there before.'

'Before what?'

'Before I woke up.'

'You didn't do this?'

Dylan said nothing, his head bowed and his breathing heaved as tears fell between gasps for air. Eliot crouched and pressed the issue with less venom. 'Do you remember anything?'

Dylan sniffed and thought for a moment. He hesitated before speaking. 'Just the smell of cinnamon swirls.'

Eliot glanced sharply at Tony, who walked away and silently gathered a set of handcuffs. There was a look held between them, and quickly after, agreement.

Eliot spoke softly. 'Dylan.'

Dylan forced his head up. The last thing he saw was the tattooed arm and the pale ham fist coming fast through the blur of his wet eyes. Then the lights went out.

14

An Unlucky Boy

Paracetamol with a chaser of hot instant coffee. Adam turned his eyes from the white-washed walls that teamed up with the harsh LED lights to assault the retinas. He buried his nose over the lip of the bamboo paper cup to mask the nauseating stench of antiseptic cleaning fluid, deodorisers, and sterile air of the ventilation system. His stomach twitched again when he thought about the ten bodies undergoing decomposition through the double doors. He shifted in the plastic seat where the pathologist had left him with the promise of returning in twenty minutes.

The crinkle of his newspaper against his side was a welcome distraction. He withdrew it from inside his jacket and thumbed through the pages.

The headline was on the topic of new funding to combat knife crime in Sunderland announced by the council. One million had been pledged in a new scheme called *Knives Down - Jobs Up*. Looks great on paper, he thought. As did all simple solutions to complex problems. People liked simple, and they liked money. Throw a handful of spare change at it, and the politicians can sleep without a conscience while they gather more votes on the back of another useless policy. Besides, the problems of Sunderland were just a regional problem, after all. No impact on the capital or the major cities. In the end, one million was not even close to what was needed. Knives don't just appear in society. A cocktail of broken families, broken justice, bad parenting, street gangs, and overpopulation all go into the shaker before a knife is pulled.

Adam skipped twelve pages of gossip columns. The next story went on about the aftermath of Storm Lucas, which had claimed the lives of more than one thousand people on the island of Bermuda in 2039. The reporter has asked a 'top expert' what coastal cities in the region need to do to protect themselves from the onslaught of global warming. Adam sighed and moved slightly, momentarily giving his back some relief from the hard, plastic seat.

He flicked idly on. Film reviews, book reviews, new music. He delved into the lesser-read middle pages, where small stories were given only a quarter of a page or less. A name caught his eye in a column entitled 'The Twisted Ladder.'

The name sent him back in time: 'Professor Cole', an old pharmacy school lecturer who he got on well with as a student. They had remained friends since, and he even unofficially consulted the professor on cases from time to time, especially if a new drug hit the street. This week's title: 'Pharmacogenetics: what is it and could it cure cancer?' He decided that was more up his street.

Researchers at Newcastle University have announced the results of a landmark trial, which they believe could be the key to unlocking a new arsenal against cancer and other life-limiting conditions. Part of pharmacogenetics is the study of how quickly drugs are broken down by different people depending on their genes.

'The idea isn't new. Basically, some people are what we call rapid metabolisers,' said senior researcher, Professor Cole, 'they break down drugs much quicker than say moderate or slow metabolisers. Which means they clear the

drug more quickly and would therefore benefit from a higher initial dose for the same condition.'

But the researchers have been looking at this from a new angle when it comes to cancer. With things like chemotherapy, we all think of side effects such as hair falling out, vomiting and exhaustion. But what many people don't know is that a lot of chemotherapy drugs are not active in the body until they are broken down into what scientists call their 'active form' by molecules called enzymes.

Professor Cole explained, 'Normally, when a drug is broken down into the active form, it's also partly broken down into a range of metabolites which aren't useful. But by working with geneticists from across the world, researchers here have been able to alter the genes within cancer patients so they can create new enzymes which more efficiently and accurately breakdown chemotherapy into their active forms.'

In addition to this, genetic advancements mean researchers have been able to ensure that the required enzyme only exists within the tumour itself, so the drug is only converted into its active form where it needs to be, and keeps it there. Patients in a recent trial have shown a twenty-fold increase in the effect of three different anti-cancer drugs prompting funding for wider research.

Adam mulled the idea over and smiled at the work of his old teacher. Impressive stuff, no doubt about it. He allowed himself to hope that even he would live to one hundred and flicked on to the sports section for something lighter. For five minutes he immersed himself in the world of football transfers and tactics, horse racing results, and boxing. A glimpse through the paper window into a seemingly parallel universe compared to his own life. The things people complained about beggared belief. He was saved from the swelling anger of a footballer demanding over £1 million a week by the appearance of the pathologist.

Her head sat on a pencil thin neck and showed only the faintest traces of make-up. Her eyes were large and her brown hair was tied back into a pony tail that fell to the top of her spine. She wore a white coat and trainers with some kind of cushioned sole support.

Standing awkwardly and slightly duck-toed, she spoke, 'Detective.'

Adam's back twinged as he rose, his lower muscles almost as stiff as the seat. He released the groan that yearned to escape his lips and considered the pathologist again. She was a nervous type, thought Adam, and new. He tried to remember if he'd seen her before, but nothing came to mind.

Adam followed her through the double doors into the large, airy room of the morgue. Only half the lights were turned on, dousing one half of the room in shadow. Washed in cold light on the far wall, the bank of metal drawers that served as temporary coffins stared back in five rows of five. One in the centre was open, and the body pulled out. A tag around the toe read C. Lang.

'Blood burst through the vessel when the needle went in,' said the pathologist, as Adam approached. *So much for small talk*, thought Adam. He scanned her name tag. Dr Selhurst, and a photograph of her, smiling faintly. The name still didn't ring a bell. She went on. 'Extravasation. Not surprising. That's where the blood comes out of the vein but stays under the skin.' Adam decided not to go down the *I know, I used to be a pharmacist* path. Better to save the time and play dumb. Dr Selhurst began packing up a few items on a nearby bench. Adam turned his attention to the body before him.

The pale lump of unfulfilled possibility lay on the metal drawer tugged out from the wall of death. The vicious bruise was there just as the AI crime scene had revealed, right where the forearm met the upper; the brachial artery. Although the wound was faded, it was far more horrific in real life.

She caught the slight shock in his double-take. 'Surely *you're* not surprised by that?' She took off the white coat, which revealed another name badge pinned to her pale blue shirt that read: Hello, I'm Lisa! in friendly font.

'Sort of,' Adam admitted. 'Bit nasty isn't it, even for a botched junkie hit? Is it infected?' He glanced back at the body.

'No. But it's not that unusual. Quite a bad one, yeah, but not unheard of. Tox report was pretty clear though. Wasn't much for me to do if I'm honest.'

'Was it though?'

Lisa turned sharply, taken aback by the attack on her judgement as Adam went on. 'There wasn't that much cocaine in the blood.'

'True,' she said, straightening up. 'But drugs are broken down a lot in overdose patients before they pass. See it all the time. Besides that's not the main thing.'

Adam frowned. 'What is?'

'When we decide on cause of death, it isn't just the tox report. There's also the symptoms to consider. The post-mortem showed clear signs of breathing difficulties, dilated pupils, heavy sweating, the list continues in my report. Every symptom of crack cocaine overdose. Also...' she motioned to the body before them. 'He's a known drug user. That can't be ignored. All of it forms the decision based on the information we have.'

Adam lingered over the boy for a moment. The clock in the corner of his glasses read 17.15. He removed Luna and pocketed her, earning a suspicious glance from Lisa.

It didn't need to be recorded. It shouldn't be recorded.

The pathologist loitered, clearly impatient to leave. With the tone and false smile of a bar tender calling last orders, she cleared her throat. 'That everything then?'

Adam hovered a moment longer, in part only to spite her. He took one last look at the pale young face of the boy. He saw an unlucky boy, not a bad person. Someone dealt a bad hand and forced to play it at a table where everyone else was cheating. In another life, if there was such a thing, Adam hoped he was having a fairer crack of the whip. Parents who cared, a good neighbourhood. A good life.

And yet, the drawer closed on Charlie Lang.

15

The Smell of a Cinnamon Swirl

In the cellar of the bakery on Grey Street, orders from the secret menu of Bright and Sons were attended to under the moonlight.

Cakes, brownies, and cookies were the easiest. Batch baked. An array of weighed and measured ingredients lined up on immaculate benches. Self-raising flour, eggs, golden caster sugar, water, vanilla essence, milk, icing, softened butter, cocoa powder, chocolate chips. And last but not least, ground cannabis sativa and indica. Hybrid forms grown and tailored to the customer's request. Not the brain slapping hash that filled the streets and knocked you clean out. Bright and Sons provided something rare, something controlled. The connoisseur's choice.

Tony cut each plant under the warm lights that dangled above the farm. Each leaf snipped with a pair of nail scissors and the care and attention of a midwife cutting an umbilical cord. His infatuation with perfecting his blends was vital to the success of the business. Theirs was ultra-high quality, bordering on pharmaceutical grade. The only thing they were missing was the official paperwork. The exacting manufacture and quality assurance processes were filed away in the alphabetised cabinets of Tony's mind. Nothing tangible existed in the way of records on that front.

Upstairs, Eliot turned the fruits of Tony's labour into baked goods that masked the taste better than most. The outcome was batches that looked no different to anything sold on the counter. This meant that if they were ever found, appearance alone would not betray them. The health inspector was none the wiser, and the 5-star food hygiene rating shone on the wall by the door, framed and polished. Bright and Sons had the supply, and a colossal demand to match. Besides the online sales, Eliot sold some select batches directly in the small hours, driving a van to an agreed location. Brands were removed, nothing to tie it back to the shop. Masks were worn, fake names were used. The fewer the merrier, people they had worked with for years. From here, the fresh sweets trickled down the supply chain into the open mouths of students with too much time and free cash.

The dirty money paid to the Bright brothers was washed through the laundry of the business books from both branches of the bakery as well as takings from the daytime delivery vans. The key was consistency, and crucially, moderation. No more than twenty percent over the legitimate takings. Not one penny. Any more, and the dogs would come sniffing, noses to the ground and down into the cellar. Buyers occasionally asked for more. What was a few more boxes? Eliot saw that they never asked again. Give an inch to these fuckers and they snatch a mile. More is never enough for men like them.

Eliot allowed the low tones of a midnight radio channel to play over the hum of the ovens. Tony sat and watched his brother work away with what had become an impressive efficiency. The larger brother had poured himself a glass of ale and took the occasional measured mouthful here and there. Entirely at home, enjoying it even. Like some kind of TV pastry chef. Slapping down dough, weighing, pouring, mixing, piping. Baking four different products in multiple batches. There were no recipe books or sticky notes littering the table. All timings and measurements were held in the neural cookbook of his brain. He would have his own Christmas best-seller if only it were legal.

On the central oak table stood the pièce de résistance of the batch: a three-tiered wedding cake.

'Looks good,' said Tony, pointing to the sweet masterpiece.

Eliot smiled and pinched some stray icing into place. 'Bit loud though, isn't it? Doesn't really blend in. And who wants a weed wedding?' he laughed.

'That's the point,' said Eliot, topping it off with a statue of a bride and groom. 'Who the fuck expects a weed wedding cake? It's so over the top, it's invisible. Plus, it's obviously not goin' to an actual wedding. They'll break it down and sell the slices. This just helps answer any unwanted questions.'

Tony nodded to himself. He noted Eliot take some further pointed care with the icing. As always, the icing had to be just so. It was entirely at odds with the general appearance of the big man. After all he'd done with those muscles. And here he was, icing a cake with care in the small hours.

'How's Dlyan?' asked Eliot.

'The process is underway. It takes time.'

Eliot's phone buzzed.

'I'll be there in twenty. Out the back.' He hung up and turned a stone face to Tony. 'There's another one ready. I'll call you in a bit.'

Eliot approached a middle-aged woman under the security light behind the old nail factory. The conversation was hushed. A bag was exchanged, money flashed briefly in the light. She shuffled away and ducked her head down.

Eliot climbed into the van and watched.

'She's normal,' he said into the phone resting on the dashboard.

Tony grunted back down the line in the usual half listening manner he adopted when someone spoke to him while engrossed in some lab experiment. Eliot always phoned him. Partly an attempt to make him feel like he was leaving the bakery. Partly for company. Mostly because even over the phone, Tony was a good judge of character. He could pick them best.

'Single mother. A nurse, actually,' said Eliot. 'Even runs a football team. Holds down a normal life, her kids don't even know about her addiction.'

'She'll do nicely.'

He watched as the solitary woman reached the arch beneath a bridge, pausing to find her keys beside a parked people carrier. Eliot checked the road again to make sure it was clear.

* * *

Dylan's mind danced between memory, imagination, and the space in between. A montage of images spiralled on, spat out of some crazed projector in his head. The crinkle of a plastic curtain. A bright light and a soft chair. The blindfold went over his face before he could catch anything else. One thing stood out clearly: the smell of cinnamon swirls. Then the white hot pain in the arm, and the blackness that truly gripped him. A blink of sleep later, the chill of the park on his spine, the blindfold gone, the wet leaves stuck to his back, the moon peering through the hedge above. Shivering in the dark. Dylan sobbed quietly.

16

Play Now, Fish Later

Adam stepped out onto the grey concrete car park and climbed into his car. The cold air whipped at the warm skin where Luna had rested on the bridge of his nose. He watched the pathologist applying lipstick in the rear-view mirror of a Mercedes as it drove itself out the carpark. Adam took out his lighter, flicked it open, and knocked back a pill. He snapped the lid shut and dropped it in his pocket, feeling calmer knowing his mind and body would be soothed in twenty minutes or so. The closing steel drawer flashed in his mind's eye. He made a decision, and spoke it to the car. 'Call Maddie.'

'Calling Maddie,' replied the car's computer.

Her chirpy voice came through the speaker. 'Hello.'

'Are you free tomorrow night?'

'Erm, yeah, don't really know anyone here yet,' she joked. 'Why?'

'We need to go somewhere. I'll send the ticket to your phone,' he said, ignoring the quip.

'Ticket. What for?'

'You'll see.' Adam hung up.

***

The drive home was uneventful and earlier than usual. He wandered into the living room and slumped onto the couch, allowing the noise of his mind to settle in the soothing silence. Clara was nowhere to be seen. *Probably just in traffic*, he thought. *Or was tonight spin class?* That was when he heard the giggling upstairs.

Adam smiled to himself. He loved an opportunity to surprise her on the phone with one of her friends. He moved cautiously up each step, tracing the familiar path he knew created the least noise. Halfway up, Clara's voice carried down the stairs. A tone that somehow set his hair on end.

'No, I'll be there,' she said excitedly. 'Okay...seven? How the hell am I supposed to...?' There was a long silence until Clara spoke again, reluctance lingering on her tongue. 'Alright, alright. Yeah, see you then, bye.' The faint undertone of flirtation hovered in the air. He moved to climb the stairs but stopped at the sound of his phone on the coffee table in the living room. It could be worth answering. Maybe something to do with the case. His head decided, and returned to find the number was withheld from some call centre spam.

The thought of Clara's conversation clawed a new hole in his tired brain. He decided to announce himself and shouted up that he was home. The call was met with shuffling from above, and Clara emerged into the living room.

'Oh, it's you,' said Clara. She smiled, as calm and normal as she always did. 'What's it with these early finishes?' she laughed, reaching over the couch and kissing him on the cheek. 'You must be getting better, DCI Morell?'

'I heard you talking as I came in,' said Adam, kissing her back in his usual tired after work manner.

'Oh. Yeah, just Kat from work. Wants to organise an office girl's night out.'

'Ah nice. Where's she thinking?' he asked, flicking the TV on.

'Just a new bar in town. In the Bigg Market.'

Adam decided to play completely ignorant. There was something there that his gut could not let go. A slight hesitation, the glance out the window in the answer. Something unnamed, yet...off. That being considered, technically there was nothing to go on. No hard evidence. He would play now, and fish later. He grinned and held out his hand, gesturing for her to sit beside him. She snuggled into him and he flicked the TV over to a football match. 'Forgot this was on! I could get used to these early finishes,' he said.

The rest of the evening slipped away into the sloth of TV, snacks, and sleep. At 10.30 p.m., Adam said he was going to bed and set his alarm for 5.30 a.m.

By 6 a.m., the next morning, he was in the car and sliding off down the road. But instead of heading to the office, he pulled into a nearby cul-de-sac, on the route out of their housing estate, and parked on the kerb. Power off. At 6.45 a.m., Adam was beginning to doubt his senses. Was this an overreaction? Probably.

The sunrise bleached the edge of the morning sky gold. Then, as the street lights were thinking about turning off, Clara's Mini drifted by the opening onto the main road.

Adam shifted the car into drive and tailed her at a distance, letting two cars slide between them. Within ten minutes they had made it to west Newcastle. The neoclassical elegance of the town centre was reflected in the rising, minimalist progression of self-cleaning glass, steel and sharp carbon fibre of the newer buildings. The HMRC headquarters were nestled somewhere in this district.

Adam slid to the side of the road and watched through the steel mesh of a multi-storey as Clara's car slipped itself into a parking space on the ground floor. She climbed out and tapped her phone against the payment machine that had logged her registration plate as she entered, and walked for ten minutes into Grainger Town. Adam lost her while he parked his own car.

By the time he'd found her she had picked up two coffees and some pastries. He took a discreet vantage point behind a hive of cyclists locking up their bikes in the endless public rack of chaotic metal. Clara took one coffee for herself and handed the other to someone in the street.

He was sharp-dressed; tailored suit, black leather gloves, well built with thick, curled hair, and olive skin. His jaw seemed frozen into a smile from the moment she caught his eye. Clara laughed once or twice, flicking her hair back over her ear. She only did that when she was nervous. He said something to make her laugh and then they walked on, back into the district of glass and steel.

Adam followed, keeping a hundred yards back, blended somewhere in the stream of pedestrian traffic. Eventually, the bright foyer of the seven storey HMRC building loomed.

He watched them stop outside the tall glass front doors. The man in the suit hugged her. She hugged back, and they parted. The man headed down a side street and Clara disappeared into the building, through the security turnstile and out of sight.

17

22 Holograms Chasing a Ball

The holograms kicked into life and the crowd roared. Twenty-two players walked out onto the pitch in front of a full house of eighty thousand seats. The real match was taking place in Paris: The Champions League final featuring Real Madrid versus Juventus.

Across the country, stadiums fitted with holographic projectors beamed the players in Paris onto the pitches of the UK. Only those with bets on cared much about the score. No British teams in the final made for a neutral match. But football was football, and with tickets half the price of an in-person match, it was a worthwhile Saturday evening investment followed by a few more drinks on the town. A hell of a lot better than watching it in the pub or at home on TV.

Adam and Maddie sat nursing pints through a slow start to play. They were perched halfway up the stands, wedged between a family of four and a group of young lads using the match as a good excuse to pre-drink before a night out.

Adam had taken the time to shave back to a millimetre of stubble, unable to bear the incessant scratch that came with a growing beard. Maddie had pushed her raven hair back with a headband, but otherwise they were dressed more or less as they would for the office, with the addition of large coats suitable for late autumn in Newcastle.

Maddie sipped her pint as the virtual ball soared over the bar and the cheers died prematurely. 'I still can't believe the force are paying for this. Jake and I pay through the nose for tickets. Well...Jake does.'

Adam snorted. 'Like I said, officially, we're here to keep an eye on *him*.'

They gazed to the left, where a group of VIP boxes took over the stand. In the middle, one box dimly lit and less crowded than the rest revealed the hulking silhouetted figure of Luke Marshall.

'But there's a massive police presence here. It's not like he can do anything.'

Adam shrugged. 'I know, but we barely see him at all. This is a rare chance, and the truth of it is the department needs to look like it's made some progress. Couple of photos, write a report and we're done. Plus, it's a free ticket to the match. And to be honest...'

'What?'

Adam ignored the question. He thought about Clara, and how the real joy had come when he knew he didn't have to spend another night pretending not to suspect anything in front of her.

'What do you reckon, then?' Maddie said, pointing to the scoreboard.

'I'll say 3-0, Madrid,' said Adam, switching his plastic pint glass to his less numb hand.

'Oh, want to put your money where your mouth is?' Maddie said, tilting her head.

'Already have,' Adam said. He flicked his phone into life and showed a bet of £10 placed on a 3-0 victory for Real Madrid.

Maddie raised an eyebrow. 'Twenty to one odds,' she muttered, 'not bad....ooof.'

The words slipped out involuntarily as they did for most when a football strikes the post. The dull thud fired out the speakers and died in a wave of 'ooohs'.

'Grab a few photos,' Adam said, nodding towards the boxes.

Maddie subtlety adjusted her augmented glasses and zoomed into the distance. In the private boxes, a group of suited men and dolled up women sat watching the match. The private security lurked around, never once looking at the match. Maddie focused in on the shadow of Luke sitting at the centre.

Her glasses read: Luke Marshall: 70% match, as they scanned the figure doused in shadow. Beside this, one of the few confirmed images of him loomed on screen. She grabbed a few snaps of what she could. Just as she turned to the match, Luke's phone lit up as he scrolled, allowing a brief half-light on his face. The match indicator rose to 85%. Maddie felt a shot of excitement as luck fell in her favour. She captured the image and sent it to Adam.

'That's as good as we'll get,' said Adam, scanning the picture. He considered the cold silver and gold eyes that held venom even for his own phone screen. Malicious beads nestled in a vile face that, even resting, housed its own detestable, conceited smugness. He knew the image was useless, but at least they had something more than shadows for the report. 'Anything we can get is useful.'

'Weirdest stakeout I've ever been on,' said Maddie.

'Most fun though?'

Maddie paused. 'Yeah, probably. How did you know he would be here?'

'Magic,' he said with a grin.

Maddie rolled her eyes. 'How did that low life know?'

'Lowlifes speak to slightly 'higher lifes' and so on. Mostly it's because there's so many of his scumbags here, one of them must have let something slip. Hard not to brag about being in the top box. But Luke would have known that. He just doesn't care.'

A huge cheer erupted and the stadium burst into life. 1-0 to Real Madrid.

Twenty minutes later, the half time whistle pierced the air. The huddled stream of punters shuffled through to line up against the endless wall of urinals and relieve themselves, ready for more. Queues formed for pies and pints. Knee joints were straightened and legs stretched, backs pushed forwards and cracked.

Adam waited for Maddie outside the toilet. They queued for another pint and then headed back to their seats.

He put his hand in his pocket to check for his lighter and met the sharp edge of an envelope.

'Who the fuck has left this here?' said Adam, reaching for it. Maddie pressed her lips together and shook her head.

'Not a clue.'

He instinctively looked at the group of lads beside him.

'Who the hell are you lookin' at?' shouted the smallest and furthest of the group. He was barely out of school, definitely the youngest, and brave because he had four people between him and Adam.

Adam gave his cold stare, but that seemed to only spur the rest of the group as wry smiles formed on mischievous lips. He shut them up immediately by flashing his badge.

'Go on, do something, big man.'

The lads reluctantly dropped their masks and faced forward, slowly and awkwardly trying to absorb themselves in small talk and pointing to players that were re-emerging onto the pitch.

Their clueless faces told Adam they had nothing to do with the envelope. The family to the other side of them still hadn't returned. It was unlikely to be them, either. In theory, it could have been anyone on the way to the toilet or the bar. One of three thousand people.

The envelope was sealed with a strip of tape. Adam peeled it away with a gloved hand to preserve any DNA and allowed the contents to fall casually into his free hand. A single note.

'What is it?' Maddie said.

Adam held it between them, shielding it with his body, and read it out quietly.

Charlie Lang was murdered.
Duke.

The family returned and Adam quickly slotted the note back into the envelope and carefully tucked it into his pocket.

He and Maddie focused their augmented glasses back onto Luke. He was still sat as he had been, glaring at the pitch.

'Could it have been him?' Maddie muttered, taking a sip of her drink.

'Maybe. Although Duke doesn't ring a bell. Do you know a Duke?'

'I wish.'

'We should check the cameras.'

'Yeah. Get onto it...' Maddie rose to move. Adam tugged her arm gently. 'In the morning.'

She looked at him. 'If we act now, we can do something.'

Adam said nothing.

'You don't think we'll find anything?'

'I know you won't. Listen.' Adam spoke in a hushed voice. Maddie sat down close to him. 'This is nothing even near to anything you've done before.' He rubbed the back of his neck. 'I don't know what, but there's something very off with these deaths. Check the cameras if you really want to, and then you can text me when you've found nothing.'

Maddie hovered for a moment. Torn between Adam's logic and proper procedure. As always, the latter overruled and she disappeared for half an hour. When she returned, Adam was a pint ahead. Her face gave nothing away as fans stood to allow her to shuffle back down the row.

'And?'

'Not a thing. But there's plenty of blind spots.'

She braced herself for the impending I-told-you-so. But another goal from Real Madrid lifted the crowd to their feet as their players ran to celebrate in a corner of Paris. The whistle blew ten minutes later and the same players fell to their knees.

Barely anyone waited for the trophy presentation. No one wants to see another team collect a prize, and besides, the nightlife of Newcastle was calling.

In the night air where the crowd began to thin, Adam could feel himself breathe easier. His head cleared a little. Enough to bring Clara back to his mind. He wasn't ready to go home yet. She would still be awake. He suggested a trip to a bar instead.

As though she were reading his mind, Maddie responded. 'Wouldn't your wife have something to say about you going to a bar with another woman?'

He paused. 'Clara does what she wants, apparently. I think she's...' The thought blew away in the wind. He shrugged. 'I'm going. It's up to you if you want to join me.'

They ended up in a pub just off High Bridge. The ceilings were low, old, and crooked. A 17th century shell that moved with the times. Projector TVs, live music, packed bar. Adam and Maddie found a table on a balcony above the throng. A few couples dressed for a night out eyed their heavy coats and winter wear but left them to it.

Maddie pulled on her augmented glasses for a bit of light scrolling. Adam put his Luna in the case. A text alert appeared on Maddie's phone. She turned to him and grinned.

'You don't like new tech, do you? AI, AR, that sort of thing.'

Adam wheeled out the neutral stance. 'I think it can be useful.'

'Come off it, you don't have a new phone. I mean, you still manually drive your car!' Maddie's smile dropped as she read the melancholy in Adam's eyes. 'What?'

He spoke softly, just within her earshot. Mostly to himself. 'That's because a self-driving car killed my daughter.' He stared down at his pint glass and turned it slowly. His gaze returned to Maddie, and his voice rose to something closer to normal. 'Malfunctioned, came off the road, and the brakes failed.'

A train of goosebumps carried the chill down Maddie's spine even before she could fully process the words. 'Oh, my Go—'

Adam spoke as through he was remembering every moment as it happened in real time. 'The car had a choice, driven by AI. To drive onto a grass verge and run over my daughter, or hit a wall and probably kill the couple inside the car. She was three.' He took a deep breath and another swallow of beer. 'What was it they said? *The programmed logic of the car dictated one life is worth less than two.* After that my wife and I didn't really, you know...and a few years later I met Clara. In a car crash, of all places.' Adam pulled out his lighter. Maddie watched as he opened the top, flicked out a pill and swilled it down with a slurp of golden liquid. His voice was now more matter-of-fact as he left the memory behind like a helpless hitchhiker, consciously ignored. 'That's where I got these, by the way. Back injury from the car crash,' he said, following her eye. 'And so no, to answer your question, I don't trust new tech. Not one bit.'

Maddie traced the pills being tucked away into his left side jacket pocket and made a mental note to find out exactly what they were, although it was obviously some kind of painkiller. Maybe tramadol or morphine. Now was not the time. 'I'm so sorry,' she said.

'Cheery drink, this turned out to be. Never bringing you to the pub again.'

Maddie grinned. Adam forced one and stood up.

'Where are we going?'

'You're going home. As for me, I'm going to look into the files to see if we have anything on Duke.'

They parted outside. Adam hailed a taxi for her, and waited until it was out of sight before going back inside.

He asked Luna to search for Duke as a first or last name. One or two profiles were fished from the digital abyss. One dead and another in prison. Solid alibis. He gave it up. Too many pints and pills to think properly.

Somehow, his feet carried him through town. Flashes of bright 3-D holographic advertising swirled in his opioid mind. Lights and sounds of bars, the whir of electric cars. He found his way to the yellow lights of the Metro underground train, and ten minutes later to the quayside of the River Tyne. He was leaning over a railing, gathering himself when he saw it. A group of women walking out of a pub. On the back of an uncovered shoulder was the twisted ladder of a double helix tattoo. A thought turned in his head, searching through the opium fog to reach his attention. Eventually, it met the mark of his mind's eye. The twisted ladder.

The thought lead to another and eventually landed on a question. Only one person would be able to help him with that.

18

A Crazy Idea

Not many consider Newcastle a city of science. Hen nights, stag dos, and partying would come to mind for most.

As far back as 2005, its scientists were the first in Europe to successfully clone a human embryo. Since then, many global advancements in stem cell research to treat everything from Parkinson's to dementia came from an area less than two square miles in the unassuming party city of Newcastle-Upon-Tyne. The science culture in the city bubbled silently under the radar of popular opinion. Beneath the surface, a network of advancements between different institutions, including the NHS and Newcastle University led the way in genetics. Solving problems others could not. For instance, 3-D printed organs had answered the call of millions in need of transplants. But body parts are not the same as car parts. As a foreign invader, the body rejects most 3-D prints. Each person is unique, and that uniqueness is written in DNA. Only genetics can solve the true problem. And in 2034, by applying genetic manipulation to 3-D printing, organs that would once have been rejected were fully accepted by the host. Tailor made, cooked up from a recipe written in the genes.

The shadow of the King George VI building loomed over Adam. He was grateful for the cold air that seemed to cool his hangover as it washed over him. Outside, the plaque read: School of Pharmacy. His old stomping ground hadn't changed a bit. Inside, he traced the corridors without the need to think. He wandered on autopilot through the main building and into the high-ceilinged reception, which unusually was nestled at the back. Adam waited by the narrow window as the receptionist continued to type. Her long, red hair brushed the old keyboard. The familiar smell of the original parquet floor somehow comforted his swirling brain.

The receptionist looked up. Slightly taken aback by the untidy jacket and dishevelled face that accompanied the police badge. 'Can I help you?'

'I'm here to speak with Professor Cole.'

'He's in a lecture, I think. Let me just pull up his time table.' She flicked the touchscreen and found a glowing blue calendar. 'Yep, he's busy for the next thirty minutes but should be able to see you after.'

'Thanks. Room seven?'

'Er...' The receptionist searched the screen again, and re-emerged with a raised eyebrow. 'Yes, that's right.'

Adam nodded and strolled off before she could ask how he knew. Cole would never give up lecture theatre seven unless he died in it. Even then he would probably haunt the place.

He reached the oak doors, with brass handles dulled and scratched by five generations of hands. Inside he heard the dampened tones of the eccentric academic, his voice rising high and suddenly low as he explained something probably quite boring in the most exciting way possible. He hadn't lost a beat. Adam smiled as he plonked himself into a chair outside and checked the coast was clear before taking another pill. Drug abuse in the school of pharmacy. The irony wasn't lost on him, but the ache in his back had soldiered on since his crash, and now the pain receptors screamed for relief almost as much as his craving. Almost, but not quite. Adam had admitted long ago that the creature of physical pain had morphed into a far more insidious monster of mental dependence.

Adam rubbed his neck. Charlie Lang returned to the forefront of his thoughts. He ran over his idea. Thankfully, the sullen faces of hungover students were a common sight for university lecturers. Adam would be no exception.

The students filed out and Adam caught the tall, stooping figure of Prof Cole. Grey-haired, thin lips, blue piercing eyes. Still sporting his brown dogtooth suit.

'Your thesis was handed in ten years ago, Morell,' he said nonchalantly, without breaking stride.

Adam jumped up and stumbled slightly in following. 'Yeah, I still remember the heart palpitations from the energy drinks. Got a first though didn't it?' He grinned.

'On tuberculosis, wasn't it?'

'Yup.'

The old professor stopped and turned on his heel with a smirk. 'What can I do for you, Adam?'

'I need a word.' He knew the professor loved to speak about his cases. On the odd occasions Adam consulted him, his eyes lit up with the glow of something more exciting. Something juicy to apply his knowledge and finely-tuned mind to.

'My office then,' he said, gesturing to the end of the corridor.

They moved into the well-lit, high walls of the spacious office. Nothing but the computer and holographic screens were younger than 1940. Cole took a measured glance at Adam before pouring a whisky for them both and gesturing for him to sit on an oxblood, high-back Chesterfield. 'Looks like you could do with one of these.' Professor Cole raised his glass. Adam did the same and swallowed a deep draught of the amber liquid with hidden relief.

Cole rested a hip on the edge of his desk. The same old twinkle in his eye that meant he was ready for the question. 'So, what is it?'

Adam wasted no time. Cole always had the decency and shrewdness not to ask more questions than he needed to. And so far, he had never betrayed his confidence. An unspoken agreement reserved for unofficial business. Nothing written down, no cameras, no recordings, no minutes. 'It's just an idea,' he began, taking another slow sip. 'But...I need to know. Is it *theoretically* possible to change someone's DNA so they overdose on a small dose of a drug? Say, if they were to slow down the elimination of the drug? Or maybe even create a toxin as a by-product? I saw the article in the paper about your research. The twisted ladder. If anyone's an expert in DNA alteration and pharmacogenetics, it's you.'

Cole snorted. Adam knew he would have hated being interviewed by the press. He was old school as academics go. No industry affiliation. Science for the sake of science, plain and simple. He was probably dragged into the interview under some sort of last warning. The professor tilted his head and stared up through a long, high stained-glass window that let through a shaft of bright sunshine above the wood panelling. 'It's an interesting question. Theoretically, I suppose it would be. Can't see it getting past the ethics committee, mind you. But I suppose it could be done.' He folded his arms, drumming his fingers across his elbow. He pinched his forehead, almost knitting his eyebrows together in the middle before releasing it. 'I think making someone hypersensitive would be more likely than a toxin though.'

Adam's mind jumped at the comment. 'How would that work?'

Cole scratched his chin and looked back at Adam. 'Well I'm not sure of the details around exactly how the procedure would work. It's certainly possible, especially with today's technology. I suppose they would have to upregulate the receptors somehow. If they could code DNA to make more receptors for a drug than it's supposed to have, and code the enzymes to stop it from being broken down then...'

'You would have something that's effectively an overdose,' said Adam, giving away more excitement than he intended. His head fizzed with possibilities as it combed the cold cases with new hope, landing on Charlie Lang.

The professor paused. 'Is this for one of your cases?'

'Yes.'

Cole waited momentarily, then acknowledged the lack of elaboration with a gentle nod. The unspoken agreement. He finished his drink, sprang up and paced across the room. 'You don't look well, Adam. When did you last sleep?'

Adam snorted derisively, looking away into space. 'A while ago.'

A thin smile drew over Cole's lips. 'You're an addict chasing addicts, Detective Morell. I do hope the irony is not lost on you.'

'Believe me, it isn't. Thanks for the whisky.' Adam stood and placed his tumbler back on the silver serving tray. 'Good to see you, professor.'

A few moments after Adam left, the aging voice called after him down the deserted corridor. 'If this is important to a case, the big question isn't really if it could be done. The question is why?'

For once, Adam felt he knew a lot more than the professor.

19

Nothing Drives Courage Like the Fear of Death

Pearce stabbed the mocha button on the machine. A short, impatient hiss emerged from somewhere within. The cup snapped into the holder and out poured his third of the day. Excessive even for him. Anything to ease the bubbling tension was welcome. DI Morell rarely requested a meeting. When he did, it usually brought sleepless nights and paperwork.

Adam found Maddie at her desk in the office. He led her into a quiet meeting room and ran over his meeting with the professor, leaving out no details other than the prickly point of his own addiction. Then they headed to the canteen for lunch.

'It doesn't prove anything,' said Maddie, scooping up a mouthful of lasagne. Not quite the lunch rush, they sat alone among the sparsely populated tables.

Adam picked up a tall glass, brim-full with orange juice. Somehow, he always craved it on a hangover. 'I know. But it would explain everything. The deaths, even the tox report.'

Maddie gave him a quizzical look. 'There was cocaine found in his blood...'

Adam shuffled forward and rested his elbows on the table. 'Okay. Listen. The death of Charlie Lang was labelled overdose because *some* cocaine was found in his system, fair enough. But it wasn't sky high, agreed?'

Maddie nodded reluctantly.

'So the diagnosis was made based on the fact that he produced the symptoms of overdose, like dilated pupils and breathing difficulty, as well as the presence of *some* cocaine in his blood. The pathologist even said the fact he was a known addict is also taken into account. But we *do* know that the purity of the crack was tiny. So how could it cause an overdose?'

Maddie sighed and stared at him seriously. 'And you think it's through genetic manipulation?'

Adam knew how crazy it sounded. But he also knew there was method in the madness. 'I'm saying nothing else can physically explain it. How else could someone who has taken a low amount of crack cocaine die of a drug overdose? If someone stops them from breaking down the drug and increases the amount of receptors so they become hypersensitive to a low dose. That's how.'

Maddie twisted her fork through her food, staring into space. 'We don't know he took a low amount, that's just based on the sample Magic gave you.'

Adam sighed and ran his hand through his hair. 'Look. I know what it sounds like. But addicts are dropping like flies, overdoses are sky rocketing in the city and the pattern fits across all of my recent cold cases. There wasn't a huge amount of any given drug in any of their bodies when they died. The diagnosis is made on the presence of some level of a drug, the symptoms of overdose and the fact they were known addicts.' He picked up his orange juice and took a swig. 'It even explains the lack of norcocaine in the tox report. If there was only a small amount of cocaine then there's barely any chance of finding any norcocaine.'

A small group of uniformed officers drifted by the table. Maddie waited until they passed by. 'What about the note?'

'This would count as murder. Whoever sent that probably thought he was poisoned. What if they aren't a million miles away? Gene therapy, and the next time you take whatever it is you're addicted to...you die.'

Maddie raised an eyebrow as he downed the orange in one.

'You'll get heartburn.'

'Already got it.' He massaged his chest with a palm and stifled a burp.

'So, do you think Pearce will buy into this?' she asked with a sigh. A creeping concern was burrowing in her consciousness for the man sat before her. She couldn't deny there was some logic in the idea. But seeing was believing in her world. The part of her that had originally thought the case would only last a few days was now truly dead. Clearly this bee in Adam's bonnet was here for a while longer.

'Dunno,' said Adam. 'I'm hoping he'll see something in it. Enough to keep him off my back for a while. But it's protocol to inform him anyway, so you'll be happy about that at least.'

Maddie rolled her eyes as the truth made a hard landing. She tapped her water against Adam's drained glass. 'I'll cheers to that.'

Half an hour later, Pearce glared at Adam over a sandwich. Somewhere above, the lingering smoke of a cigarette was yet to escape the room through the open window. He recounted the story as he had to Maddie.

'Quite the story,' said Pearce, juggling a cigarette and a napkin while wiping his sticky BBQ-sauce-ridden fingers. 'One for the record book of wasted bloody police time. Even if I did believe this...whatever the hell it is, you don't even have any bloody evidence.' He squeezed the napkin and thumped it into the bin beside him.

Adam closed the door. 'I know. It's an idea, but the note is worth chasing up, surely?' Adam flicked the envelope on the desk, now encased in a clear evidence bag. 'Forensics didn't find any DNA, prints or threads on this. Could've been from anyone. But everything is linked; the bruises on their arms...look, I know it's a long shot but surely, it's worth exploring? Why rule it out?' He leaned forward, face inscrutable, glaring into Pearce's eyes, applying as much subtle pressure as possible.

Pearce hesitated, then shook his head firmly.

'Because we don't have time for long shots. I want nice and easy, watertight, where the evidence is stacked in our favour. I want to not look like a bloody idiot in front of a judge while a case is thrown out in front of us.'

'It is possible. I've spoken to an expert. A prof—'

'Adam!' The natural gravel in Pearce's voice churned into a growl. The vein in his right temple bulged, filled with the special reserve of anger that waited at the end of his tether. 'Look at yourself.' He stood up and checked through the window to the main office. A few faces peeped over monitors or through holograms. Pearce closed the blinds and Adam heard him try to hide a deep breath. He returned to the desk with a hushed voice that still held the venom. 'Do you think I don't know about your *pain* problem?'

Adam felt his pulse rising. He felt the weight of the lighter in his pocket pressing against his heart. How much did he know?

Pearce sighed. His voice returned to something softer. Perhaps the softest he could muster. 'What happened to your daughter was...' Pearce searched the air '...horrendous,' he said sincerely. 'But this is a professional environment. For your own good, you're off this case. And if you don't get clean in the next month, I swear on my life I'll write you off, forever.' He glared at Adam and said nothing more, indicating the meeting was over.

Maddie watched as Adam flicked open the door to Pearce's office and stormed across the main floor out of the room. She gave it a few minutes and then followed.

Adam was tucked behind the wheel of his car, staring at the grey road beyond the gate, and at the same time somewhere entirely different. A white car flashed across his mind, onto a grass verge. A blur of yellow, the scream of brakes, the cries, the silence. Her yellow jacket, stained red. The pale face in his arms, soft and beautiful. An empty face still full of innocence. Always the same set of images, and once they started, he was never able to stop them flicking through his mind until the internal film had spent its reel.

The rasp on the window dragged him back. The door clicked. Maddie climbed in quietly beside him. The tear on his cheek lost somewhere in the stubble. For a moment, he didn't recognise her. Half his mind still sitting on a grass verge seven years ago.

He heard himself speak; a flat, defeated voice. 'The case is yours.' He pulled out his lighter and tipped a pill into his hand. There was no point in hiding it.

'Tramadol?' she asked, grateful for the chance to delay the awkwardness of the situation, and at the same time address the other elephant in the room.

'Codeine, originally. Now something stronger.' He swallowed the tablet, and felt the dry smooth muscle of his gullet massaging it down towards his stomach.

'Maybe it's for the best.'

'You don't believe it either, then?'

Maddie gave him a faint squeeze of the hand. 'I didn't say that.'

***

Traffic officer Helen Doors felt her attention drifting as she surveyed the A1 motorway. The grey monotony of the road, the warmth of the car and the twelve-hour shift all pointed to sleep. Coffee was her only ally. She wore the compulsory Day-Glo yellow peaked cap and was glad of the tinted windows to hide it. The rest of the uniform had modernised over the years, but the traffic cop hat stuck like trapped wind.

She watched without interest as the flow of self-driving cars drove by in almost perfect harmony. Stopping distances were matched, no one pulling out unnecessarily, everyone indicating. Behind the wheel, commuters and families paid less attention to the road ahead than they had when she was a girl — talking to their kids in the back seat or sometimes brazenly scrolling through their phones. She clocked their registrations through the car's automatic number plate recognition device on the dash and inputted the offence. A letter would be on their doormat in three weeks. The system had also picked up, logged, and charged two cars for driving without either tax or insurance. The fastest speed she'd clocked in the last hour was a peep over 70 mph. Probably a slightly faulty speedometer. Hardly worth the chase, and certainly not worth logging. Especially when she was fully intending to drive home at eighty herself. There had to be some perks to the job.

Stifling a yawn, she poured another cup of coffee from a thermal flask. As the rim met her lips, a rush of red and black whipped by. The heads-up display on the windscreen read 120 mph. She grinned, flicked on the blue lights and sped down the hard shoulder up to eighty, before merging with the traffic and firing up the siren. Computer systems of the cars around her recognised the emergency service vehicle and drifted away, clearing a clean path for Helen to slam on the accelerator.

* * *

Ten minutes earlier, somewhere between a corner shop and oblivion, Stevie lay in a damp sleeping bag. He drifted from his sleep — the winter chill nipped his nose and pulled his eyes open to the reality he longed to escape. For an addict, sleep is the real sweet relief. He tried to heave himself up, succeeding on his third attempt, and stared at the floor while the headache stamped across his brain. He slowly stuffed his sleeping bag into a rucksack and stooped to collect the small change dropped into his baseball cap, before he clambered around the side street into a battered red Citroën parked across double yellow lines.

The car was dented, uninsured and untaxed, but the ten-year-old whip was still reliable enough. He shoved the rucksack in the back and slipped into the driver's seat. An alcoholic, a heroin addict, and a dealer, he spent money as fast as he earned it.

He set the car to automatically crawl several streets, still reeling from his drunken sleep. Somewhere in the back, discarded bottles and cans slid around the foot wells. On his fifth sporadic turn he was in a maze-like housing estate. That was when he noticed the black prowler filling up the rear-view mirror. *Probably just the drink,* he thought to himself. *Gear makes you tetchy, Stevo. Gear makes you tetchy.*

He took hold of the wheel, de-activated the self-drive and forced himself to take six random turns, never into a cul-de-sac. But on the sixth successive random turn, the car followed like a shadow.

He pushed the Citroën out onto the main roads and down onto the motorway, following the speed limits as they stepped from twenty to thirty to fifty and then seventy. With each increment of acceleration, the prowler matched.

On the open road, he waited for an opportune moment. One where he was momentarily out of the line of sight. A mammoth yellow Ford pick-up slipped in behind him. Without hesitation, Stevie floored the accelerator, weaving frantically between the traffic, undertaking and whipping onto the hard shoulder. As expected, with every move, the car followed, although he fancied a slight gap opened. He racked his brain for who it could be. Ten names came to mind, but this was serious. Whoever they were, they weren't dropping in for a chat. He wiped the cold sweat from his eyes and gripped the steering wheel with white knuckles, partly for control, but largely to keep his own failing body upright.

Blue lights flashed far behind. Too far to help. He fixated on the wing mirrors and the rear view. Another slalom through a series of lorries and he was slightly further ahead. He slipped off the next exit and flew across a roundabout in a chorus of road rage and beeping. Nothing drives courage like the fear of death.

The Citroën slipped onto an industrial estate. A vast expansion of soulless warehouses built in the last decade. The rear mirror was finally clear. Stevie flicked off his lights and prayed.

The last thing he remembered was glass cracking and the airbag hissing as his face whipped towards the wheel.

Then, once again, came the sweet relief of sleep.

20

The Man in Red Trainers

Andy Verne walked and talked like an accomplished gangster. His deep scouse growl fired out a reliable machine gun of curses, and flattery followed just as easily. He was loose enough with his money and clever enough with his tongue to earn the ear of valuable friends at The Warrior's Arms, one of only three boozers on the Nine Acre's council estate. He drank but never used. His clockwork routine ran with military precision. Very few things disturbed his business around the estate. Although, no one could say for sure what exactly his business was, not to the police at least.

He donned new trainers regularly, always bright red, a hooded vest, and designer joggers. Tattoos seeped from under his vest and round his bulging shoulders, betraying the edge of a winged angel that stretched across his back and cut around the front into the claws of a demon, gripping the edge of his chest.

A mid-level guy, he'd done well to carve out a place for himself since his mysterious arrival twelve months ago. But he calmed the pricked ears and sniffing noses with his charisma and genuine stories of the scene in Liverpool. They saw another working-class lad who knew the score. Never put his nose in where it wasn't wanted, and eventually, he was just another hard face in the crowd. He drove a slick car which no one dared to touch. He wore the bright red trainers for consistency — to be noticed and then blend in with the repeated familiarity.

Andy Verne was also an elite undercover police officer; twelve months embedded in the life of Newcastle's underbelly. The reason they brought him from Liverpool: no one knew him. Low risk of an old school friend or neighbour from his real life giving the game away. Easy, considering he wasn't even from Liverpool. That had been his last assignment away from his real home in London. His real name was Sean, but the scouse mode of Andy Verne was now his default. He'd been using the accent for so long he sometimes accidentally used it on calls to his wife.

Only four other people were supposed to know about Sean. His two handlers, the superintendent, and Pearce. For obvious reasons, the less the better.

* * *

Maddie Evelyn had slipped on her gym gear, and threw on a large hoodie to shield her face from the wind and prying eyes. She took the X21 bus to Salisbury Close in Green Meadows. At 2 p.m., only the occasional pensioner used the bus. Maddie eyed an old woman undertaking a well-practised and clearly arduous procedure of standing up, ready for her stop. Gripping the walking stick just right, testing its hold, then shifting her weight forward and lunging up. At her age and condition, failure at any step would mean some kind of broken bone. A leap of faith if there ever was one, just to get home. An old soul trapped on an estate that had changed immeasurably from housing a neighbourhood full of decent, hard-working people, a neighbourhood with a promise that social housing would be the answer. To them, it was a ripe, exotic peach that turned bad and rotted over time. A place that had slid from home to hell in sixty years. Over time, crime infected most streets like a bad cold. Many didn't bother to mow the lawn, clean the gutters, wash the windows. Kids didn't play games in the street unless it involved a fight. As always, places don't ruin things, people do.

Maddie allowed the old woman off before her. A weak smile came back. A smile that wasn't sure whether to trust the simple act of kindness. The bus pulled away. Maddie readied her earphones and jogged through the red brick and pebble dash jungle. No augmented glasses today.

She passed a small group of kids playing truant, and a mother pushing a pram, holding the hand of a four-year-old. She returned to Stainmore Street, where Magic lived, and settled in a bus stop shelter down the road. She sat there for thirty minutes and let two buses arrive and depart before moving on to the park. The central play area was being used by the mother with the baby and toddler. She rocked the pram and watched the four-year-old bouncing merrily around the twisted steel playground frame drenched in graffiti. To him, this was the world; too young and happy to realise his bad luck. This playground was pure joy. What could be better than a swing on a sunny day? One day he would learn, and it would be time to choose a path. Maddie hoped it would be the right one. The mother looked tired, but she looked dependable, well dressed enough for the area. There was hope there.

Maddie sat on a bench and waited for 3 p.m. A few lads walked by trailing a cloud of vape. Their ecstatic laughs and glazed eyes suggested some kind of arrested development. They spotted her as they approached. Her long, thin legs, tight with the leggings, the pretty face protruding from the hoodie not doused in a ton of make up like the other girls around the estate. A novelty.

'Eh lass, fancy a drink?' said the nearest. Both looked like they had been dragged through a sportswear shop and grabbed whatever clothes came to hand, likely funded by a sweet mixture of dole money and theft.

She pretended to ignore them; her earphones still lodged in her ear but turned off. A shadow crowded her vision as they gathered either side.

'Hey, c'mon just a couple of drinks.' He nudged his mate with a burst of boisterous laughter.

Maddie casually reached into the pouch of her hoodie and felt the cold can of mace greet her with a handshake. One friend she could count on.

'Why would I want to go for a drink with you?' She looked him dead in the eye.

He smirked. 'Why wouldn't ya want a bit o this?' he gestured to himself and his wily friend sniggered.

'Because you're a fucking loser. Who spends their Tuesday jobless in a shitty tracksuit wandering round a park?'

The smirk left their faces.

'Do you know who the fuck I am?' His shoulders went back slightly as his chest came out. The stance widened. The attempt to make himself more intimidating ultimately nothing more than a reflex to a damaged ego.

Maddie knew he was likely a nobody in the bigger picture. He might do a bit of dealing, maybe recently threw a few fists in public, so within this square mile he might be mildly important, but ultimately, he was nothing more than a prime candidate for a case study into the failing of modern Britain. Inevitably he would end up as a blurred face on the news or a mug in a mugshot. She held his stare and remained otherwise entirely unmoved.

He moved sideways and pulled out a knife, gesturing it to her cheek. Maddie flinched and moved slightly back. The cold steel whispered by her skin as he toyed with it.

They stood for a moment. Maddie seethed as she scolded herself. Allowing this to happen was beyond stupid. She hadn't expected a reaction this quickly and cursed herself for not being more cautious. To move the mace would mean getting a nasty cut at least. She tensed her jaw as he traced the blunt edge of the blade around her cheek.

'Gorgeous you like, aren't ya. Never seen you before, have you Davy lad?'

'Nah, must be new round 'ere like.'

The blade moved up and flicked her hood back.

Maddie did everything she could to control her breathing. The mace would be about timing. About waiting, and hoping they would distract themselves for the split second she needed. She could feel his hot breath, tainted with the stale notes of alcohol and cigarettes.

'Where do you live, darlin'?'

A crunching of footsteps behind them saw the knife slip up the man's sleeve and just as quickly a smile appeared on their faces to the woman who walked by with her son and baby. She gazed at Maddie for a moment and for a second Maddie saw the pity in her eyes, and yet there was something about her look that said she wasn't surprised, like she'd seen it before. A moment's glance at the man with the knife and she flinched away and hurried on down the path, gesturing the boy to follow. He danced along merrily behind the pram.

Maddie moved. The mace seal broke nicely. The man with the knife screamed as the spray doused the eyes in burning mist. He reeled back, slashing with the blade.

Maddie jumped sideways. Not quick enough. A slight nick to the arm sent the adrenaline into overdrive. She winced and trained the nozzle on the other man, Davy, who had tensed up and backed off, eyeing the can primed in Maddie's hand. Weighing up his options.

'What the fuck is going on 'ere then?' The scouse growl spat from behind. The red trainers and black beard of Andy Verne approached with his dog, an alert Staffordshire Bull Terrier.

Davy stuttered out nothing in particular. His allegiance was to survival, to the hardest man in the room, whoever that may be. Someone to stand behind. That person was now Andy.

'Ere, you two are always fucking dickin' about in the park. Looks like yous have both been done up by this one here though. Wait until this gets round, eh lads.' He strutted towards them and laughed, ignoring the screams of the blind man and nodding to Maddie. 'Nice one love.' Then he paused as he spotted her cut. Davy said nothing, almost awaiting instructions from the big man.

'Are ya thick? Get fuckin' movin', now!' Andy barked. The dog growled instinctively, sensing the threat in his master's voice. He motioned to the blinded man who had now stumbled further away, still fully engaged in nursing his streaming eyes. 'Take this twat with ya.'

Davy backed off, keeping his eye on both Maddie and Andy, then turned and walked away, guiding his blind friend away by the sleeve. When they were a while down the path, he called out.

'We'll get you, ya bitch.'

Andy Verne spoke with a very slight London east end twang. 'DS Evelyn,' he said quietly.

'Impressive accent.'

'Yeah, it's getting old, to be honest. Anyway, I can't hang about. What d'ya want?'

'I think you know.'

21

Telling Tales

As with all autumn nights, mother nature tapped her watch impatiently, and the sun obeyed, descending over the horizon earlier and earlier. Maddie watched the final rays bounce off the dusty window panes of the old pub.

Inside, the irony of The Silver Lining's dreariness was not lost on her. She had found Adam easily enough. He wasn't allowed to disable the tracker on his glasses and even if he tried (which he probably had), he wouldn't have figured it out without breaking them.

The regulars perked up at the sight of Maddie as she removed her augmented glasses. She was used to turning heads. They at least had the respect to look away after she caught them gawping. She smiled faintly to herself and ordered a gin and tonic. Then she made a beeline for a stained-glass booth in the corner where Adam sat beneath a picture of bygone soldiers. She slid into the seat opposite him, facing the bar. The regulars seemed more settled at the sight of a newcomer now that she was with someone. Even if it was that elusive guy who always sat in the shadows. They also knew their chance at 'making a move', as microscopic as it was, had now gone completely.

Adam gave her a faint nod. Heavy bags pulled at his eyelids. 'Checking up on me?' he mumbled, barely glancing up from the pint on the table in front of him.

Maddie noted four empty glasses. No doubt there were two less pills in the lighter-come-container he kept in his inside pocket.

'Thought I might find you here,' said Maddie softly. Adam said nothing and continued to stare down into his liquid escapism, picking up the thread of some interrupted thought or memory.

Maddie went on, 'I'm sorry, Adam. I really am. Although, you're not doing yourself any favours in here.' She looked around at the regulars who had almost melted into the tired furniture, mechanically supping their beers. She felt a wave of sadness. 'You shouldn't be here. What would Clara say if she knew?' Maddie leant over the table separating them.

Adam grunted and looked up at Maddie with bloodshot eyes. 'She's playing away. At least, I think she is. Can't prove it yet.'

Maddie sighed. A rush of frustration came over her. 'Well, if you got rid of that lighter, stopped coming in here and maybe actually followed orders, your life wouldn't be such a car crash.'

Fuck! Her hand went to her mouth. She knew as soon as she spoke. 'Sorry. I meant... that was a poor choice of—'

'Yeah, that's you, isn't it? Thought you might be different.' He snorted and shook his head.

'What do you mean?' Maddie sat back into the floral tapestry seat.

'You're smart, Eveyln. Smarter than the rest in that so-called police force. Your problem is the book. All you're bothered about is getting back to London with a clean record and a nice promotion.' Maddie pursed her lips as Adam went on. 'What? You think I wouldn't know about your situation?' Maddie leaned forward again and spoke through gritted teeth.

'Is this about the Lang case? You want me to follow your story about some kind of genetic manipulation? You can't just...there are rules, Adam.'

'There it is. Text book, that's what your nickname should be. Fucking box ticker. Rules...' He almost spat the word. 'Open your eyes, Maddie, there *are* no fucking rules here. How do you know who to trust? By following the rules you're trusting the police force, the system. People like Luke Marshall *own* the system.' He shook his head at the thought. 'Look at Magic for crying out loud! My best informant is a bloody drug dealer who I keep out of prison in exchange for titbits of information.'

Adam glared at Maddie in silence for a second, before she broke the stare and took a sip of her drink. 'If you knew nothing else about this department, that would be enough to know the rules are done. And don't think it's any different in London, by the way. Think your boss Chrissie Richards doesn't have any skeletons in her closet? Trust me, I've heard things...'

Adam swilled another mouthful and turned over his right hand. The lighter was nestled in his palm. He rubbed his thumb over the poppy embossed on the front and became lost again in his own thoughts. Maddie sat nervously, her own thoughts racing.

'What's with the poppy? Is it a Remembrance Sunday thing, from your army days?'.

Stalling, thought Adam. Maybe a chink in the armour. He spoke more softly. 'I suppose it is partly. And obviously poppies make opium, so there's some irony with the pills. But mostly it's because Poppy was her name.' Her eyes dropped to the lighter once more.

'Your daughter?'

Adam swallowed the ball of pain that swelled in his throat whenever he said her name.

'You know, the two behind the wheel were both known dealers. Went down a year later for possession with intention to sell.'

Maddie fell silent.

'Listen,' he went on. 'If you've nothing to say, then leave me alone. Doubt your boyfriend would be happy to know you're spending another evening in a pub with me.'

Maddie was stifling her own tears. Adam felt a tinge of guilt somewhere deep within. A blunt feeling, numbed by the alcohol and opium playing tag team at dulling his senses.

'Yeah, we're erm. We're having a break. Permanent one probably. Long distance just isn't me and Jake barely responds to my texts, anyway.'

Adam nodded his understanding and the stone face broke slightly into something that resembled sympathy.

'Sorry. Suppose we've all got secrets.'

Maddie sighed and took two shot glasses from a passing waitress, doing the rounds for extra tips. 'That's why I'm here,' she quipped. 'This isn't the table of the drunk lone junkie, it's actually the table of shit relationships.' She held the shots in the air.

Adam cracked a smile and took one from her hand.

Maddie's eyes crinkled in the corner. She took a deep breath and sank half her shot. 'Listen, I'm not naive. I know how it works. It's just, it's not how it's supposed to work. Certainly not how my dad always made it seem working for the Met. I know he was probably sugar-coating the whole thing. It's just...if I tell you what I know, one black mark and a clean record is gone forever. I don't know if I can.' She finished the shot and shoved the glass towards the rest of the collection.

'I suppose the question is, what could happen if you don't?'

Maddie swallowed hard. 'It's possible someone could die.'

He nodded slowly. 'Not much of a decision then?'

'I know. I, it's just I shouldn't even know it, anyway. The whole thing is fucked up.' She covered her face with her hands.

'Maddie, it's your decision.'

She stared through her fingers at the poppy pill case sat on the table, and the augmented glasses folded away in the shadow of the wall. She took a deep breath, withdrew her hands, then she spoke.

'I know who Duke is.'

Adam lifted his head. He forced himself through the stupor of the drugs to a place clear enough to think.

'Are you serious? How long have you known?'

'Only today for sure. Duke was the nickname of my ex from a few years ago. I thought it could just be a coincidence. He didn't even put the note in *my* pocket and last I heard he was in Liverpool. But then I remembered, I thought I'd seen someone similar in Green Meadows when we visited Magic. Just a glimpse. He's grown a beard and his hair's longer. So, I went to check. Got into a bit of a scrap with some idiots. And there he was, walking that bloody dog, same time he used to. Like clockwork.'

Adam was silent for a moment as he rubbed his stubble, then said: 'Thank you. For telling me. We need to set up a meeting. What's he doing in Green Meadows?'

Maddie said in a hushed voice, 'he's an undercover. From London, did his training in the Met.'

'Did he say anything? About Charlie?'

'No. He said he would only speak if you were there. Somewhere private.'

'Remember the stakes here. It's like you said...someone could die. Charlie might not be the last. He certainly isn't the first, if I'm right, and if this guy knows something then we need to try.' Adam peered around the booth to check no one was lingering nearby. 'And...if it helps in some way, you can't really break the rules if the system is already broken. Can you?'

Maddie nodded. She flipped her phone so it was facing up and typed.

Can we meet? He's in — send.

The pair looked at each other for a few seconds in silence, then both their eyes were drawn down to the phone lighting up on the table....*9 pm, I'll drop a pin.*

A moment later, the pin came through, a precise location tacked onto the map. It sat somewhere in the middle of Jesmond Dene.

'Nice spot to be fair,' said Adam, raising an eyebrow. 'Maybe he's trying to rekindle some of the old romance?' He grinned for the first time.

Maddie reactively gave him a playful kick under the table. 'Shut it.'

They spent the next few hours in the pub. Adam decided he would switch to drinking lime and soda. And in the subsequent hours he sobered up, and the opioid loosened its steadfast grip on his senses. He felt some semblance of clarity and more comfortable than he had in a long time. Perhaps it was meeting someone who knew his story and didn't seem disgusted by his ongoing waltz with drink and morphine? He noticed a small change in Maddie as well. A subtle opening up. Like she'd been keeping herself locked away and projecting the 'perfect' cop, while inside the real person, with problems and flaws yearned to be heard.

Adam came back to the table at around six, with another lime and soda and a lemonade for Maddie.

'Should've seen the looks that lot gave me when I ordered this,' said Adam, throwing his eyes to the regulars perched on the bar stools. She glanced at the array of body shapes, from grotesquely fat to sinewy thin, all figures and sizes spread across eight bodies. She gave them a wave and a smile. They shifted and turned back to their conversations.

'Don't antagonize 'em,' laughed Adam.

'What's their deal, in here every day?'

'Alcoholics. Plain and simple.' Adam shrugged. 'Some of them hit the pies hard as well, and the thin ones stay thin because they barely eat. Plus, smoking increases your metabolism and suppresses your appetite, and some of them smoke like chimneys.' He looked over at the bodies. 'They sit in here and put the world to rights. Plough themselves with pints, pop out for the occasional cig, and wait for death. Worse places to wait, I suppose.'

At 8 p.m., they made their way to the car. Maddie felt the right thing to do was to drive it manually. They stopped in a car park beside Jesmond Dene. The leafy green of the Victorian wooded valley melted into nighttime shadows. The air was crisp in the strange two-mile park, a stone's throw from the city. One minute's walk away and you were on a street with dog groomers, cafés, and pubs. Slip through a set of stone and iron gates, and there it was. Like going through the wardrobe. The place was something of a tourist attraction, with its own waterfall, overlooked by a quaint arched stone bridge that spanned a river. A million shadows and secluded spots ripe for a quiet word. No one around except a lone figure stood among the trees.

Andy Verne gave a short sharp whistle as Adam and Maddie passed by on the well-worn path of the river bank.

He had changed his clothes to a set of jeans, a jumper, jacket, and a baseball cap. The red trainers were swapped out for some black indistinguishable shapes in the darkness below. He beckoned them through the tree line into a small clearing.

'Thanks for coming,' Maddie whispered, approaching him.

He nodded. 'Let's get this done.' The sharp scouse accent was nowhere now. His head turned to Adam. 'DI Morrell.'

Even with only the faint splash of light from a lamp by the river, Adam saw plainly the strained lines of undercover work written onto his face.

'Duke.'

Duke raised his chin, but otherwise was clearly in no mood for pleasantries. He checked once more for passers by and launched straight into it. 'Magic Coyne sold Charlie the gear and I'd already tested it before you. Same conclusion. Street garbage quality.' His gaze remained on Adam. 'But there's been some rumours going about...people going missing. A day or two, ya know, and then back like it was nothin'. Picked up nothin' but a nasty scar. Barely any memory. You know what I'm talkin' about.' He shot a knowing look at Maddie. 'Then usually, give or take another day, they're dead. Overdose. But, and this bit is where it really pricked my ears. Word is some of them keep banging on about a lab.'

'What do you mean?' Adam said quickly.

Duke shrugged. 'I don't know, I suppose like experimentation.'

Maddie raised an eyebrow. 'You're kidding?'

Adam couldn't resist shooting her a told-you-so look.

'Is there anyone? With a lab?'

Duke sucked his teeth and again checked the desolate wooded park for signs of life.

'So, there is someone?' pressed Maddie.

Duke sniffed. 'Apparently the Bright brothers have one. For cooking up whatever it is they sell. Mostly weed, I think. But rumour is, they've got lab tech.' His eyes moved from Maddie to Adam. 'And the middle one, Tony, he's some biology wonder-kid. And then there's the fact that no one's seen their youngest brother in over three days. Not unusual, but the rumours are what they are, y'know. Anything looks suspicious.'

'Where is it supposed to be?' Adam asked.

Duke rubbed his hands together for warmth. 'No one knows. No one knows if it's even real or where they live. But they do own a café on Grey Street. Can't miss it.'

'Why didn't you raise this with your handler?'

Duke laughed. 'How did that work out for you? Yeah, word spreads fast.'

'Okay. So why me?'

'Because you're invested in this. Can't let it go, can ya? And you've got a reputation for knockin' down doors without the er, required documentation, shall we say. Which, incidentally, is the only way you're ever going to get close to this. If *this* even is something.'

Adam saw nothing to suggest a lie. No fidgeting, no looking away at the wrong time, no stalling his answers. And besides, why would he lie? Put himself in danger. Exposing his cover to one more person. Which left only one question in his mind. 'How do you know you can trust me?'

Duke nodded at Maddie. 'Because she does.'

22

How Do You Choose Your Last Ever Drink?

Stevie Wilks died in the corner of The Leazes pub. Propped up against the wall, one hour before anyone noticed. It wasn't unusual for people to grab forty winks after a pint. The discovery was made by the kid who collected glasses, too young to serve behind the bar, not that it stopped him. That small fact would get the bar a fine after the police took his statement.

Stevie's hands had shaken when he'd ordered, passing a fluttering, grubby £10 note across the bar. That was not unusual. His pale face clamoured with sweat, but that was also not unusual. He smelled vaguely of a man unwashed for at least three days, again, not unusual, and nor was the sickly scent of discount shop deodorant he used to thinly mask this fact. There were a few signs when the young barman came to think about it. Slurring a bit more than usual. Stumbled badly when crossing the bar. Strange for Stevie, on reflection, but not unusual for the clientele of this establishment.

Somehow, he shuffled to the bench in the corner and the golden liquid met his desert dry lips and mouth. The pale lager would be the river he would sail towards the light. The clouds of heaven or the fires of hell, but light nonetheless. He didn't mind which, he visited both every day.

Stevie began to sweat more as his heart hammered faster. The engine ticking over at higher revs than it was designed for. The odd beat missed here and there, the pistons out of sync. Then came the sudden cold and the rising heat as the dial of his body's temperature regulator span out of control.

He thought about the last two days. A blank space. Not an unusual occurrence, but this felt different. Flickers of memory. The sharp pain in the arm. The flashes of blue plastic curtain. The faintest smell of cinnamon and coffee.

Stevie pushed it aside. It didn't matter now. He was strangely calm. In the end, he knew he had lived the last ten years on borrowed time as far as the life of a junkie goes. Like a loaf of bread surpassing its sell by date, miraculously resisting any mould, until one day, the inevitable green spec appears. He recalled his first dance, and his last. Stevie thought about his last happy holiday when he was ten; the school trip to France and the sun beating on the surface of the river by the cheap hotel. He thought fleetingly about the life he could have lived. His life before alcohol, before drink carried him on the rollercoaster that followed. The girl he was supposed to marry. For a long time now, to her, he had been nothing more than a fleeting memory, and he had come to terms with that. She might hear about his death, but perhaps not — or not for a few years, because her life had taken her into different circles, a world away from the nightmare that had been Stevie's life. He thought about how sharp his mind had been, quicker than most. And how, for the last thirty years, he had wasted it on slogging through the day, too focused on receiving the next fix to prove useful for much else. He thought about the dreams he had as a boy and the warmth they gave, the possibilities of a life ahead.

The usual withdrawal symptoms of anxiety and suspicion fell away in his last dance with booze. The buzz faded, but rather than the empty void that usually followed, a spec of light and serenity filled his body. As he felt his organs shutting down, he smiled, took a last glug of lager, and sailed the golden river towards the sunset of his final breath.

When his body was finally noticed, the young bartender gave him a sheepish nudge before feeling the dampness on the cold face. He called over the owner and the small crowd gathered. An ambulance was summoned. Someone tried to do CPR and succeeded only in breaking two ribs. But Stevie Wilks was long gone.

The paramedic confirmed the death with two fingers pressed to the carotid artery of the neck. The police were not far behind, and the crowd thinned rapidly in their presence. The police constable relished the chance to walk into the known crime den and close it down without any backlash. He ignored the daggers and poisonous glances that flew his way, and passed the message onto his sergeant through his augmented glasses. The chain of command was followed up to Pearce, who grunted his acknowledgement of the email.

A few minutes later, he passed the message to DS Maddie Evelyn.

23

Out of Order

Adam chose early morning for the door knock. This wasn't some two-up-two-down shit box on Green Meadows. He would need to knock politely and talk his way in.

He knew the Bright brothers would have to create the illusion of innocence. Of having absolutely nothing to hide. Any whiff of suspicion would need to drown in the aroma of pastries, coffee, and cakes.

Unless...they had nothing to hide. The thought brought an icy chill to the bones. It crossed through the background of Adam's thoughts like a bad extra on a film set, out of place and ruining the take. It all depended on the quality of the intel. And on that front, Adam had once again put his trust, and now his reputation, in the word of the street. Duke might be a cop, but when it came down to it, his information was based on street hearsay.

Adam and Maddie slept in the car, taking it in shifts to watch the café across the street. No one had entered or left since the gaggle of gossiping employees (most verging on retirement age or past it) had locked up at 7 p.m. Time would tell how much they knew.

'No wonder they make great cakes,' said Adam. 'Looks like he's got a team of grandmas working for him.'

Adam kept his custom of pulling the relevant files before knocking on a door. Luna displayed two of the Bright brothers. Dylan and Eliot. The first file was thick with various drug charges since the age of seventeen, a brief stint in prison, more petty dealing and using since then. When all was said and done the gaunt face of Dylan Bright was nothing more or less than the face of an addict. Through the eyes of many, a criminal, a menace, and drain on society. The other view, Adam's view – he was unwell, in need of medical care, a product of his environment and a few bad choices. Capable of a life beyond addiction. Capable of giving back. Adam knew this from experience.

The image of Eliot Bright accompanied a much shorter list of offences. Some violence in his youth, possession of cannabis, and not much more. Nothing for the last ten years. Adam zoomed in on the mug shot. The shrewd face that sat atop a mountain of muscle belonged to a criminal. Just one too clever to get caught. Call it intuition or experience, he was certain of that fact.

The third brother came up with no hits. Other than the affiliation to his brothers by way of his mother's womb, Anthony was clean.

Maddie's watch lit up on the hour at 7 a.m., beside a reading of her heart rate: a cool sixty beats per minute. She had fallen asleep quicker than Adam could only dream of.

He watched for the next half an hour as the gaggle of staff re-entered the building. The looming figure of Eliot followed a few minutes after. At 8 a.m., the sign on the door was flipped to 'Open' by a wrinkled hand.

Adam nudged Maddie gently. 'It's time,' he said. He noticed the heart rate monitor climb to ninety as she woke, registered what was happening and unclipped her seat belt.

'Morning to you too,' she grumbled, after clearing her throat.

They walked across Shakespeare Street to where it intersected the head of Grey Street.

'Want me to wait at the back? In case they leg it?'

'They won't,' said Adam. 'If Duke is right, they couldn't run and risk the lab being found. It would only bring more attention.'

Adam remembered to add some of the chirpiness he assumed an early morning coffee go-getter might wear before pushing through the plush glass door of the café come bakery. The first customers. One member of staff was covering the counter.

'Can I speak to Mr Eliot Bright, please?' said Adam, smiling.

'Oh, er, yeah, what's it about?' asked the woman, sensing the formality. 'You the health inspector?' She pushed a pair of pointed thick-rimmed glasses up her nose.

'No, no. Actually, we're from the police.'

Her eyes lit up at the sight of the badge. She hid her excitement poorly. 'I'll just get him.' The grey perm disappeared into the depths of the building.

Adam felt a quiet tension bubbling. There was no knowing for sure how Eliot Bright would react. *Maybe Maddie was right?* The thought was banished. He felt confident in his gut, and the big man didn't disappoint.

Eliot Bright appeared with a warm smile. His lumbering frame ducked through the door and towered over the counter. Somewhere behind him, the perm of the old lady hovered.

'Mr Bright. I'm DI Morell, this is DS Evelyn. Mind if we have a word?'

'Be my guest,' said Eliot. He was clearly adopting his soft café voice. Suppressing the boom lurking within those lungs. 'Why don't you come into the office.' He gestured to the door behind the counter.

'I'll just wait here,' said Maddie. 'Wouldn't mind a coffee, actually. Didn't have the best sleep.' She turned her gaze to the board displaying an eclectic choice of beverages.

'Certainly. Gwen, do you mind?'

Gwen clearly didn't mind, and beamed back at Maddie. A chance to be part of some action beyond the humdrum of the day-to-day business. A chance to ask a few prying questions on behalf of the ladies of the bakery. And to a detective, no less.

Adam's instinct told him then and there, if there was something shady going on, Gwen, and probably the other regular staff, had absolutely no idea. She was clearly chomping at the bit to inform her colleagues that the police were here. Already relishing the thought of hogging the spotlight in the tea room. If she knew even the faintest whisper of a hidden lab, so would everyone in her book club, and eventually, so would the police.

Adam followed through the door behind the counter. Eliot blocked most of the narrow passage that followed. The air grew warmer and richer with the smell of fresh baking. A door appeared on one side labelled 'Staff Only'. It opened as another of the permed ladies emerged from the small cloak room and cleaning cupboard. They stood aside to let her pass. On the other side of the passage was a cramped office space containing a battered computer and paperwork. About the right size for a small business. Eliot entered the office, allowing a view beyond to where the passageway ended, with a large open kitchen cooking up the soothing scent of freshly-baked bread. A few more employees shifted about the stone floor.

'Only the one chair, sorry,' said Eliot. The giant man in the apron looked almost comical in the cupboard sized office. Adam thought about closing the door, then decided that would probably make it even worse, so lingered in the doorway.

'Nice watch, business must be doing well,' said Adam, nodding to the Rolex dangling from the thick wrist.

Eliot chuckled. 'It's a fake, if I'm completely honest. Bought it in one of them Turkish markets on holiday in Marmaris.'

Not a bad answer, thought Adam. A sharp lie. The watch was as real as the platinum ring on his little finger, and gold chain bracelet on his other wrist.

'Listen, I'm sorry to say, but there's been a few accusations about your brother.'

'Which one?'

Adam suppressed the urge to laugh. *As if he didn't know.* Another quick lie, a play for time. 'Dylan. You don't happen to know where he is, do you? No fixed abode, according to our files. He's a hard man to find.'

Eliot grunted. 'You're tellin' me.'

'So, no idea where he is, then?'

'Not seen him for a few days,' Eliot replied, rubbing his forefinger over his top lip.

Adam nodded. 'Did he seem okay?'

'What do you mean?'

'Was he unwell?'

Eliot simply shrugged, smiled, and bit his tongue.

One benefit of Luna was it kept people calm. Smart criminals don't want trouble. Constant filming means any aggression is caught, and the evidence leads to a conviction in court. So, in a way, the whole conversation had been his version of the ideal answers. Towing the line. Adam decided to take the first step to finding the truth. He took the glasses off, powered them down, and pocketed them.

'So, I'll ask again,' said Adam. 'Was he unwell?'

Eliot said nothing for a moment, taking his time to consider the detective further. He decided this one had shown him a courtesy. He would return the favour in a small way. 'You know fine well he's a smack head. He's never well.' He shook his head. 'Why? Is he in trouble?'

'There's been some suggestion that he's working with Luke Marshall's crew.'

Eliot shook his head firmly. 'That's bollocks.'

'It's just a question.' Adam gave him a glimpse of the stern eye he reserved to remind people that his politeness was not the same as weakness.

'He wouldn't last ten minutes with them.'

'Well, maybe *he* thinks he would?'

There was a moment's pause. Adam knew the oiled cogs of the man before him were slipping through the gears, whirring within the machine as he weighed his options.

'Up to you, big man,' said Adam.

'You don't believe me.'

'Not really...'

'I'm not asking. I know you don't.'

Adam felt his short fuse beginning to burn. He changed tact. 'You don't mind if I take a look in the back room, do you?'

Eliot gestured with a mammoth hand. 'Be my guest.'

Bold, thought Adam. Could have asked for a warrant. The bad extra on set walked across his mind's eye again. The seed of doubt. He pushed it away. There *was* something here. This feller was smart, no doubt about it. A few years Adam's senior, he was a world above Magic Coyne. Asking for a warrant would have showed his hand.

Adam nodded and walked briskly into the large stone kitchen. He felt the presence of the giant following behind him.

Maddie was already there. Scanning the room. Her eyes fixed on a broken fridge in the corner nestled among some boxes. Gwen busied herself with weighing ingredients, oblivious to the snooping. She looked even more like a grandma than before. Showing her granddaughter the tap-your-nose secrets of the rolling pin and oven.

'What the—' The soft café voice slipped as Eliot paused to rein in the temper and re-phrase his question. He turned his glare on Gwen. 'What's she doing back 'ere?'

Gwen's cheeks turned red. 'Sorry, I...she said she just wanted to see how it was made. Didn't see any harm.'

'Go. Now. Come back in an hour.' The other two employees stopped and exchanged a look. 'You two, as well. And flip the sign to closed on your way out.'

The three women sheepishly removed their aprons and left quietly. Eliot waited until the bell rang over the front door before he spoke.

'No way to treat your staff,' said Maddie, raising an eyebrow. 'She seemed lovely.'

Eliot's jaw moved as his teeth ground beneath the muscle. Adam caught him taking a brief glimpse of the fridge in the corner. 'You need a warrant. Show me one, or get out.'

'Could do. Or we could just place you under arrest. Say you attacked us. Isn't that right DS Eveyln?'

'Oh, yeah, easy,' said Maddie, trying to seem natural.

'You're bent then?' Eliot spat. 'Scum.'

'It's an art form,' said Adam, waving away the insult. 'She's still learning, though.'

Eliot paused. His eyes darted. Adam broke the silence. 'So, you can either show us what's in that fridge now, or after we've charged you for assaulting an officer.'

The big man froze. He sighed heavily. Too heavily, as though breathing a world of worries in and back out again. When he was done, he calmly grabbed a large wooden bread roller.

'Maddie, go!' Adam dived at Eliot, spearing the tree-trunk-sized waist. Eliot reeled and brought his elbow down on Adam's back. He moved to swing the rolling pin, but Adam was up, and sent a handful of flour towards his eyes.

'Fuck!' Eliot bellowed, tossing the heavy roller as though it were a pencil, taking a chunk out of the wall. The back of his dinner plate hands rubbed at his powder-filled eyes.

Adam turned, expecting to see Maddie on her way out. She was, in a manner of speaking — halfway through the fridge door — not the exit.

Adam quickly followed her, edging through the frame into the moist drafty room beyond. Iron fingers took a fist full of his jacket and held him there. The face of Eliot Bright glowered at him. Filled with a strange mixture of fire and fear.

'Don't...' his voice cracked, betraying his desperation. 'You don't have a warrant. I'll have your jo—'

CLICK.

The sound was gentle and final.

Eliot glanced at the handcuffs securing him to the handle fitted to the false back of the fridge. He released his grip on Adam.

Maddie and Adam stood back at the top of a spiral staircase.

Eliot breathed deeply. A tear stung the corner of his eye. He let it go. The sound of his cursing was muffled by the hand that wiped his face.

Adam nodded. They descended the stairs. The smell of weed smacked the senses on the third step down. The site of it came on the ninth. And before them was revealed a vast underground drug farm. In the corner, an array of lab equipment was being tentatively protected by Tony Eliot wielding a crow bar, trembling.

'Holy sh—' Maddie's words fell away. 'How the hell?'

A loud clang fell down the staircase. Eliot Bright sauntered down the last few stairs behind him. A tired man in almost every sense, tired of hiding secrets, tired of the life he'd chosen, almost dragging each leg. The door handle was in his fist, still attached to the handcuffs. Adam tensed again. Ready for a second round. He felt Maddie do the same. Then, briefly, Eliot nodded to Tony, and the thin, slick-haired man dropped the crowbar. The game was up and they knew it.

Adam moved over to the lab area. He recognised some of the equipment from his university days. Centrifuge, microscope, fume hood, temperature-controlled cupboard, ultra-cold freezer. Plant cuttings and pots were arranged on one bench, and soil brushed neatly into small heaps. On the other side of the room, a narrow camp bed, microwave, toilet, and fridge were plumbed and wired.

'Where's Dylan?' asked Adam.

Eliot frowned. 'You're not interested in...this,' he said, waving his arm to the room.

'I never said that. But I'm more interested in Dylan.'

There was a moment of complete silence.

Through a door halfway along the wall, a light flickered, followed by a thud. Adam ran towards it and pushed through to the crumpled shape of Dylan Bright sleeping on a mattress with little for company beyond a glass of water, a bucket, a few slices of bread, and a toilet. His hand was cuffed on a long chain to a pipe fitted to the wall. A TV played the news quietly. Dylan Bright whimpered.

'I'm calling it in,' said Maddie.

Suddenly, Tony and Eliot twitched. One for the crow bar, the other for a pair of scissors. Maddie sensed it as soon as the words came out of her mouth.

'No!' Adam blurted. 'We're not calling it in.'

The Bright brothers froze.

'Why?'

'Because...he hit the nail on the head.' Adam nodded to Eliot. 'The team can't be trusted.'

'They've kidnapped their own brother,' Maddie said, looking at her partner like he had taken too many of his pills.

'It's for his own good,' said Adam.

Maddie frowned.

'The equipment isn't here, Maddie. It wasn't them.'

'What wasn't us?' protested Eliot. This convinced Adam further. There was genuine confusion behind the cold eyes and beard. Perhaps those eyes weren't so cold.

Adam pointed at Maddie. 'You know what it's like. Someone in the station finds out and all of a sudden there's a leak. Before you know it, we're clinging onto nothing.' He turned to Eliot. 'You're trying to get him clean, aren't you?'

Eliot nodded. 'Believe me, we've tried everything. This was the last resort, and he's getting there to be fair. Almost a week in now.'

'What is it, crack?'

Tony nodded. 'And the rest.'

'Have you given him anything? To wean him off?'

'Why?' asked Tony.

'Have you given him any?!' Adam said louder, taking a step closer to Eliot.

'Not a thing.'

Eliot stepped into the room and examined the shivering shape in the bed.

Adam crouched beside Dylan. 'Because one more hit and he's a dead man.'

24

Somewhere Between Grey Street and Oblivion

The ebb and flow of consciousness had been playing with Dylan for the last four days, swinging a pendulum between the agonising pain of reality, and a place of sweet relief where the lights slowly faded into sleep.

Awake, the cold sweat was always the first convincing sign he was no longer dreaming, opening the floodgates to dread and worry. After a moment of nauseating panic, he remembered where he was. The adrenaline rush drifted away and he suddenly became aware of his aching muscles, and the swirling pool of vomit coiled in his stomach, waiting to strike. The toilet in the corner had been cleaned, and the mop had wiped up what hadn't met its mark, leaving the signature scent of bleach hovering over the whole experience.

The coil unwound itself violently and without warning, sending a feeble cup of bile and undigested bread into the bucket beside him. The dregs dribbled onto his sweatshirt. *Was that a new sweatshirt?* He didn't remember buying it. Somewhere in the abyss, his clothes had been changed. How long had they been like that? He turned towards the wall and curled up, tucking his hands into his face, breathing slowly. Each breath a minor victory. A step forward. A slight whiff of soap clung to the skin of his fingers. He kept them close, anything to mask the acrid, soulless stench of bleach.

After an hour or so of agony, uncertainty and fear, the pendulum swung, the feeling came, and the light of his mind waned into oblivion. Not a deep sleep. That would be too easy. This was something weak, lingering just beneath the rippling surface of slumber. Here, the same dream appeared at some point or another. The crinkle of a plastic curtain. A bright light and a soft chair. The hollow tap of an empty paper coffee cup placed onto a table in front of him. For a second, he saw the logo of the Bright and Sons bakery. The blindfold went over his face before he could catch anything else. A little too tight. He asked for it to be loosened, but nothing happened. The light burned again. Then, the smell of cinnamon found his nostrils before the sharp pain in the arm. Finally, the lights went out in his head and the dream shifted elsewhere, or dragged him back to life. Repeated, over and over.

More than once he had awoken to find the room coated in black plastic. The hallucinations came and went as they pleased. A demon in his head playing with him on a set of strings. A blink, and Luke was there, stood by the door under the glaring light bulb, watching. Another blink and he was gone. Replaced by the sobbing man, tied to a chair with the screwdriver in his thigh and a hood over his head. The first time, Dylan had watched as Luke reappeared, and with a malicious smile and flourish, removed the hood from the man in the chair as though revealing the prize on a TV game show. The hellish, bloodied mess stared manically with one eye. Somehow still sobbing quietly despite the bullet having torn away a quarter of the skull. After that, Dylan always closed his eyes tight, like a young boy afraid of the monster under the bed. Still, the whimpering of the man continued, incessantly begging for help until at last the pendulum swung and, mercifully, sleep took Dylan.

His mind swirled with the hands of the clock for four days before anything resembling reality found its way his through his ears. The voices and visions continued; though none that convinced him they were anything more than his own tormented thoughts. Not until the fourth day. An unfamiliar deep tone, like a jagged knife that cut each word deliberately. Something about a boy. Dylan's focus slipped briefly as sleep tugged on his leash. His own hand swept across his cheek and rubbed harshly at his eyes, forcing consciousness on himself. The voice went on.

'I know exactly what it sounds like. This is evidence.'

Dylan heard the silence of his brothers' contemplation. The snort from Tony, and his fast retort.

'Genetic manipulation. Why the hell would someone do that to Dylan?'

'I don't know,' said the voice.

Eliot spoke, worried, 'This isn't exactly concrete. How did you even get this?'

A phone vibrated, then a woman spoke. Her voice was more tightly wound and southern. Unable to conceal a sudden sense of urgency. 'Adam, we need to leave. We shouldn't...'

'There's no reason to...'

'There's been a, well, it's police business. I have to go.'

A discord of scraping chair legs as someone stood and two others followed. Dylan slipped into the dream again, finally yielding to the pull of the pendulum. And there, once again, came the smell of cinnamon.

25

Frère Jacques

A new message waited in the encrypted inbox. Black-gloved fingers danced over the password and the screen lit up. The white glare was the main source of light in the room. Only the cheap desk lamp stood by an armchair in the corner offered a shy yellow counterglow. This stood atop a stack of books on birds and gardening, which reached up to the arm, offering its service as a side table. A plastic foldable table stood adrift in the centre of the room, on top of which a pot of purple orchids fought for the scraps of artificial light. In the drab and sparsely-furnished industrial room, with metal pillars, barren wooden floor, and flaking walls of painted white brick, the orchids looked obscenely out of place. The only other piece of furniture was an immaculately made bed, wearing grey sheets folded with deliberate precision.

The occupier, a tall man, with sharp narrow eyes tucked under thick but trimmed black eyebrows. His jaw was hard and square, set below high cheekbones. The hair was trimmed on the back and sides, fading up to a set of thick, tidy curls. He wore a tailored navy blue linen suit and black tie over his olive skin.

The man closed his old 2030 laptop without another look, dousing the room in darkness, fought only by the little desk lamp atop the pile of books. He placed the laptop down beside him on the bed in a slow, almost robotic motion. An arm reached underneath the bed and he withdrew a small brown leather satchel. He lifted it like a museum curator and placed it beside him, smoothing the sheets where they wrinkled.

The man whistled a clean and practiced rendition of 'Frère Jacques' quietly. He had a fondness for nursery rhymes. They soothed the unconscious mind as they had when he was a boy. He whistled them to all of his victims, especially the ones in the most distress.

The clasps of the satchel were carefully unclipped. He reached within and withdrew a pouch of thin cotton tied with elastic. The man removed the elastic and rolled out the cotton to reveal three needles loaded with clear liquid, sealed with a sterile plastic cap. He examined one, peering through the thin cylinder of liquid at the light of the reading lamp. Satisfied, he placed them back in the pouch, refastened the elastic, and moved it to one side.

The last notes of the nursery rhyme ended and he reached again into the satchel and withdrew a fully loaded handgun, polished to the point where the black surface caught even the smallest hint of light. Beside this, he placed a handsome flick knife with an ivory handle that curved in four loops to double up as a fierce set of brass knuckles.

On detecting a faint spot of dried blood on the blade, he withdrew a white cotton handkerchief. He tongued the cotton until it was sodden and then set about rubbing at the mark. Slowly the white material stained as the blade shone. He held the handkerchief out as though it were infected and dropped it into the satchel.

With a sharp flick, the blade twirled around a forefinger, making the loop five times before being caught in a smooth grip. It slotted perfectly into a sheath just under the right arm, fastened to the chest. The gun went into a holster fastened to the left side of the chest, also under the arm. The man practiced withdrawing them, pulling the gun and then the knife from their houses in two fluid motions. In less than two seconds they were both ready, the gun poised to fire under the itchy trigger finger of the right hand, and the blade interlaced within the fingers of the left.

Methodically, he returned the weapons to their case. The clasps were re-sealed, and he slid the satchel back under the bed. Then he lay back, motionless, eyes closed.

A muffled whimper fell through the air. The man's nose wrinkled; his thick eyebrows frowned slightly. The leather gloves rubbed their fingers together and he sat up. Again, crying seeped from the cupboard. He moved over and withdrew a polished key on a retractable keyring fastened to a belt loop of his trousers. He slipped the key in the lock, twisted, and pulled the thick wooden door. On the floor of the cupboard, curled up and shivering with panic, a woman flinched, hiding behind an arm. Her eyes squinted, starved of light and now blinded by the luminescence of the feeble desk lamp as though it were the sun. A sense of renewed dread filled her as she stared up at the sharp silhouette, which stood unfeeling in the doorway.

The man moved away and returned with a bottle of water, which he dropped beside the desperate soul.

'Toilette iz in one hour,' he said. The woman jerked in some kind of recognition. The man smiled with a warped tenderness. 'I know zat you are scared,' he continued. 'You know, when I am feeling...uneasy, zer's somesing I use to calm me. You know, perhaps it will work for you.' He nodded encouragingly.

With a thin smile, he moved over to the plastic table where a small ornamental musical box stood. He lifted the light wooden lid and out poured the tinkering, gentle rhyme of 'Frère Jacques'. The man took a deep breath, as though he were breathing in the sound. When he breathed out, the manic smile revealed the truth of the beast within. He stared at the woman and gestured to the music box as though her problems would melt away in the melody.

From the cupboard, the cries continued, muffled. The desperate sobs of someone lost in the hands of a madman.

26

Acceptance

The combined assault of scents wafting down from the warm bakery, the stink of weed, and stale air of the basement proved effective at churning the swirl of nausea that bubbled in Maddie's stomach. She paused at the top of the iron spiral staircase — a piece of metal snagged her jacket. She tutted, releasing some of her anger with a rip on the material. Getting out of the underground farm and lab, she took a deep breath and rested her back on the cool brick wall beside the door to the broken fridge. Tilting her head back, she closed her eyes for a second as she tried to control the sickness washing over her.

She thought back to the conversation downstairs. Adam had explained his theory. The Bright brothers had not laughed but simply waited for him to finish, nodding occasionally. Clearly the first they'd heard of it. Probably wondering why a cop was trusting them with this information. *Why indeed?* They had said Dylan was missing for two days before he ended up in a park. But that isn't close to hard evidence. It's not even on the same continent as hard evidence. She remained unconvinced. And the longer this case went on, the more the rules would have to bend, and with each bent rule, the thin golden thread holding up her exemplary record would fray a little more.

She swallowed hard at the thought. *How had it come to this?* Always the model pupil, an unyielding champion of the rules and without the faintest blemish to her name. Here she stood, in the grey area of right and wrong. No man's land. Unexplored territory, where her past experience and training offered little to no light out of the grey wilderness.

She listened for footsteps on the stairs. None came. At least Adam had the sense to leave her alone for a moment. She pushed through the false fridge into the kitchen, with its rustic heavy stone floor, long benches, and a thick, almost medieval table straight from a banquet hall.

Who were these men? The Bright brothers. She considered them one by one. The youngest first, perhaps the simplest. A petty offender by all accounts of his record. An addict, not perfect, but probably not inherently malicious. Now tied to a locked room at his brothers' behest. She had peered through the small square glass into a prison cell, albeit a clean one, with food and fresh water within reach. She puffed her cheeks and forced out a lungful of stress and tension. Still, it felt wrong. Was it a room or a cage? There had been some signs of care in there. The place was clean enough, the bed appeared comfortable, and there had been a creature comfort in the form of the TV. So perhaps Adam was right, it was more a hospital room and less a cage.

Unless, of course, it was just the cage of generous captors. Easier to keep a comfortable guest quiet. Perhaps a blood sample would reveal God knows what cooked up from the lab. She paced the long stone slabs of the floor, staring at her own shoes.

Her thoughts shifted onto the middle brother, Tony. The self-proclaimed agoraphobic. Intelligent, without a doubt. The conversation had been enough to show it without the letters after his name. Clearly the brain behind the set-up downstairs. She thought about those sharp eyes, untrusting of what they saw. But were they untrustworthy themselves?

And then there was the eldest, and perhaps the most complicated. Eliot Bright was a large puzzle in every sense. Behind that geordie accent, thick beard and gruff larger-than-life persona, Maddie suspected there was a sharp and deep mind. Not academically sharp like Tony, but smart. A reader of people, a nimble social dancer, a heavy thinker. For a moment, Maddie also fancied there was a kind heart. Far from flawless, but a light shade of grey. Therein lay the rub. She stopped pacing and leaned against a worktop, staring through a decadent, three-tiered wedding cake without noticing it as her thoughts wandered on.

The discovery of Dylan left her with few choices. The safe option (at least for her) was to bust them. The discovery of the basement itself was reason alone for that. But if the Bright brothers were not behind any alleged genetic manipulation experiments, and Adam was right, then maybe now wasn't quite the right time...and then there was Adam. She lowered herself down to the warm stone floor adjacent to an oven, her back against a cupboard door.

Adam had played his hand. Now it was her turn to show the cards. There was no reason for him to risk anything unnecessarily. He would probably lose his job if he was wrong. But then, *he* was obviously unstable. There was no water tight reason to trust the Brights. Sure, none of the lab equipment pointed obviously to anything associated with genetic manipulation. But that was based on Adam's assessment alone. And who knows what that would look like when the technology itself could be cutting edge? But then who was to say this was where they did it? Maybe they had another lab? A warehouse...anything. Medical tech had come so far in the last twenty years they could probably do it in a small storage unit.

Maddie reached up and took a bite out of a cinnamon swirl from a tray hanging tantalisingly over the counter directly above.

She took out her phone and swiped to a new message which had been a welcome excuse to leave the basement. Another overdose confirmed. Forwarded by Pearce. The profile of Stevie Wilks popped up with photos attached. She scanned through them. Nothing. More nothing. *Wait*, there was maybe something. The final image where the shirt had slipped. She pinched the screen and enlarged the image. Another bruise. Exactly the same as the one in the virtual crime scene on Charlie Lang in Green Meadows.

'Holy shit,' she whispered through a mouthful of sweet, warm, cinnamon pastry. Maddie read on to a report from earlier in the week. A high-speed pursuit. She checked the date and almost dropped her phone. Suddenly, her worry trebled, and yet at the same time her thoughts became clearer. In an uncertain corner of her mind, at least some part of the decision had been made for her.

'What is it?' Adam asked, concerned. She hadn't heard him coming as he emerged sheepishly from the fridge. Ultimately, he knew the decision for this case rested with her.

Maddie held up the photo embedded in the e-mail and said nothing, waiting for him to cross the room, and the penny to drop. He approached with a look of tense trepidation. His mind rushed to the worst. Had she called it in? Even reported him for turning a blind eye?

As he took in the image, the tension melted away, replaced by a tinge of excitement. Adam shot her a look. A smile threatened to cross his face. She allowed one to form in the corner of her mouth.

'And there's one more thing.' She scrolled through the email to double check her thoughts. 'Stevie Wilks' car was flagged driving at high speed away from a vehicle known to belong to associates of Luke. And you'll never guess when?'

'Two days ago.'

Maddie nodded excitedly.

'So, does this mean...'

'I believe you. At least, I believe it enough to follow this further.' She couldn't prevent the smile from spreading, mirroring his own. 'Oh, shut it,' she snapped. 'There's still no evidence this is genetic. But there's undoubtedly a pattern. If we do this. IF, I want them checked out properly,' she said, pointing to the basement. 'We need to question them more.'

Adam took a deep breath of relief.

'Agreed.' He held out his hand and pulled her up. He pulled a little too enthusiastically and Maddie collided into his chest. For a brief moment, she could smell the warm aftershave. For an even briefer moment their eyes lingered until, uncertain, they each stepped away.

Adam gave a small cough and shrugged. 'Sorry. You were a bit lighter than I expected.'

'Erm, implying what?' asked Maddie, mock angrily. Inside, she was grateful for something to brush over the moment, whatever it was. Her head was swimming with the shock of the case, the basement, and now that.

Adam rolled his eyes, equally thankful for the chance to play it down.

They descended the spiral staircase back into the cavernous basement with its stone arches. Again, the sight caught Maddie off guard, making her do a double-take. A drug farm and a lab, all underneath a city centre bakery with five-star reviews. There was something genius about it.

Eliot Bright eyed them with suspicion. He wanted the answer from the horse's mouth. Neither he nor Tony had moved from their seats, forced to await their sentence like prisoners in the dock. Desperation forced the words from Eliot's mouth.

'You stayin' then?' he asked Maddie gruffly.

Maddie stared at him hard and spoke with authority in her voice; clear and calm. He needed to know she couldn't be walked over. And despite his seniority, she needed Adam to know the same. 'We'll do this your way,' she said, looking at Adam. 'But I want the cameras wiped upstairs. And you're going to search this place fully — I want to know every detail. I want know what you're doing, what you've done, and most importantly, what you plan to do. And by the way, that will be exactly whatever I say.' Her steady gaze landed in turn on all three men before her.

Tony Bright lit a cigarette. Through the plume of smoke, she could see his eyes assessing her. Disliking the situation with every fibre. To be at the whim of two detectives, with their hands firmly on the rug beneath their feet. But Maddie also saw something that was reflected in equal measure in his brother's face: acceptance.

27

What the Tax Man Doesn't See

The UK's illegal drugs business is worth well over fourteen billion pounds a year. For that kind of money, you could easily build over two dozen state-of-the-art hospitals. An ever-growing pie and a thousand vultures circling for a slice. All three of the Bright brothers understood this. They had their fingers firmly in the pie, in one way or another. They knew how it was made, what ingredients worked best, and what temperature was needed.

Both Adam and Maddie had every intention of understanding their particular recipe for success.

'I'll get some coffee,' said Eliot. Maddie tensed and glanced at Adam. He nodded back his understanding and fired Eliot a stern yet simple look; I'm coming with you, and don't try anything. They knew he wouldn't. Deep down, the Bright brothers were locked in handcuffs of their own making. The knowledge of the room itself was an axe hovering over their neck. The room they had worked so hard to build and protect. However, within the criminal underworld more than anywhere, you can never really trust anyone completely.

Eliot and Adam emerged five minutes later with a tray of Bright and Sons' finest flat whites.

'The best. Jamaican blue mountain,' Eliot announced, as he put the tray down.

Adam raised an eyebrow. 'How much change would I get for forty quid?'

Eliot chuckled. 'Not much.'

Adam took a sip. He pursed his lips and admitted to himself that it was delicious. But outwardly he maintained a stone exterior.

'Not bad.' The words forced through his teeth like a schoolteacher having to acknowledge the accomplishment of a detestable student. He decided he would let at least half of it go cold and pushed the thought aside. Despite their pretence of hospitality, Adam could sense impatience in the room. Before Eliot could follow up, he continued. 'I want to see the books.'

Tony pulled a computer tablet from a drawer and placed it on the table in front of Eliot. He signed in and slid a spreadsheet into hologram mode so that it projected a fifty-inch translucent image from the tablet, floating weightlessly in the air.

'This everything?'

Eliot grunted. 'Everything official. The only records that we keep are for the tax man.'

As Eliot took him through the books, Adam felt the pang of dread he expected Clara felt when faced with a bottomless spreadsheet. He pushed her from his mind as the sting of their problems instantly found its mark.

In terms of the books, everything was in order. Official income could be accounted for through the sales from the real bakery and café, plus the second branch in Ponteland. Income exceeded outgoings, taxes paid in full, all up to date.

Maddie traced every column and slowly nodded her satisfaction. 'That accounts for how you keep away the taxman's sniffer dogs, but what about the unofficial business?'

'The safest place of all, bonnie lass,' said Eliot, tapping his head. 'In here.'

'Run me through it,' she said sternly.

Eliot heaved a deep sigh through his heavy frame. He took a generous swig of coffee, as though the recently boiled liquid were a glass of apple juice. Then he closed the tablet and pulled aside a piece of paper.

'I want it on there,' said Adam, pointing to the tablet.

Eliot hesitated and glanced at Tony, who was lighting another cigarette — the ash tray beside him mounting with stubs that attested for his worry and suspicion. Eliot opened another blank document on the tablet hologram and began to type.

'How far back?' he asked, his fingers hovering over the keyboard.

Maddie interjected. 'Five years.' That was the protocol. She would have at least that done by the book. Something meagre to point to if this all blew up. Eliot looked at Adam hoping for some leniency.

'You heard her,' said Adam, glancing at Maddie. She waited until Eliot turned his frame before giving Adam a subtle nod with a weak smile.

Eliot began to type. Large but nimble fingers accustomed to the finesse of cake decoration and baking lent themselves to the subtle art of filling a spreadsheet. For ten minutes straight, he seldom made a mistake before twisting the hologram slightly for them to see. He then split the hologram into three larger screens.

'First sheet is the shrooms.' His eyes met Maddie's. 'We've got a thousand growin' at any given time, and boxes more dried in a temperature-controlled room at the back which keeps them good for a year. Tony grows them, and I bake them into various things. We sell 'em off, minus the overheads of electricity and we're clearin' a quarter of a million a year.' He pointed to the final number, written in bold.

'How do you sell them?' asked Adam, taking an unconscious gulp of coffee.

Tony interjected. 'The dark web, mostly. Dealers buy them anonymously and then the rest is up to them. We're just the supplier.' He shrugged.

'And the weed?'

Eliot stretched his back, which proceeded to crack seven times like a burst of distant machine gun fire. He glared at Adam, trying to read the poker face. Maddie was clearly too nervous to be lying, that much was obvious. This was beyond anything she'd done. But was he being led into a trap by the confident, amiable nature and calm green eyes of DI Morell? Why was this detective so willing to let this slide? Yes, he had them in his grip, but would he squeeze them for everything they had? It happened. Cops with too much power, and not enough feeling.

Eliot dragged the next spreadsheet through the air. 'Weed's the biggest part of the business. We produce less, and the heat lamps use more juice, but it goes for more so we clear about half a mil a year.'

'How do you cover the electricity in here? Why hasn't your bill been flagged on the system?'

'Because it's not on the system,' said Eliot cooly. 'And even if it was, it wouldn't be that bad. We're a busy bakery so that muddies the water. But we stay off the grid thanks to a shed load of solar panels on the roof, which Tony upgraded. Twice as efficient as the ones you can buy off the shelf,' he added with a touch of pride. 'I can take you up there if you want to see them?'

'I do,' said Maddie. 'Later. For now, I think we know all we need to about this place. But I do want those spreadsheets, in full.' She reached over to take the tablet but Eliot held it firmly. Adam leaned forward. Eliot was quick to raise a calming hand of apology. He sighed and spoke.

'There is...one more thing.' He nodded to the last remaining spreadsheet. But instead of reaching for the keyboard, he stood and wandered over to a stack of shelves.

'Eliot!' exclaimed Tony. His mouth moved to speak again, but found only a wordless sigh as his older brother shook his head.

'There's no point hiding it Tony.' He gave him a reassuring smile and proceeded to remove a box of empty plastic trays used for sorting mushrooms. His thick forearm disappeared into the shelving and emerged grasping a chunk of stone from the wall, which he dropped into a tray. The hand moved back to the shelving.

'Stop!' Adam yelled. 'Slowly.' He had jumped up and was now approaching Eliot. The big man removed his arm and held both hands up. Then he stood back and motioned for Adam to reach in himself.

'Be my guest.'

Adam sank his arm elbow-deep into the cold hole in the wall behind the shelves, and pulled out a blue plastic bag. Eliot walked back to the table and Adam followed, tipping out the contents. Two things cascaded from the plastic: a small bag of sealed, sterile intravenous needles, and another of brown powder.

'You're fucking kidding?' said Maddie, looking to Eliot for an explanation.

'That's the only stash you'll find of that stuff,' he replied, regarding the brown powder with a hint of disgust. 'We don't deal it. I want to make that clear right now. We give it away for free to one or two folk who want to wean themselves off. We check them out first, make sure they aren't goin' to blab, and that they're not goin' to fall off the rails easily.'

Maddie furrowed her brow, turning the thought over and drawing a blank. 'Why?'

'Harm reduction?' said Adam.

Eliot pointed. 'Got it in one. Treatment.'

'Well...explain,' Maddie said impatiently.

'Our most recent client is a nurse.'

Maddie shook her head disapprovingly. 'Client?'

'Client,' said Eliot sincerely. 'She's got kids, and she's been addicted to heroin for about five years. She's a stable user. A functional member of society. But she could feel herself slipping so we brought her into our little programme.' He shoved the heroin back into the plastic bag. 'It's as simple as this, she's a good person, she wants to stop but won't go to the doctor for methadone because then she'll be struck off as a nurse, and worse. So, we offer her a clean needle and a supply of quality product, checked by Tony in the lab here. Been doin' it for a while. Got some people completely clean as well. And this nurse, well, she's already lowered her dose.'

Maddie closed her eyes, took a deep breath and rubbed the bridge of her nose. When she opened them, a new determination shone through.

'Look, you have to be the weirdest dealers I've ever met.' She caught Adam's gaze, who appeared to be at ease and almost amused by the idea. Maddie decided to deal with it later and move on. She grabbed the tablet and the ghostly screens vanished. 'We have bigger problems.' She nodded to the door, behind which Dylan remained shut away. 'Right now, I want to know more about Luke Marshall.'

The air grew immediately tense. As though he was there in the room, or listening in the shadows. Eliot cleared his throat. 'You think *he's* involved in what happened to Dylan?'

Adam looked at her with equal concern.

Maddie shrugged. 'If it's not you, then I think it's possible. Who else has the money and ability to pull it off?' Tony came closer, sitting down opposite Adam. Maddie continued. 'It's obviously a relatively simple procedure. Slip them a needle. The nasty bruise is explained away as just another junkie injection site. Then the next time they take whatever substance it is they're addicted to; they drop dead. It's almost murder by suicide. The perfect murder.'

Eliot rubbed his jaw and moved over to a line of kitchen-style cabinets above the lab workspace. One was inlaid with oak and gold trim. Inside, bottles of whisky, wine, rum and vodka were lined up.

'Poison?' he grunted.

'Whisky,' said Adam.

Maddie shook her head.

Eliot poured himself, Tony, and Adam a glass of scotch and passed them around.

Adam gently sniffed the peaty aroma of the highland waters before sipping. The warmth washed his mouth and burned his throat. With this coating applied, the next sip was delicious, as was the way with whisky.

'I'll assume you know a bit about Luke, given your job,' said Eliot, tilting his head back and taking a drink. 'I know him better than most.'

'Really? How?' said Maddie, leaning forward in her seat.

Eliot drained his last swallow. 'I'll skip the basics. I don't know exactly what you have on him, but anythin' you've heard is either completely true or not far off. It's hard to exaggerate with the bastard.' He looked into his empty glass and laughed. 'He's like a poltergeist. I heard last year he travelled to Istanbul to personally hunt down someone his top bloodhounds had declared 'unfindable'. Luke found him.'

'So how do you know him?'

'We used to be mates. In school. Even then, he was sadistic. I knew somethin' wasn't right with him when we were about eight. He tore the head off a squirrel. Just ripped it off, laughing. Threw the thing away like a toy he was bored with and went on with his day. That was just the start. Stealing, fighting, you name it. But he was popular y'know, and at that age, I didn't think on it too much. It's not like I was a saint either. We started goin' to the boxing club. Sparring partners. That was one thing I saw him take seriously. Boxing coach loved him, but I gave as good as I got, don't you worry.'

He refilled each glass with a generous pour. 'They should have expelled him from school, but he was making good headlines. National awards in maths, languages, philosophy. Even fuckin' violin. Which kid from a council estate plays a violin?' He shook his head as though the thought still beggared belief. 'He didn't even try; it was like he just knew things. Girls loved him, of course. At least the ones who like to live dangerously when they're young, and there's plenty of those.'

He let out a laugh, staring at the table and into the past. A fond, reminiscent smile crossed his face, and then faded just as quickly. 'We grew up. When we were seventeen, he asked me if I wanted to go out that night. Said he needed a hand with somethin' and there was good money in it. So, I went along. He drove to this druggie house. Introduced me as his friend to these dealers and said we were there to help out. I couldn't back out. So, I spent the night shifting a load of pills in clubs I was too young to be in, shitting it. By this time, Luke was gettin' to the point he was built big, way taller than your average teenager. We both were, I suppose, but I was a bit slower. Made me look like a mouse at the time.'

Adam watched the thin semblance of joviality in Eliot's face suddenly flicker out. He spoke now in the serious, cold tone of someone reliving a nightmare.

'At the end of the night, I went into a back alley to meet him. There was a scuffle, some moving shapes. That's when I saw someone begging on the floor. I couldn't make them out. All I could see was that Luke had a gun in his hand. The feller from the druggie house eggin' him on. It was an execution, an initiation, not a fight. It wasn't until they ran off that I saw...' The words choked, and the big man was clearly having trouble fighting off the swell in his eyes.

Tony stubbed another cigarette into the smouldering pile of the ash tray. His pale face somehow a shade whiter. Eliot coughed and cleared his throat with a deep growl before speaking.

'There were four of us. It wasn't until the police knocked on the door an hour later that I found out who they'd shot.'

Eliot took a heavy breath through his nose. The knuckles of his right hand whitened around the glass.

Adam and Maddie felt the same sense of foreboding, waiting for him to reveal their secrets in his own time. Finally, Eliot spoke again.

'Sam was our eldest brother.'

'Your *brother*?' Maddie repeated, unable to hide the horror in her voice. She flicked through her phone. 'I didn't...there's nothing in our files...'

'Sam never got into any trouble. Nicest soul there was. No charges were pressed, and officially, they still haven't been if you take my meaning,' he said sternly.

Adam interjected before the look of uncertainty of Maddie's face could manifest into a problem. 'This is off the record, for now.'

Eliot considered Adam for a moment, then nodded his satisfaction before going on.

'My dad was in prison. He knew about the sort of men Luke was falling in with. Besides, he was too fucked up to do anything even if he could. They made their message loud and clear the next day. A bouquet of flowers arrived with about a hundred others. This one had a bullet fastened to the tag. Even if we could have done somethin', they'd have killed everyone, including my mother. And Dylan was still just a little kid. Even if they didn't want to get their hands dirty, they could still have me pinned for dealing.'

Tony stood and took a few steps away. Avoiding eye contact and standing with his back to the table. He lit another cigarette, looking out over the cannabis plants as though he were surveying a sunset after a long day in the fields. He spoke without turning.

'That's the only reason he lets us operate,' he said.

Maddie probed further. 'What do you mean? You think he feels guilty?'

Eliot snorted. He interlaced his fingers and leaned forward, allowing his bulk to rest on his powerful arms. 'Guilty? He didn't bat an eyelid. No, I think he likes me to watch. See how well he's doin' and what I could have had, y'know, if I'd followed him. And if I had followed him that night, then Sam would still be...'

Eliot rubbed his mouth, leaned back in his chair and let the thought evaporate. He spoke now with a clearer, calmer voice. But Adam noticed a subtle quality to it bordering on numbness. The true sound of a man with nothing to lose, having just poured out his heart faster than he poured whisky. That was a feeling he understood. And his instinct as the eldest living brother spoke was that Eliot Bright was a decent man, for all his faults, and if he was to get anywhere with this case, a man worth listening to. He hadn't moved since Eliot told his story, allowing him the time to talk. He did the same with renewed patience as Eliot went on.

'The thing about him is, he's a born strategist. A genius without a conscience is a dangerous thing. Maybe even the most dangerous. You lot keep waitin' for him to slip up, pin him on something concrete. He never will. If you want to bring him down, then you need to break the rules. Like you did today.'

Maddie shifted slightly. The basement fell into a strange silence, with only the hum of the heat lamps for company. Adam felt the elephant in the room climbing up his throat. The question that had to be asked. He didn't sugar coat it. There was no point.

'Why did he kill Sam?'

Tony blew out a long slow plume of smoke, and with that came the long train of thoughts that had clearly simmered for a long time in the cauldron of his sharp intellect.

'Rumour was he had accidently started flirting with one of the dealer's girls. But that's not a reason really, when you think about it, is it? I *have* thought about it, almost every day. Why would a seventeen-year-old shoot a grown man? The answer's simple.' He dropped the cigarette, stubbed it out with his shoe and turned to face them. 'Because he enjoys it. Because he could. Because he knew there would be no consequences, and because he could finally take his first real step into the world he would one day rule. Killing Sam was the door and he walked through it with a fucking smile.'

Tony smoothed back a handful of his slicked black hair and breathed out. He locked eyes with Eliot for a second. There was a fleeting moment of unspoken understanding. Like neither had ever discussed it until now. Maybe they hadn't, thought Adam.

Maddie finished her coffee and placed the cup on the table. Adam had watched her controlling herself as the conversation had twisted into an ever-darkening maze.

'I'm sorry, for what happened to your brother,' she said sympathetically. 'But we need to know what happened to Dylan, and we might not have long. There could be others out there. If there is someone experimenting on people, we need to find out who.'

'Since you knew him, do you think Luke could be capable of doing *this?*' said Adam, pointing to Dylan's room. 'Killing is one thing, but this is something else.'

Eliot nodded. 'Oh aye, he's capable alright. Funds aren't a problem either. But the only problem is I can't see why?'

Maddie stood up. 'That's for us to worry about.'

'Fair enough.' Eliot shrugged. 'So, what next? The staff will be back soon.'

'They don't know about this place, do they?' asked Adam.

'Not a clue,' scoffed Tony. 'They're a nosy bunch, but no one in their right mind would open a fridge that said *out of order* and then push through the back of it.'

Maddie pulled out her phone and made a quick note. 'Good. Next I want you to show us those solar panels,' she said, gesturing to the ceiling. 'And then you're going to carry on as if this didn't happen. Life in this bakery shall continue.

Don't try to contact us. We'll be in touch. Oh...' she pointed to Dylan's room, 'and obviously don't let him have any more heroin. When he's able, tell him everything, but do *not* let him leave this basement.'

* * *

A new message waited in the encrypted inbox. The man they called Jacques clicked and a pair of green eyes stared back from the laptop screen. Six-foot, brown hair, wide shoulders, a controlled amount of stubble. There was a wildness to him. Were it not for the police officer's badge he was holding, he would have thought him some kind of mid-level gangster. Leather jacket, casual T-shirt, jeans, and scuffed boots. But it was the way he carried himself. An ease, a confidence, a certainty that he now saw in the handsome face.

He clicked to the next image. The green-eyed man now in his car, holding a lighter adorned with a poppy. Perhaps a soldier? He wondered which regiment for a moment. He needn't have bothered. It was all in the file, but he liked to test his judgement. His gaze slid up to the name at the top of the profile.

'Detective Inspector Adam Morell. Northumbria Police.'

The note below the image was absolute.

'Take alive to the place where it happens.'

He fancied this one might give a good chase. He half-hoped he was wrong. After Istanbul, there could be no more mistakes. The gloved finger clicked a key and the file corrupted itself, never to be read again.

28

The Side Without Any Rules

The morning sun crept its orange and pink fingers over the horizon, framing the skyline and bouncing off the smooth River Tyne. As the pair drove back to the station, Maddie was quiet, and Adam didn't try to make conversation. He knew she would need time to let her thoughts settle. He had mastered the art of turning a blind eye. The Bright brothers were no different to Magic. A useful bit of leverage. Eventually, she broke the silence.

'The heroin,' she said. 'You're okay with it?'

Adam shrugged.

'They're trying to help a few people quit smack, or at least use it safely, free of charge. It's not exactly our biggest concern.'

Maddie nodded, unconvinced, and faced forward, staring off into the distance. Adam noted her uncertainty and went on. 'Actually it's not a new idea. Back in the 1920s it was legal in the UK.'

'What was?'

'Heroin use. Used to be called the British System. Basically it allowed a long-term prescription of opioids to addicted patients. Worked very well until the Americans came with the so-called war on drugs. Portugal actually decriminalised opiates in 2001 and that worked wonders for the same reason.'

'So you're a narcotics detective in favour of legalising heroin?'

Adam thought for a moment, then nodded. 'Yeah. On prescription, obviously. But yeah, without a doubt. If it works, it works.' He shrugged at her look of disbelief. 'What? It's not like we're doing a great job of stopping heroin use are we?'

Maddie rolled her eyes and sank back into silence. Adam sensed that her thoughts were swarming again. A tug of war raging between the choices in her mind.

When they reached the station, they agreed Maddie would go in first and Adam five minutes after to help avoid any questions from Pearce. A fine rain fell as if to spite the sunny day. She said goodbye and left with wetness in her eyes.

Adam felt a tinge of guilt at having dragged her into this. But in the end, the choice had been hers. She could have left, called in a team. Would've been one of the biggest busts the city had known for a few decades at least. But that would have been the wrong thing to do. The wrong thing for Charlie Lang and Stevie Wilks, and all of the others in his file that was not quite cold. Adam respected her more for it. It's usually never easy doing the right thing.

He spent the rest of the day chasing up number plates and doing dog work for various cases across the team. Some extra punishment from Pearce. That took him until exactly 9 p.m. Nothing like boredom to make you aware of the time. Then he swung by a McDonald's for dinner. He ate more than he should have, and rasped on the door of Magic Coyne's mother's house feeling sick. She gave him the usual poisonous sneer, and Magic climbed into the car an hour later in Green Meadows. Today's Hawaiian shirt was bright yellow, sporting palm trees and hibiscus flowers.

Adam asked if he had heard anything else connected to Charlie. Magic was easier to read than a toddler's picture book, and through the cursing and moaning it was clear he knew diddly squat about Charlie. But the rumours about more people going missing and then winding up dead had reached his dreadlock-covered ears. Adam listened as he skipped over the scarce information he had on the subject. Despite inconsistencies in his flaky scraps of intel, there was one solid undertone: fear. Plain and simple.

Adam felt a tingle in his spine. First Stevie, now this. Finally, months after his first suspicions, he felt like a cop chasing a lead rather than his own paranoia.

The house was quiet when he eventually returned home close to midnight. As usual, Clara was asleep when he came in late. Exactly as he'd hoped. He watched her sleeping for a second. The black, smooth outline of her phone on the bedside table whispered to him. He thought about opening it, curiosity goading him, but decided against it.

He took a hot shower and made a mental note to shave. Sliding into bed, Clara didn't stir. The sheets were cold. Perhaps colder than normal because of what he suspected of the woman next to him. He still didn't have a good reason to react, and yet her gentle breath was suddenly like a dripping tap. He got up and went downstairs. She wouldn't ask too many questions — it wouldn't be the first time he had collapsed on the couch after a late one.

When he awoke at 3 p.m., there was a note on the coffee table that read:

'Sausage rolls in the fridge x.'

Adam allowed his feet to swing down onto the soft rug.

'Shit!' He snatched his phone. Dead. That explained why the alarm failed. Weeks of lost sleep had finally caught up to him and claimed its inevitable victory. He rubbed his eyes and thought about the day ahead. At least what was left of it. Yesterday morning re-played in his mind. The story of Eliot's childhood with Luke had re-stoked the fire and left the feeling that some progress was being made for the first time in a few years. Luke was now in his sights more than ever. His picture had been pinned up on the board for so long he was almost part of the furniture. Like a magazine left on a coffee table for so long, you stop noticing it.

Adam was not worried about the Bright brothers. An unusual trio, but not the real problem. He knew Maddie wouldn't be able to shake the concern in the same way. He thought of her for a moment, the tears in her eyes when they arrived back at the station from the bakery. He wished he had said something comforting, something that resembled gratitude, or that he cared.

The grip of tiredness had loosened. That always gave him confidence in the day. Less likely to miss anything. Before he did anything else, he trimmed his stubble, brushed his teeth, and got dressed.

He plugged his phone into the car and waited for it to come to back life. Ten texts and five missed calls, all from Maddie. He could almost hear her panicking. Most of them simply asked where he was with increasing concern. He responded: 'Alive and well. Slept in.' The rest he would deal with when he arrived. Ignorance was bliss. But there was one more thing to deal with now. Pearce would have his balls for being late. He did the only thing he could; phoned the office and conjured his best grovelling sick voice.

'Hi, it's Morell. Sorry I haven't called yet, Karen. I've been absolutely zonked out. Yeah, yeah feels like the flu. Been going round, yeah, that's probably it. Okay, okay, you're a star, thanks a mil.'

And that was why he had always said, 'Hi,' to Karen.

His thoughts turned to Clara as he glided the car by her office block half an hour later. He knew there was little chance of seeing her. Above everything else, no matter what turn the case took, nothing compared to the feeling that dug into him when he thought of her. Whatever it was, it would have to be dealt with. Sooner rather than later.

The parade and buzz of the beginning of the rush hour home was in full swing. The autumn sun burned at its lowest point of the day. Students, builders, office workers, pensioners all wading into the pedestrian river that filled the streets. Adam knew the Bright brothers wouldn't expect him to return this quickly. But he wanted them to know who was in charge. That he could do what he wanted, and they had to obey.

He parked down a side street and read his remaining messages. The next few hours were wiled away by answering emails in the car within view of the Bright brothers' café. The place ticked over with a steady stream of customers. Nothing to raise any alarm. Eliot made no appearance, at least not outside. Adam was comfortable they were keeping their end. But since he was hungry, he stretched his legs, turning right and meandering across the perfect sweeping road of Grey Street. He pushed through the glass doors and joined the long queue. Eliot clocked him after a minute. Part of Adam laughed at the thought of these people eating above the biggest weed and shroom farm in the north, probably in the country. The audacity of it. Right in the city centre. Luke had helped them stay secret, no doubt about that. Probably collecting a greedy cut from his old friend. Something Eliot would never admit to. And something he had conveniently left out of his story.

Adam reached the front of the queue. 'A flat white please, mate, and a chocolate muffin.'

'Coming up,' said Eliot cheerfully. Through the jolly inn keeper persona, Adam sensed the searching eyes and seething bitterness at being checked upon like a child in a playground. He served the coffee without another word. Adam leaned in as he took it.

'Business okay? All ticking along nicely?'

'Can't complain, yeah. Although it could always be better.'

'Too true. Thanks, mate, see you *very* soon.' Adam winked as he picked up his order and turned away.

He sipped the coffee outside and took out two morphine pills before devouring half the muffin.

The cold metal flip lighter made him think about the other poor sods lost to this case. How many didn't they know about? How many had they got to? How many bedraggled living corpses were just one hit away? At least Dylan was safe. One saved. Adam swallowed one pill and put the other back in the lighter.

He looked up to Grey's Monument at the end of the road. Built to commemorate the Great Reform Act of prime minister Charles Grey, the 133-foot stone tower met at the intersection of Blackett Street, Grainger Street, and Grey Street. Adam wandered up the curved bend of Grey Street towards the tower. Bars and restaurants hummed with the bustle of late-autumn nights.

It wasn't until he approached the foot of the monument itself that he noticed he was being followed. Was he getting paranoid? Probably. Had he been sucked too far into the wrong side of the game? The side without any rules. He took a glance back and saw a tall, suited man, mostly a silhouette against the night. But he could see the intent in his stride and the strength of his figure. Adam pretended to browse a book shop and waited as the figure walked by him at a distance towards an alleyway. He was following. Adam knew it. And worse still, he didn't linger by the monument as an amateur would have. He would be in the alleyway, waiting, watching.

Adam picked up the pace again and chanced it on the Metro, Newcastle's underground train network. He took a glance back before descending the steps below street level into Monument Station. The man was illuminated briefly as he emerged from the alley and passed under the sign of a Spanish restaurant. Curled hair, tanned, sharp features. Not enough time for more detail.

The sickly artificial lights of the Metro were almost violent on the eyes. A holographic AI ticket conductor answered the question of a tourist looking for directions. Otherwise, the station was fairly quiet. A few students, a small family, and a couple of loitering teenagers.

And then one more passenger, descending the stairs from the other entrance. The face rang a bell instantly. A face that sat right beside Luke on the whiteboard at the station: PJ.

Adam glanced back up the stairs and saw the legs of the tall man beginning to descend. Leather gloves. The faintest bulge under the arm where the tight, long overcoat betrayed the gun. Not enough time to see the face as PJ approached.

Adam hopped through the holographic ticket conductor and over the barrier. He bounded down the escalator shaft that dove into the bowel of the city, slipped past a group of old timers and burst out onto the platform heading east. Mercifully, the sign read: Whitley Bay — Due.

Seconds later the hollow tunnel sighed and the tracks gave a faint rattle as air swelled down the line. The headlight eyes of the white and yellow steel train appeared from the black warren of tunnels into the light of the platform. Adam watched as carriages slid past, holding a few passengers each. Rush hour had come and gone.

A large group of student girls ready for a night out chatted on the platform, clutching water bottles that almost certainly contained vodka lemonade. Adam was grateful for their presence. Luke's hounds wouldn't do anything with a crowd like this. And not with this many cameras. Another figure dressed in a suit was waiting at the end of the platform. For a moment, Adam weighed him up. Was he waiting for the train, or Adam? PJ emerged beside a family and the group of old timers, oblivious to the chess match unfolding.

Adam had no choice. His only option now was the train.

He stepped towards the nearest door and waited for it to open. A few passengers stepped off and he took a seat with his back to the window, facing into the carriage.

PJ stepped onboard to the left, one carriage in front of Adam.

Seconds before the doors beeped closed, Adam saw the tall man enter to his right, taking a seat in the carriage behind. The main lights of this carriage were broken, and with only a faint, cold strip of emergency lighting, the man was a shadow, watching him.

29

Hide and Seek

Adam sat as calmly as he could in full view of another CCTV camera and showed his face to it clearly. Then he made a point of keeping his eye on each of them in turn. He slouched and let his face rest into the indifferent expression of the underground commuter. He needed to avoid alerting other passengers. They were the main thing keeping the two men away. Any sign of trouble would make the commuters shuffle into a distant carriage or worse, force a mass exodus. But despite his appearance, Adam prepared himself for fight or flight. Feet firmly planted and hands out of his pockets.

The tall man stared pensively. An eery silhouette, like a fisherman on a riverbank, line cast, just waiting for the chance to strike.

PJ watched Adam for a few minutes and then relaxed into his phone. No doubt providing an update to Luke. Almost imperceptibly, PJs leg bobbed nervously over his high platform trainer. The worst part was, PJ probably thought he looked good. That had been the way with many gangsters for decades, streetwear. Dressed in sports gear or gym wear at all times. It's comfortable, no doubt, but Adam felt the class had gone. Even his own battered leather jacket and jeans looked more presentable. The other man *was* what Adam would describe as classy. His suit had clearly been tailored, the tie pristine over the crisp, cotton shirt. The black overcoat fitted neatly, yet the bulge of the gun had stuck out like a sore thumb to the trained eye.

Platforms trickled by, and the handful of passengers filtered on and off. Overall, the numbers stayed on the low side. At one point, a group of lads, maybe twenty or so years old, huddled near the tall man, obscuring him further. They took one look at the suit and were ready to take the piss. Adam heard the crack as the man stood and swiftly broke a nose with a rising elbow. A yelp was swallowed by the snap of the vicious headbutt that followed.

One of them shouted and the others echoed, 'What the fuck?' The rest backed off as one of them fell into an armlock. Realising the scene around him, the tall man released the arm, and the lads moved to the next carriage, nursing their egos. They scurried off at the next stop after one announced 'This is us, guys.'

Unlikely, thought Adam. They would no doubt be waiting for the next one to get to their actual destination. He wished he could excuse himself as easily.

He regarded the tall man with fresh eyes. A experienced hired killer if there ever was one. Not a regular part of the crew, hence his lack of rapport with PJ, but regularly on the payroll of the international organisation under Luke's boot.

The train had moved out of the underground tunnels onto the overground lines. The stations of Howdon and Percy Main sauntered by, and Adam glanced at the train map above the standing handrails and weighed his options. The line was on a loop. He could wait until he was back at Monument or Central and leg it to the police station.

The key would be surprise; running when they least expected it. Even through the tall man's scuffle, Adam had slumped like he was spending Sunday on the sofa, and maintained the position for the last four stops. PJ had long stopped keeping a firm eye on him, glancing occasionally. Despite the darkness, the tall man in the suit had maintained strong supervision. The faceless black profile of his head had barely twitched, but even he had begun to glance here and there as impatience and uncertainty breathed down over his shoulder. A sign of nerves, perhaps?

The stop for Meadow Well was announced. On stepped a group of eight teenagers who stood between Adam and the suited man. PJ still had full view from the other side. The doors closed, and Adam glimpsed the suited shadow through the forest of chatting bodies, oblivious to the two killers that flanked them.

The rattler moved on down the line, and Adam maintained his disinterested pose. For all they knew, his plan was to ride the train until morning. He thought about calling in back-up. That would force their hand. Not a good idea in a cramped space.

As the station for Tynemouth appeared, Adam noticed the teenagers shift, blocking the eye line of the suited man entirely. PJ's eyes still coveted his phone for the most part. The screen lit up. PJ read the message, lifted his gaze across to Adam and grinned. *Who was on the other end of that phone? Luke? Almost certainly.* In his confidence, PJ turned and looked nonchalantly out of the window. Strange how quickly arrogance destroys a good plan. Adam saw his chance.

The doors pinged, the teens were moving to leave. Adam launched himself in front of them and pelted down the platform. The crucial three seconds it took for the two men to react had turned into seven by the time they got through the teenagers.

The train had halted at the open aired platform. Tynemouth was easily one of the oldest and grandest stations, covered in a long, pointed glass roof and propped up by the original Victorian, cast-iron pillars.

Adam searched for the fluorescence of a police jacket. The platform offered nothing but shadows as he burst through the station and out onto the main street.

The long high street ran straight, with the sea at the far end that was trimmed for a mile by gold sanded beaches. Both sides of the street were lit with pubs, restaurants, cafés and small supermarkets. There was enough going on in Tynemouth for a night out without having to even travel into the city, and many didn't.

Adam craned his neck back for a second and saw the two dark figures in full sprint after him.

He spent a lot of time in Tynemouth when Poppy had died. Especially at the old lighthouse. Something about the solitary spot and sea calmed him. He saw it now, beyond the black metal fence that led down to the beach. Without looking back, he descended the steps and climbed onto the long concrete pier that forever flexed a strong arm against the waves. The sea was rough, even for a spot that regularly saw surfers. Several white walls of water rose and washed over the concrete as he pounded on.

The pier seemed like a marathon. Adam cursed every pint and cigarette he'd ever had.

Another glance back and the two men were closer now, perhaps forty yards. That was enough. Finally, the shadow of the lighthouse swallowed him as he slipped around the other side and vanished.

The two men ran into an empty space and exchanged a look, neither particularly familiar with the other. There wasn't an ounce of fondness in the cold faces as they wordlessly considered the situation. But the orders were clear: work together.

Only the inky sea lay before them under a starless sky. They glanced over the edge, down to the black, barren rocks. No one would have survived a jump. If the rocks didn't take them, the biting cold of the turbulent sea would kill all but an expert swimmer. And after running the best part of a mile at full speed, Adam Morell was not that person.

Above, the lighthouse lamp turned on its axis, sweeping the horizon and the beach in its never-ending circle. A small door hidden in a deep stone arch was bathed in the warm light, and then thrown into darkness as the lamp continued on.

PJ moved, but the tall man held up a hand. The leather strained against the controlled, white-knuckled fist beneath the glove. From his pocket, he withdrew a fingernail sized device. He moved it towards the lock. Within the last few inches, it jumped from his fingers with a metallic clunk of a heavy magnet. He raised a sleeve, revealing a smart tattoo of a jack-in-the-box on his forearm. He flicked at the ink handle and the jack jumped out of the box soundlessly. PJ watched as the man smiled, like a child lost in his own world. As the jack jumped, the metal device glowed white hot and the door handles either side fell away.

The tall man withdrew a thin ski mask and pulled it over his head. Only the cold eyes shone through. Two obsidian black holes in a pool of shadow. He nudged the door open and wandered in to the circular room.

PJ had seen smart tattoos coded to the usual stuff: phones, heart rate monitors, temperature monitors. But this was beyond bespoke. The jack-in-the-box was probably coded to a few other devices. However, it only made him even more wary of the man they called Jacques.

At the centre of the room, a spiral staircase twisted through several floors up into the sky. The lamp could be seen twirling at the top. Save the re-wiring, and an updated lamp, the lighthouse had barely been touched since the nineteenth century. A battered wooden table and chairs hosted a set of abandoned playing cards and hi-vis jackets from maintenance men, who rarely visited the automated lighthouse. The next floor revealed an old galley-style kitchen with a generous seating area preserved for tourists. Likewise, the second floor housed a few traditional beds, and the top floor the lamp itself.

PJ tried a set of light switches without success. He waited in the bedroom as Jacques climbed to the top floor, whistling a nursery rhyme. PJ had heard him do this before. Living up to his poxy nickname.

Jacques took no interest in the dark sea view and began to climb down, continuing to whistle the nursery rhyme, 'Frère Jacques'. He shielded his eyes from the lamp. His foot paused on the first stair and the whistling stopped as he heard a groan, and then silence. He drew his gun and descended.

Adam waited in the centre of the room, PJ's arm was twisted and locked in his fist, an inch from breaking the bone, and PJ's own gun held to his head. PJ surrendered any pretence of calm as the cool, carefree look melted from his face and raw panic took its place. The desperate panic worn by the face of a human shield. Adam stared on, still surfing the wave of adrenaline, and numbness of the poppy pill.

'What do you want?' he sneered.

'Your number 'az come up,' said Jacques quietly. The voice was strange, muffled slightly by the mask, with a high, almost whispering edge to it. And yet somehow it carried, piercing the gloom over the sound of the waves.

PJ tried to break free, Adam twisted the final inch and cracked his wrist. The younger man let out a scream.

Jacques gave a faint chuckle. 'It's always good to 'ave a challenge, uh PJ?'

Adam edged back each time the great lamp swung away, dousing his half of the room in complete darkness. Inching towards the wall, he needed a moment where the tall man's attention dropped for a second — where the black eye of his gun nozzle would dip an inch or two. Enough time for his one and only plan to work.

The foghorn blared through the thin window and filled the room, as though answering Adam's prayers. The gun dipped. Jacques was momentarily distracted for a crucial fraction of a second. As the light swept away from him, Adam kicked PJ across the room into Jacques and flicked the heavy lever switch behind him. The lighthouse lamp died completely, snuffing out any remaining dregs of light apart from the ray of moonlight trickling through the narrow window.

Shots came, coughing flashes of light and splintering wood. Adam dived and the shots followed his noise. Then the stillness. Cloak and dagger in the pitch dark. Hide and seek with fatal consequences. Adam crouched low, back against the wall, doing his best to control his breath. In addition to one in the chamber, he guessed around three bullets were left in the magazine. The other man probably had the same or less.

He could hear the light trainers of PJ, the ruffle of the nylon jacket. He would be scrambling for the stairs. Not the man in the suit; the professional. The man who had made every effort to conceal his identity.

PJ clanged down the metal staircase, grunting in pain until he reached the bottom. He wrenched the door open and spilled out into the night air, cradling his arm. Vomit knocked on the door of his stomach. *Who to call? Not*

Luke. What would he tell them? He eyed the small side door with terror and braced his ears for the finality of a gunshot. Whoever came out of the front door would decide his fate.

He didn't ponder the question much longer. The crash from above signalled the end. The sickening, gut-wrenching scream was swallowed by the sea below. Too dark to tell who it was.

PJ hid behind a concrete buttress within earshot of the door. He heard the footsteps emerge.

'Jacques?' he hissed. Nothing. Not unusual for the suited man to blank him. 'Oi, Jacques, is that you, lad, for fuck's sake?'

The gun on the back of his head said it wasn't. 'Fuck. Man, listen, we were just doin' what we were told.'

Adam could almost hear the pistons of PJs heartbeat steaming at full pelt.

'By who?' ordered Adam. The shard of glass in his arm dripped blood onto the floor.

'Who do you fuckin' think?'

'I need to hear a name,' he barked, gritting his teeth through the sharp pain in his arm.

PJ whimpered. The tough man who had carried out executions, now a boy once again. The tears fell and he didn't even try to stop them.

'He'll kill me.'

'Maybe.' Adam let the words fall and the chill settle into PJ's bones. The reality of his choice dropped its full weight on his mind. 'Or...maybe you could tell them your friend told me. Right before he went into the North Sea.'

PJ sniffed and snarled, 'Fuck you, I'm not tellin' you nowt.'

'You know what I'll write in the report? I'll tell them that you two pulled guns on me, chased me here. I stole a gun, threw one man out the window and shot the other at the front door because he pulled a knife on me.'

'I haven't even got a fucking knife on me.'

'Lots of things get lost in the evidence room.' Adam pushed the gun a little harder into PJ's skull.

'They'll pull CCTV.'

'No cameras here, son. Probably one of the only places in the city. Probably why I brought you here, when I come to think of it.'

'Please, just...'

'NAME?' Adam shouted.

The gun cracked and PJ winced as the sonic boom slammed his ear drum. He fell to the floor clutching his ear. A trickle of blood poured through his fingers. He felt Adam drag him to his feet and saw the barrel of the gun previously aimed at the back of the head.

'Alright, alright. Fuck.' The tears came again. He shivered in the brisk North Sea air and struggled to stand with the agony of his broken wrist and torn ear drum. 'It was Luke who sent us.'

Silence filled the pier once again. Adam sighed in relief as the name finally landed. No closer to anything he could call evidence. This kid would never testify. But a step closer to the truth.

'Close your eyes and count to sixty.'

PJ sniffed. 'Please don't kill me.' Sobs jerked his chest and shoulders. 'I, I never would have done this. You don't know what it's like growing up how I did. It's dog eat dog. No chance of getting out. And you don't know what it's like around *him*. I did what I fucking had to and I hated every second of it.' PJ wiped his running nose and thought back to the boy who used to like toy cars until he became old enough to listen to men who worked for Luke. Men who did unspeakable things. Small things which didn't seem too bad at first, but in the end, here he was. 'Please, don't...'

PJ did as he was told and counted down from sixty, took a deep breath, and turned around to an empty pier.

30

C.O.W.A.R.D

The hound didn't move an inch. The black pointed ears stood on end. Alert. Unflinching. The muscle of its thick hind quarters stretched across its back. Even the neck bulged with raw power. PJ knew a dog only had one way to release raw power, and that was through the jaw. Through a set of vicious teeth, loyal to nothing more than the next meal. As much as people like to think otherwise, that was the truth of dogs when it really came down to it, especially working dogs. Could you call this thing a working dog? Robot was more like it. The perfect diet and military levels of discipline. PJ had seen that raw power first hand. He had seen it tear at the throats, arms, legs, and even the unmentionable parts of men and women.

Once, he had read about how dogs used in warfare experienced their own version of PTSD. Not this thing. No unarmed man stood a chance. The strength of a Doberman's bite is just shy of a wolf. Once the teeth sink in, they aren't coming out unless you can stick something sharp in its brain, and the dog is free to rag doll whichever poor bastard is on the other end.

PJ sat in the dog crate and stared through the bars into the psychotic eyes watching in the corner of the room. He felt like the gazelle on a wildlife documentary. Only, a real gazelle never had to wait before its predator, watching those hungry eyes.

Still, anything was better than catching the other set of eyes. Those belonging to the other, far more intimidating beast in the room. Currently, they were trained on a port decanter.

Luke Marshall took a clean glass from a stacked, ceiling-high cupboard, and poured himself a generous measure of the blood-red liquid.

For the one hundredth time, PJ scanned around the rest of the office in search of an escape. Even just a weapon, a pen on the hulking mahogany desk that sprawled almost the entire width of the room. He knew within himself that what he was really looking for was a chance. Something to hope for.

Warm air raged out of the fireplace, where Luke had intentionally stacked the logs far higher than needed. Sweat saturated PJ's clothes. The room had no windows for the air to escape. For anything to escape. The only way out was right by a dog called Gun.

'What do you think?' said Luke at last. He turned and sipped the vintage. In his left hand, he held out a dog collar.

PJ said nothing.

'I asked a question.' He glared at the younger man.

PJ nodded.

'Thought so. A whimpering dog in a kennel needs a collar. Look here.' He crouched and held the collar close to the bars. 'Even had it engraved for you.'

The brass name plate shone back at him. The letters spelled out in the glow of the flames: C.O.W.A.R.D.

'Not the gangster nickname you dreamed of, is it? IS IT?' Spittle flew from his enraged mouth.

PJ shook and backed against the wall of the cage. 'Please...'

'You're alive for one reason only, boy. Because you're gonna help us kill him. And if you do that exceptionally well. If. Then I might let you live.'

Luke stared up at an oil painting on the wall. The style was old, nineteenth century. In reality, it was a cleverly framed dynamic AI screen mimicking Saïn or Turner or something in between. A Tuscan landscape stretched out in a blanket of olive trees and barley fields. Somewhere, a windmill turned slowly. He picked up a tablet and swiped. The oil painting shifted; the Tuscan landscape replaced by a view of Tynemouth lighthouse under a grey sky. Blurred oily waves crashed against the pier and brushed up the side of the white column before receding back into the North Sea.

PJ thought about the night before, just as Luke had hoped he would. His gaze closed in on the small window halfway up the lighthouse. There was no doubt that Jacques would have had a panoramic view of the sea as he flew through the glass. The scream played again somewhere in his memory. He swallowed, but there was nothing there to swallow.

'Thirsty?' asked Luke. He opened a door at the bottom of the drinks cabinet. The white light of a fridge burst out into the otherwise flame-lit room. Luke took out a tall glass bottle of water and closed the door. Condensation ran down the side. 'Good stuff this. Imported from Sweden. None of the chemical shit they stuff in the tap water now.'

He turned the bottle around in his hands, admiring it like it was one of his rare, first growth Bordeaux wines. 'Pure and clean from a place which isn't vastly overpopulated. It's overpopulation that causes bad tap water. Recycling the sewage over and over and over again. A cocktail of chemicals is needed just to make it safe. Did you know that?' Luke laughed to himself, his eyes still on the bottle before moving his gaze to PJ. 'Course you don't. If it doesn't involve a video game, alcohol, or drugs, you're an idiot, aren't you?'

He stared at PJ as though he were a freak in an old travelling circus. A penny to gawp at the freak. The look went through him. The silver and gold eyes somewhere else and yet present. Like he was contemplating the very existence of PJ.

And PJ felt a familiar feeling in the presence of this strange man — once again knowing there was a much bigger picture, and he could only ever see part of it.

Luke turned away and poured the cold water slowly into a fresh glass whisky tumbler.

To PJ, the experience almost passed in slow motion, like he was filming a TV ad for luxury water. Right now, he would take it over any bag of white powder. The tumbler was held out in front of him, but PJ simply waited. He had seen Luke playing with people like this before. Like a child with a toy. Enjoying the torture. He had seen men and women begging around this point, pleading and promising anything and everything to be free and keep their skin. It never made a difference. Luke would do what he would do, and nothing could stop it.

He knew everything he was going to do before he'd even walked through the door. It was like a sadistic destiny that couldn't be changed no matter what you did. That was the second most terrifying thought. The first was Luke's real weapon. His favourite toy in the chest: uncertainty. How would it end? He may want him to call the detective, or he may have been messing with him. The only thing to do now was wait, and he was damned if he was going to beg. Begging to the detective was one thing, because he, at least, was human. But not Luke.

'Not want it?' said Luke, gesturing again.

PJ said nothing.

'Take it. I need you alive.' He opened the door of the cage and held it out. PJ hesitated, and then reached. The dog growled.

'Actually. That's a good point.' The growl stopped; the glass was taken back. PJ watched the dog now and half wished the cage was shut. The psychotic eyes were fixed on the glass. 'He needs it more than you do.'

Luke tipped the glass into a dog bowl. The hound prowled over, and with one last glance at PJ, lapped greedily at the cool water.

'Tell me,' said Luke, smiling at the beast. 'What happened last night? And this time, I want the truth.'

PJ sighed. 'I told you. We chased him down to the lighthouse. He beat us in, hid somewhere and jumped us. He threw Jacques out the window. I went at him. Got a few knocks in, but he...I underestimated him. He got a lucky shot in, I mean. When I woke up, he'd done a runner.'

Luke rubbed his mouth. 'Hmm. I've seen you kill men twice your size with your bare hands. Why did this man beat you?'

'Like I said. Lucky shot. Can't win 'em all, can you?' PJ shrugged.

'True. True,' he muttered with mock sympathy. 'For you. I can't remember being beaten since I was ten. So, that's it? Nothing else? Where did he go?'

PJ feigned thinking hard. 'I don't know. Like I said, I was out for a bit.'

The lie came easily. And he spoke convincingly, like a beaten man. A man with nothing to lose. Because he was both of those things.

Luke drained the port and smacked his lips.

'It's a shame, boy. It really is.'

PJ felt every muscle tense against his will. His pulse soared. His heart beat like a battle drum. He knew this was it. Whatever was coming, was coming now.

Luke bent down and patted the dog as it finished the water. He took something out of his pocket and placed it on top of the cage. In the dark corner of the room, PJ could only see a box shaped shadow above him. Then Luke lifted the lid and out spilled the melodic notes of Frère Jacques.

With each note, PJ's heart sank. The box never left Jacques's pocket. Which could only mean three things. They found the box washed up on the beach, they found Jacques's body washed up on the beach, or…

"Ello, PJ.' The Frenchman always struggled to pronounce his name. Even at two letters long, he couldn't quite wrap his tongue around them as he couldn't with so many sounds common to other languages. But that mattered now less than ever as he strolled through the door wearing a vicious smirk. Between Gun, Luke and Jacques, it was difficult to tell who was the most unhinged.

He stood next to Luke, who simply watched PJ for his reaction. Both men stared at him like a pair of wolves after cornering a lamb.

After a long silence, Luke finally spoke. 'Would you like to do the honours?' he asked Jacques.

The Frenchman nodded, the fire in his eyes rising up like the flames in the hearth.

PJ fought for the only thing he had left: dignity. He would not cave in easily. Whatever pain came, he would die without screaming or crying.

'Ferme tes yeux,' said Jacques, pointing two fingers in a V-shape at his eyes. PJ glanced at Luke. Waiting for the translation.

'Close your eyes,' he whispered, before sitting back in the leather chair.

PJ did as he was told, still suppressing any sign of panic despite feeling certain he was about to faint.

After an age, he felt the shadow of the assassin lean over him, blocking out the heat of the fire. The notes of the nursery rhyme still clicked in the air. Musky aftershave tainted the atmosphere. Then the pressure started around his throat, then a snap. And with that, the pressure stopped.

PJ forced open the lids of his eyes and stared at the two men stood watching him. He followed their eyes to his throat. His own fingers were not far behind and felt the dog collar.

'We still 'av work for you, PJ. But your time will come. Don't worry about zat.'

31

Solitaire

The bleeding had just about stopped by the time Adam got home. He had slipped into a taxi two streets back from the beach and flipped his badge at the driver.

The warmth of the seat pushed some life back into his bones. The adrenaline wore off as they reached his house and he held the vomit back just long enough to make it through the side gate to the back garden — depositing it behind the hydrangeas before stumbling back around through the front door into the warm hallway. Clara moved from the kitchen.

'Oh, my God! You're...you're hurt. Adam, what happened?' She raised her hand to her mouth before dashing towards him.

Adam waved her away and slouched down onto the sofa. Some glitzy game show host was throwing out hopes and dreams through false white teeth.

Clara held back for a second in shock, Adam's response halting her momentarily before she approached him on the sofa and helped him remove his jacket. The coin-sized shard of glass fell from his arm onto the floor. A stream of blood followed, trickling from the cut onto the carpet. He looked down and then back up. Colour drained from his face.

'Holy sh...I'll, I'll get the first aid kit.' She ran upstairs and fumbled around, emerging again with a green box adorned with a white cross. She opened it on the coffee table and went to work. It wasn't the first of Adam's wounds she'd dressed, and he barely needed to talk her through the steps. The cut was worse than he thought. Although the leather jacket and shirt had applied enough pressure to cork it, the blood leaked out again. Still, it wasn't hospital worthy. At least, it wasn't worth the questions.

After a few minutes of wrestling with antiseptic wipes, swabs, and bandages, the bleeding eased off and the last wadding was fastened in place with tape and wrapped further with a clean dressing.

When she kneeled back onto her heels, his blood had stained her shirt and her faint breathing eased.

'Adam, I...can we talk?'

Adam was slipping into sleep as she spoke. He had barely made it home, lost a pint of blood, and the adrenaline had eaten the scraps of energy that remained. He couldn't have this conversation. Not now. Not until he was in much better shape.

He grunted his thanks and stood up using the arm of the sofa as a crutch. With a glance back at his wife still kneeling in his blood, he climbed the stairs and collapsed on the bed.

At around 2 a.m., he woke, wearing a clean T-shirt and boxers. He couldn't remember if he had changed himself before bed, or if Clara had done it. Adam moved his hand to the shape beside him. Sound asleep. She was always beautiful. But still, the face that had brought him so much joy now only gave way to pain. He had to know, and there was one way to find out. Everything inside him said not to do it. The nuclear option. But in the end, if it was true, what difference would it make?

Adam crept around her side of the bed. On her right arm, the white rose tattoo she used to unlock her devices called out. He gently caressed it, barely touching the skin. She didn't move an inch and Adam tip-toed into the office in the next room.

The laptop had unlocked and the pale light of the screen called to him. Adam paused and strained an ear for a moment. Nothing but the whir of the laptop fan played his ear drums. He sat and clicked through to Clara's work folders, opening a few files at random. All financial accounts and spreadsheets. He meandered through photos and found himself browsing the happy albums of their last few holidays. Rubbing his forehead, he felt a sense of shame. Nothing was here. It didn't mean she wasn't cheating, but it was supporting evidence she wasn't. Feeling panicky about being caught, turning his head every two minutes, he swivelled the chair to face the door. He went to recent downloads and took a last stab at a folder entitled AND Waterfall Ltd. All files were encrypted. Not unusual. Company sensitive info being passed out externally, in this case to a HMRC inspector. They had a right to encrypt.

Adam took a look at Clara's emails, at least one hundred from AND Waterfall Ltd, all encrypted. Again, not unusual, but a little over the top, maybe. Or was it? He felt his judgement clouded by his own paranoia. Emails from the man she was with? What better way to hide them?

He glanced up from the screen. With the contrast of the bright screen against the gloom, it took him a few seconds to notice the eyes glaring at him in the doorway.

His heart flipped as he donned a weary smile and swiped shut the windows, closing the laptop.

For a moment, the piercing eyes said nothing, then he saw them soften alongside the faint outline of a smile.

'Everything alright, darling?' she asked.

'Sorry, yeah, just couldn't sleep. Bit of solitaire on the laptop. Couldn't find mine.'

'It's in the drawer.' She pointed to where Adam's laptop was usually kept.

'Ah, yeah. Duh. I'll remember next time.'

Adam passed her in the doorway and gave her shoulder a gentle squeeze, catching the scent of her perfume. He moved across the landing and was about to head for the bedroom.

'How did you get in?'

'It was already unlocked,' yawned Adam with a smile. 'Lucky I wasn't some HMRC inspector, eh?'

'Could've sworn I'd locked it,' she mumbled, searching the ceiling as she tried to recollect the evening.

Adam shrugged. 'We all make mistakes. Hey, I noticed a few emails popping up from AND Waterfall Ltd. Who are they?'

Clara rubbed her brow as though the thought of work had given her a headache. 'Just a pharma company in the science quarter. They've got so many accounts connected, offshore listings, holding companies. Whole things a bloody mess. And they won't let me meet the director for some reason.'

'Bit weird?'

'Meh, not that weird. No company wants someone auditing them. HMRC are never welcome.'

Adam nodded. 'I suppose. I'm sure you'll get there.'

He climbed back into bed and pretended to sleep. A few minutes later, she followed with a glass of water and switched off her bedside light.

The rest of the night passed slowly. Adam felt each tick of the clock as thoughts spiralled through his mind, tormenting him. Each thought led to another question. But ultimately all roads led him to the same uncomfortable conclusion — he would follow Clara to work tomorrow.

32

AND Waterfall Ltd

Adam met Maddie on Osbourne Road at 8 a.m. Sunrise was still half an hour away, but the night sky had been diluted by the blue hour of dawn. The busy main road in Jesmond sang with the upper-middle class hum of four-by-fours, and the chatter of expensive brunch bistros, vintage clothes shops and independent cafés preparing for the day.

He watched Maddie emerging from the underground Metro station under the clear sky. She seemed to know where he was parked without even glancing up.

'Morning, you feeling alright?' she asked, as she climbed in the passenger seat clutching a bread roll and coffee adorned with the Bright and Sons logo.

'What's that?' Adam glanced down at her hands, intrigued.

'What's it look like? Latte, triple shot with caramel and two sugars.' She smiled.

'How was the bakery? Anyone watching it?'

She took a sip of her drink. 'Didn't see anything unusual. Eliot wasn't even there, but yeah, all tickety-boo. For now.'

Adam could smell the sweet inviting coffee. His stomach rumbled; food consumption had been as erratic as his sleep pattern the last few days. 'Well, that's good, because I think I've got a lead.'

Maddie stopped just short of taking a sip and turned her body slightly towards him.

'Clara's been doing some accounting work for a company called AND Waterfall Limited,' Adam continued, 'she's there all week. I saw it on her calendar.'

'Who are they? Wait, you looked at her calendar? Adam—'

'Take a look at this. I mean, talk about a sign.' Adam swiped the screen on his glasses into hologram mode.

Maddie scrolled down the polished website homepage of the pharmaceutical company that called itself AND Waterfall Ltd.

She gave Adam a knowing look. One phrase leapt off the page: 'Gene therapy.'

'See what I mean?' He paused and took a breath. 'You should know something else.' Adam felt stupid for not mentioning it sooner, but the excitement of the new lead had taken over.

'What is it?'

'They tried to kill me last night. I threw one of them off the pier at Tynemouth.'

Maddie almost dropped her coffee. 'You're kidding?' Her face burned red.

'Check, someone will have reported a break in at the lighthouse by now.'

'Why the hell didn't you call?' She let out an exasperated sigh and Adam felt instantly guilty. She was right to be pissed off. He would be, if it was her out on the turbulent coastline without calling for support.

Maddie searched her phone and pulled up the police report of a broken window at the lighthouse. Her eyes widened. She began to speak, but paused and changed tact.

'Are you alright? Who was it?'

He shrugged, and looked out of the car window into the deep blue morning. 'Bit of glass in the arm, but I'll be fine. As for who it was.' Adam turned back to Maddie and put his glasses on. He pulled up the hologram, taking a swig of Maddie's coffee in the process. The profile of PJ hung in the air. His menacing mug shot a mile away from the whimpering boy that he left shivering in the cold.

'He's one of Marshall's men?'

'Knew you'd be a fast learner, Evelyn,' He smiled. 'I didn't get a good look at the other bloke. Professional, no doubt about it. Tailored suit, at least six four. Probably thirty something. Tanned. That's it.'

A cyclist squeezed between Adam's car and the Jaguar parked in front. Adam glared at him as he missed the body work by a whisker. He shook his head and turned back to Maddie. 'Anyway, Clara's having a nightmare piecing the accounts together for AND Waterfall Ltd. I had a guy look into it for me.'

'Who?'

'A guy.'

'*Who?*'

Adam hesitated. Her temper was up. Maddie was a woman who liked to have sight of the plan. This would only make things worse, but Adam knew she might not have agreed to it if he'd waited.

'Tony Bright.'

Maddie rolled her eyes and took a deep breath.

'Sorry I mea—'

'No, shush, it doesn't matter. What did he say?'

'He said he couldn't make sense of the accounts either. Which, according to Eliot, means there's no doubt the numbers are hiding something. Apparently, if Tony can't figure it out, then it can't be done, and I believe him.' He rubbed his nose and nodded at his own line of thinking. 'No wonder Clara's pulling her hair out over it. But he did find one name, links to CoL Bank, a known offshore bank account of our local international drug lord...'

'Marshall?!' Maddie exclaimed. She held her breath for a moment. Chills crawled up her arms as she revisited the puzzle. 'So, now what?'

'I need to investigate AND Waterfall. Plus, Clara needs to know it's dangerous, but they've probably got her phone and augmented glasses hacked.' Maddie nodded as he continued. 'So, a text is too risky. I'll go in, take a look around. I'm not on the case, so I couldn't get a search warrant without alarming Pearce.' Adam scratched his head. 'But you could.'

Maddie thought for a minute, hand to her head, running through each scenario, starting with the worst. 'If there's something in this, how many would be in there?'

'Difficult to say, but we'll have back up.'

'I can't call backup on this without alerting Pearce. Then he'll know that you were still investigating this and we're both in the shit.'

'I know. That's why I've got a plan B.'

Her eyes widened as Adam wound down his window and raised a hand to a small white van across the street. The lights flashed once. 'There's a reason you didn't see Eliot this morning.'

The van driver's window crept down and out popped the smiling face of Eliot Bright. Surprisingly, Dylan was sat beside him. He still looked weak, but smiled and gave a thumbs up.

'You're kidding?'

'They've been reliable so far. And if shit hits the fan, we can deny knowing them. Deny investigating them. And they can't say a thing about us without sentencing themselves to a life behind bars. Anyway, they aren't coming inside, just waiting, and if we're not out in twenty minutes, they give an anonymous tip-off to the police.'

'Is that it then?' she said with a sarcastic clap.

Adam tilted his head quizzically. 'Is that what?'

'Well you've obviously got a plan and decided to keep me out of it. Is there anything else I don't know?'

'One more thing.'

'What?'

'Not yet. I promise, it's for your own good. I will tell you. But not yet.'

Maddie tongued her cheek and turned her eyes away from Adam, towards the van. 'Fine. But I'm going with them. Your manual driving makes me feel sick. Follow behind us.'

She climbed out and crossed the street, checking twice that no one was looking before pulling open the van.

'DS Eveyln, welcome aboard,' said Eliot in his booming voice.

She nodded. 'No Tony?'

'He's not really an outside sort of bloke, y'know what I mean? Not really a ground level sort of bloke now I come to think about it.'

'I hear he's been busy enough this morning, anyway.'

'Helping out a friend with a bit of number crunching.'

'Oh, he's your friend now?'

Eliot grunted away the remark.

He shifted, allowing Maddie to climb in, with Dylan wedged in the middle.

Eliot started the engine. Maddie turned to the thin figure beside her in fresh, baggy clothes.

'I'm glad you're okay, Dylan.'

Dylan smiled. 'Best I've felt in years. Still can't really walk that far. I've got about as much strength as burnt pastry, but it beats the shit out of sitting in that bloody basement for another day.'

They drove for ten minutes into the centre of town and slid out again to the north west. Tall modern buildings loomed as they drifted through the maze of glass and concrete. The satnav stopped around the back of a brand new twelve-storey building. The road was empty, leading to the dead end of an empty delivery bay.

Adam pulled up behind them and hopped in through the sliding door in the side. Three faces turned to see him.

'Right. It's as simple as this. I'm going in, you watch on the feed, and if anything goes south, send in the tip-off with the footage from my glasses and get the hell out of here.'

'Remind me again why it's an anonymous tip-off?' asked Dylan, scratching his aching head. 'She's a cop, isn't she? Why can't she just call it in?'

'Because I'm going in as well,' said Maddie, undoing her seatbelt.

No one said anything.

The situation dawned on her. The final part of the plan Adam had kept from her. She climbed into the back and closed the door. Adam could see her anger boiling over. He could feel it in the grip that dug into his arm and pulled him to the side.

'No. It's that simple!' exclaimed Maddie, hushing her voice out of earshot of the Brights. 'I'm the officer in charge of this investigation. I'm coming in. I need to overs—'

Adam couldn't contain himself any longer. His voice lashed out with the venom that always lay just beneath the surface. 'Maddie, you shouldn't even be here! I brought these two because I knew they would want to come. And that gives you a choice.'

The small van fell silent. Adam took a breath and brushed his hand through his hair. When he spoke again, his voice was apologetic. 'If they find out you let me be involved, you're done.'

Eliot interrupted. 'But how do you even know anyone will come if we call? Luke's involved in this. No doubt he's got puppet strings on at least a few senior officers.'

Adam shook his head. 'An anonymous tip-off would bring a squad car at least. If you come in, you'll get investigated and arrested. And Maddie, as I've said, you can kiss goodbye to any promotion and take the train back to London.' He glared at Maddie, who was gritting her teeth as her face flushed. 'Maybe Chrissie Richards would bail you out, maybe she wouldn't. My guess is, best case you'd get demoted back to uniform doing dog work in the worst areas for a few years. Worst case, you're jobless.'

Again, the strange silence fell on the van. The small vacuum where the secrets of four lives were held together with a web of agreed lies. On their ability to keep each other at gunpoint.

Adam put his hand on Maddie's shoulder. 'You're a good cop, Maddie. But this is serious. If Luke is involved, and it goes south, he will find out who helped me. And there's nowhere you can run from him. If I can protect you, then I will.' He held her gaze for a few seconds before Eliot cleared his throat, breaking the moment. Adam straightened his jacket and checked his pocket for the lump of his phone.

Tears of anger welled up in Maddie's eyes. She wiped them away and finally she broke the silence. 'Tell me about the feed.'

Eliot plugged his phone into the van and a holographic screen appeared, displaying Adam's vision through Luna.

'Is it only one way?' she asked.

'Unfortunately, yeah,' said Eliot, 'so we'll see what Adam sees and hears, but he won't be able to hear us.'

'You'll need this,' said Maddie. She took out her own phone and began to type. They watched as she played around on the device for a few minutes and finished with a swipe. 'Should be with you now via encrypted email"

Adam opened the notification. 'A search warrant?'

'It's fake, obviously. I took an official one and changed some of the names. But unless that receptionist is a criminal defence lawyer, it should get you in.'

'Want a gun?' Eliot asked, as though he were offering him a breath mint.

Adam paused. Eyeing the folded towel now on Eliot's lap.

Adam watched as Maddie thought about protesting and then thought again. He considered the black metal partially covered by the fold of the towel. They would search him, that was for sure. The place had security, bag scanners, metal and 3-D printed material detectors. The gun would be confiscated and that would only raise an alarm. An illegally armed officer. Luke's problems would be solved before they began. 'No gun.'

'You sound like Luke,' murmured Dylan.

Adam gave him a look that shut him up, slid open the door and stepped out. He turned back to the three figures watching him.

'Remember, if anything happens. Anonymous tip-off with the footage. Then vanish.'

33

Below Ground

The logo of AND Waterfall Ltd was etched into a slate plinth outside the giant glass cathedral that served as their headquarters. The image comprised of a waterfall with two double helixes flanking either side of it, like soldiers standing guard. Almost as though it were waiting for him, a sheet of water suddenly poured from the top of the stone plinth and down over the name as Adam approached.

Through the revolving door that yawned open and closed, he could see little movement. A receptionist sat behind a long stone desk, made of the same type of slate that had met him outside. The desk was built to look like a dry-stone wall, with a polished flat wooden top. Behind her, the stone climbed up at least fifteen feet to the ceiling. Plants had been wedged between the stones to create a garden wall effect. LED lighting lit the skirting of the black polished floor.

As he passed through the doors, Adam's ear twitched at the sound of more water and he turned to see a twelve-foot-long waterfall pouring out of a slit near the ceiling and down into another slit in the floor. One massive clean sheet, like a wall of glass lit from below. Behind it, the company logo was again etched into the slate dry stone wall, shining through the water.

A group of employees chatted in the lobby as they entered an elevator. The doors closed and smothered their voices. Another two moved away from the reception desk through a door labelled 'Stairs'.

Adam displayed his badge at the desk to a bright-faced young receptionist, dripping in make-up. No going back now.

'Officer,' she exclaimed, and added a sickly forced plastic smile. 'How can we help you?' Her voice was overly high and friendly.

'I have a warrant to search these premises.' Adam displayed the warrant on his phone and glanced at her name tag. 'I'll need full access...Ashley, is it?'

The receptionist paused. 'Certainly, one moment.'

She picked up the receiver and waited. 'Hello. There's a police officer here with a search warrant. Okey-dokey...will do. Thanks.' She replaced the receiver. 'Someone will be down in a minute.' The plastic smile was back. A thin mask that seemed to hide some discomfort. *How much did she know?*

Adam dismissed the thought. He had bigger concerns.

Almost one minute to the exact second, someone emerged from an elevator. A squat, balding man, chubby, with thick glasses that magnified his eyes, and a thin coating of grey hair. A loose fitting double-breasted suit emphasised his rounded bulk, only a shade of grey darker than his whisps of slicked back hair. He introduced himself as Finley Caver, with an outwardly warm smile that somehow still felt cold.

'Detective...?'

'Morell.'

'Pleasure.' The man threw out a hand. He was well spoken, not from the region. 'So, what can we do for you?'

'I'd like to speak to whoever is in charge. Just a few questions, part of an ongoing enquiry.' Adam anticipated the next question and spoke the lie with confidence. 'We don't need to disclose the reason under section four.' He projected the warrant onto the wall using his augmented glasses. Finley scanned it.

'Well, I'm afraid we'll need to call a lawyer.'

Adam nodded. 'No problem. But in the meantime, I *will* be looking around.'

Finley hesitated, rubbing the sweat from his upper lip before waving an overly gracious arm in the direction of the elevator. 'In that case, allow me to escort you.'

He led Adam to the silver doors and scanned the list of buttons. Adam frowned. Where there were twelve floors above ground, there were *six* below.

Finley pressed the button for the eleventh floor. Adam shifted. He felt his heart rate rising and took a silent breath to calm it as the elevator rose. In a few seconds, the doors opened onto a wide, open plan office.

'This is the head office. After you.' The dark carpeted floor ran by a small reception desk and then beyond into the endless sea of ultra-modern cubicles. The room ticked with the sound of keyboard typing, mouse clicking fingers. Holographic screens lit the room in ever changing shades of colour as people shifted documents and scrolled through their work. Some wore virtual reality headsets and sat in meetings around the world. Present and yet entirely absent. Nodding or chatting to their corporate ghost counterparts. Adam thought the experience wasn't dissimilar to a lead that once led him to a secure psychiatric ward at St Nicholas' Hospital. All that was missing was the 'calming' music playing over the hidden speakers.

The same plant encrusted slate wall stood behind another dry-stone-wall-style reception desk.

Finley gestured to a seating area. 'Please, take a seat while I ask Rebecca to arrange someone to contact the director.' Adam nodded and sat down in a large leather chair. A few others were arranged nearby to complete a square. A neat fan of untouched books and magazines were arranged on a coffee table.

The desk was at least twenty paces from the seating area. Adam strained to hear the hushed conversation between Finley and the receptionist without success. He stood and approached, hoping to catch them off guard, but the conversation ended abruptly as Rebecca shot a false smile at Adam. *What was it with the people who worked here?* he thought, then laughed to himself, knowing the answer.

'The director is busy for the next half an hour, detective,' said Rebecca. 'But he's more than happy to see you after that.'

Adam placed his palms on the reception desk. 'Very nice of him. And the director's name?'

Rebecca turned to Finley as though she were a well-trained dog, waiting for permission to cross the road. She held the sickly plastic smile that seemed to be a trend with receptionists at Waterfall.

Finley waited until the silence was just old enough to be awkward, seemingly undecided in his response. Finally, he nodded, laughing off the uneasy exchange. He cleared his throat. 'Mr March.'

'Thanks,' said Adam. 'Right, well, in that case, I'll see the labs then, while we're waiting.' He clasped his hands together.

'Oh, sure, you don't just want to wait? We can bring you a coffee if you like? Tea?'

'I'm sure.'

'Uh, yes, right then. Through here.' Finley led Adam through the nest of cubicles and towards a door on the far side of the room. As they walked, the quiet hum almost dimmed into silence, save the voices lost in the oxymoron of their virtual reality. As for those present in mind as well as body, no one looked away from their work. Adam surveyed the strange atmosphere, and gradually a realisation dawned on him. They weren't avoiding looking at him. They were avoiding Finley.

One set of eyes, however, were fixed on him.

'Adam?' said a familiar voice. Finley showed a note of surprise but paused patiently. Adam caught sight of the blonde hair of Clara, standing and adjusting her orange dress.

'My wife,' said Adam, glancing at Finley. 'Just be a sec.' Before he could answer, Adam wound through the desks and gave her a hug. She seemed just as surprised as the rest of the room, but the smile was real. The clicking of the room recommenced at its usual level as Finley's head turned and his eyes swept the blanket of holographic screens.

'What are you doing here?' Clara whispered.

Adam hushed his voice out of Finley's earshot. 'Ah, just linked to a case. Deceased might have taken one of the drugs made by this company. Could be linked to the cause of death. Might not be but you know how it is. Need to tick all the boxes.' He glanced around the room. The workers nearby were robotically tapping away. 'Bit of a weird vibe in here, isn't it?'

'Tell me about it!' she said. 'Great to work in, though. Hardly any distractions. And the canteen is...' she blew a chef's kiss.

'Any closer to getting to the bottom of the numbers?'

'Getting there, one coffee at a time,' she said, chuckling and holding up a disposable cup. Adam glanced over Clara's shoulder and caught Finley staring at them impatiently. Finley offered a weak smile and apologetic wave of the hand. He turned and leaned on the wall of a cubicle, surveying his subordinates like a farmer watching his field of sheep.

Clara let a smile out the corner of her mouth. 'You're the first I've seen tell him what to do from what I can tell,' she whispered. Adam squeezed her shoulder and turned to leave but she pulled him back. 'Listen, I know this isn't the best time, but I'm sorry about recently. I've been a bit distant. I want to make it up to you,' she said, stroking his arm.

Adam felt a pang of hope. 'Let's talk later,' he said with a wink. 'About to get a private tour of the labs.'

'Ooh, fancy. Let me know if they've got a stash of cash hiding anywhere. Lord knows they need it.'

'You'll be the first to know.'

He moved back to the central aisle where Finley stood with the special brand of false patience particular to impatient men.

'This way, please,' he said, motioning to one of the side doors.

As they meandered through the cubicles, Adam couldn't help but wonder if he should get Clara out before he did anything. No. She was safer here, in a sea of witnesses. As powerful as he was, Luke worked in the shadows. Only a small group at Waterfall would be on his payroll.

The door led to another set of lifts. This time, Finley hit the button for the floor three levels below ground. The silent journey ended with a ping, and the doors slid open.

'Always liked this room,' he said, gazing up to the tall ceiling that could easily fit a double-decker bus. The expansive lobby was at least the size of three tennis courts.

Again, the walls were slate stone, with one feature wall where the waterfall spilled out of a slit in the ceiling. Adam marvelled at the feature and surmised that it must start on the ground floor where he came in, and descend through at least three floors. The constant smooth plane of water cut down over the wall without touching it and disappeared into another well of footlights set into the floor. Somewhere below it would crash into a pool and presumably be recycled back-up. A nice trick.

At the far side of the room, opposite the elevator, was another reception desk occupied by another receptionist. A man this time, middle-aged with a miserable resting face that somehow sprang into a vibrant smile with a zest for life at the sight of Adam. Or more likely, Finley.

'Impressive room,' said Adam, continuing to look around. 'Especially three levels underground.'

'Mm, cost a penny or two, I'll say.' Finley said, tapping his trouser pocket. 'But worth it, I think. A show of the success we're having as a company. Saving lives is as profitable as it is rewarding.'

'In that order?'

Finley guffawed. 'Ah, come now. I know there's always questions about the profits of pharmaceutical companies. *Big pharma,* always the bad guy. But research costs.'

'I can see that,' said Adam, glancing again at the lobby.

Finley fidgeted and smothered a cynical smile.

Another wall of plants climbed behind the reception desk. The extensive space was also dotted with five or six thick marble plinths that supported complex chemical structures formed out of metal.

'Our biggest sellers,' said Finely, following Adam's gaze. 'Blockbuster molecules. Each worth over a billion in profit and thousands of lives saved or extended.' Adam regarded them with causal curiosity. He always went back and forth in support of the pharmaceutical industry. But ultimately, research was truly expensive, and they did save lives. The world needed big pharma more than it liked to admit, and it always would.

Adam's eye drifted to something engraved in the centre of the room.

'The symbol, over there on the floor. What does it mean?' he asked, pointing. He wanted to play dumb. He knew exactly what it meant. But he also knew this man was pedantic. Pedants loved nothing more than lecturing someone, especially someone they consider less intelligent. If he could keep him talking, he might give something away.

'Ah, that's our logo. Come and see. As good a place as any to start the tour while we wait for the director.'

They moved over to a circular marble design debossed into the floor. Just like the others he'd seen, a waterfall flanked with two double helixes. However, this one had something extra. Underneath, some additional wording was carved below where the water foamed at the base of the logo: *Vitam Consilio.*

'Vitam Consilio...life by design,' announced Finley. 'Many diseases are curable simply by changing our genes. We can do it like *that*,' he laughed, snapping his fingers. 'And that's what we offer. The cutting edge. You'll see...ah'. Finley raised a finger and Adam turned. The receptionist nodded to Finley, who walked back to reception. The man handed him some augmented glasses which he put on immediately.

Who was on the other side of that feed? thought Adam. That was the question. He had a strong feeling it was the 'director', whoever they were.

'This way please, Detective. We'll begin the tour. I use these to help me remember the details,' he added, tapping the lenses.

They stepped out of the grand lobby and into a small white room washed with cool white light, so bright Adam's augmented glasses lenses automatically shaded slightly to shield his eyes.

'Sorry, one moment,' said Finley. He swiped at a screen by the door and the room transformed. The walls, which Adam now realised were layered with light-emitting panels, changed to black and the brilliant white lights were replaced with scattered blue patches that trimmed the base of the walls. 'Night mode. Much kinder on the eye.' To Adam, the way the blue lights bounced off the dark panels made it seem more like the entrance to some Russian nightclub than a lab. *Night Mode* could have even been the name.

A young man emerged from another side door labelled 'Changing'. Bleach blonde dyed hair, clearly a graduate of some sort. He wore a white lab coat, the top pocket bearing the same logo as the lobby floor: *Vitam Consilio, AND Waterfall Ltd.*

'Hey, I'm Richard. Happy to give you a tour.' He caught Finley's eye and his smile somehow widened as he threw out a hand to Adam. 'You'll need to coat up, sorry, just procedure.' He led Adam into the changing room where the three of them slipped on lab coats and washed their hands. Then they moved back into the small outer room.

Richard held his face in front of the scanner of the remaining door. The red light above turned green. A lock slipped and the door opened onto a long corridor. Adam wondered for a second about just how big this place was. It must have gone underneath some of the buildings nearby.

The walls of the corridor were lined with glass rooms. The odd nightclub-like lighting continued down the entire length, reflecting off the glass walls of each patient room like some kind of endless optical illusion into a black abyss.

As they walked, Adam could see the lights in each glass room were dimmed in most. All contained sleeping patients. Most were overseen by a nurse.

'This is a licenced clinical trial, of course,' said Finley quietly. 'We can provide all of the paperwork to corroborate. Dr Dubois is the lead clinician. Busy at the moment, but we have his promising young protégé, Richard here to fill you in.'

Richard gave a nerdy mock bow and launched into a speech about the trial. Most of it sounded legitimate. Pharma jargon was a language Adam spoke, and although the kid probably thought he was just nodding along while he baffled him with nonsense, he wasn't.

'...so, the vast majority of patients are people with cardiac arrhythmias. For whatever reason, their ticker is out of sync. But the new gene therapy treatment is showing promise.' Richard looked to his audience of two.

Finley nodded, encouraging him to continue.

'They have to be placed into an induced coma. Not without some risk, but it's low, less than one percent risk of complication. And the upside is a success rate of ninety percent with full recovery. And the other ten percent see at least some improvement. Well, so far anyway.'

Richard waved a little too enthusiastically at one of the nurses as they moved down the corridor. 'Even with mild improvement it means they can take fewer traditional meds. Not the handful of pills they're accustomed to. And they're able to do more exercise without getting out of breath after a few steps.' He stopped and waved a hand at the long corridor. 'This is a phase two trial, but we've got around eighty participants enrolled. Roughly fifty-fifty split between male and female. All over eighteen, UK citizens, and a fairly broad racial profile. State-of-the-art equipment. From a clinical perspective, we couldn't ask for more, really.'

They moved further down the corridor. Adam observed each room, identical in set-up.

Richard droned on enthusiastically. 'We've got 3-D printing equipment on each floor, which can print most organs as you would expect, with the obvious exception of the brain. If only,' he tittered.

They paused at the room of an elderly woman. Grey curls bloomed and fell over her face. The hospital bed was raised slightly at the head. The observation equipment hooked up to a wireless finger pulse oximeter and ECG sensors on the chest. A nurse, probably in her late twenties, was writing clinical observations onto a chart. Adam remembered those charts well. Cases like this in intensive care needed one-to-one nursing and hourly recorded observations of things like heart rate, blood-pressure, blood oxygen, and general wellness.

They moved on. Adam increasingly felt like they were treating each room like a zoo. Occasionally, a nurse gave a nod or a wave if they noticed the group of observers. Some of them sat up straight or busied themselves with diligent note taking.

'How long will they stay in the coma?' asked Adam.

'Three days, give or take,' said Richard. 'We've found it helps with recovery.'

A nurse emerged from an office with a doctor, judging by the stethoscope around the neck. Doctors always wore those in Adam's experience, even if they had absolutely no intention of listening to someone's chest, more as part of the uniform than anything else. It said, 'I'm a doctor and I want you to know it'. The pair gave a friendly 'hello' as they passed and continued their hushed conversation.

'Why three days? Feels like a long time.'

'We don't know, truth be told. Once the genetic engineering procedure is done, we've had difficulty getting them out of it any sooner. We've tried but...'

'But what?' Adam asked quickly.

Richard caught Finley's eye and his voice returned to that of the overly optimistic young graduate. 'Y'know, if it ain't broke...'

As they moved to find the door at the end of the seemingly infinite room, Adam glanced at a map on the wall showing the nearest fire exits. It displayed the web of corridors leading outward from the central lobby in six directions — with the outer rim framed with another corridor that connected each strand at the point of a hexagon. Each floor below ground level was laid out this way and stacked on top of the other.

Adam stopped and noticed that Finley was reading his phone. He wore a new kind of smile.

'DI Morell, I'm sure you're finding this all very interesting. Would you care to see another of our trials? If you're able to share more about your reasoning for this...visit, then perhaps we'd be able to better tailor the tour?'

Adam didn't like the new confidence in the strange little man. He hadn't liked him from the moment he saw him. But he had come this far and still found nothing. *In for a penny...*

'Do you have any research into substance abuse? Addiction. That sort of thing?'

Richard gave the same obedient dog look to Finley as Rebecca had upstairs. The look of knowing something but waiting for approval before acknowledging it. Finley granted the approval with a gentle nod, and Richard walked on.

'Sure, this way.'

He led them back to the central set of elevators. Adam had a feeling which button they would press.

Finley's podgy finger stabbed B-6.

'Be in hell if we go down any further,' Adam joked. Neither of the men said anything. He knew they wouldn't. It was their turn to feel uncomfortable. If they were hiding anything, which he knew they were, something told him this was where he would find it.

Finley held his unreadable resting face, with two fat hands interlocked at the fingers in front of him. Richard stared at the floor, leaning against the wall with his hands in his pockets.

The doors opened onto the sixth level below ground. Another lobby like the one above. Initially, it appeared identical. A large stone desk, heavy marble plinths displaying successful molecules dotted here and there, the waterfall and the logo on the floor in the middle of the room. As they crossed the lobby, however, Adam noticed two things; the reception desk had no receptionist, and instead of falling quietly, the water crashed into a rock pool at the side of the room.

He stared at the torrent of water, watching it froth at the bottom where the smooth pane finally shattered, ready to be recycled back up. The giant mirror of water dominated the room, and in it, Adam spotted one more thing. The logo of AND Waterfall etched into the floor at the centre of the room was reflected backwards: AND became DNA.

They moved through a door into another clinical corridor, identical to the one on floor B-3. Glass-walled patient rooms in an endless nightclub illusion. The silence was disturbed only by the air conditioning. No nurses in sight.

'After you,' said Finley.

'Please, after you, lead the way,' said Adam, holding his arm out. It was his turn to wear the false smile. He wanted the pair of them in sight now.

Finley coughed and nodded.

Richard entered sheepishly, and they moved forward, passing the glass walls with casual inspection. Again, each room was set up in a similar way. But this time, every room was empty.

'Not as much to see down here, I'm afraid,' said Finley. 'Trial only contains one participant at the moment. Quite difficult to recruit this patient population.' He let out a nervous laugh, his cool composure crumbling. 'We're looking at addicts, of course, and altering gene expression has shown enough promise. Excellent safety profile in animals. So good, in fact, that we moved to in-human studies a few months ago. Good success, I would say.'

Richard eagerly agreed.

Adam pursed his lips together and gave an impressed nod. 'Can I see them? The participant.'

'Of course.'

They moved down the corridor to where one room was bathed in the low light of medical monitors. Staring at the glass wall, Adam could only see the reflection of the men beside him. Finley nodded, and Richard, who was waiting for instruction, pressed a code into the screen beside the door. The glass wall slid sideways soundlessly. Inside, a nurse waited in a chair. The bed was empty.

'Patient must be at the toilet. This trial is less intense in some ways than the cardiac correction treatment...ah Dr Dubois.'

Adam turned to see a tall man wearing a plastic face visor. The lights reflected in blue streaks, obscuring his face entirely. A tailored suit shone through the open lab coat. No stethoscope. *There's a first*, thought Adam. He expected Dr Dubois to remove the visor. Instead, the man simply held out a stiff hand. Adam shook it and introduced himself. Only then did Dr Dubois clear his throat.

'Good to meet you,' he said with a hint of a French accent. 'Richard, you may go.'

'Thanks, Doctor,' said the young graduate nervously, leaving without a second glance.

'So, 'ow can we 'elp you, DI Morell?' He glared at Adam, who could feel a headache coming on as something began to turn slowly in his mind, like the sluggish, crawling wheels of a steam train leaving the station.

'Can you run me through this trial? I'm a bit lost when it comes to this stuff.'

The doctor removed the visor and grinned. It was a smile seldom worn, unsuited to the face, like a pair of uncomfortable shoes brought out for special occasions.

'I think you know, Adam. I think a pharmacist would 'ave a lot more knowledge.'

Adam watched the thick curls pouring over the tanned forehead. The train was building momentum.

The tingle met the neck first, then the pain was immediate. The burning electrical current ran through his nervous system. His legs gave way as the fine muscles spasmed and twitched a thousand times. A blue flash, and Adam could only watch the doctor as he crouched down to the floor, examining him like a child inspects a spider.

Adam saw it then. Too late. Those eyes. He'd seen them before, only once. Finally, the steam train was up to full speed, whistling and screaming the warning in his head. Somehow in the agony he found space to be angry at himself. Dr Dubois was unmistakably the man he'd thrown from the window the night before.

The sporadic lights of the panelled walls and medical monitors danced before him in the polished black floor. The lights slowly faded, and darkness closed in as he heard the opening notes of 'Frère Jacques', whistled calmly.

Finley broke in, his voice filled with malice. 'It's time to meet the director, detective.'

34

Throw Out the Rule Book

Maddie changed her mind three times. The feed from Adam's glasses was still black. Someone had removed them seconds after he fell.

Eliot had sat with a stone face, controlled, taking the occasional swig from a hip flask. He was staring off into a brick wall opposite. Present in body within the van, but his mind was very much elsewhere, navigating some maze of thought.

Dylan had been bobbing his leg and fidgeting with increasing intensity for the last twenty minutes, hood up, fighting a battle on two fronts: the last internal skirmishes in his war against withdrawal, and resisting the swelling tension from what had played out on the screen before them.

He broke first. 'What the fuck do we do?'

Eliot shifted his eyes to Maddie.

'Two choices,' he muttered, concluding his thoughts. 'Go in, or call it in.' He ignored the utter disbelief in Maddie's stare.

Dylan laughed nervously. 'Second one will get you both fucked.'

'We don't know that,' said Eliot.

'Don't be daft. I've told youse both. Luke has his fist around the throats of every copper with any real power. You call it in, it gets escalated, and then eventually someone on the take handles it.' Dylan's nervous fingers twitched on his free hand. In an effort to control it, he rubbed his streaming nose and sniffed hard before giving up and shoving the hand into the pouch of his hoodie. 'There'd be no back-up cavalry. Adam will turn up dead somewhere and no one will listen to your testimony once they find a load of drugs they've planted in your digs. You might even become a suspect yourself.'

Maddie could feel her own heart rate twitching at Dylan's every word as he trundled on.

'Then they'll use whatever leverage they have. You're helping Morell investigate a case he's been thrown off. Morell was investigating where he shouldn't and one drug test on his corpse and his reputation's done. Just two druggie cops caught in gangland crossfire.' Dylan burst into a coughing fit and leaned his head against the window, his energy sapped by the outburst. His voice was quiet now, but no less serious. 'You've got one choice. And you know what it is.'

Maddie and Eliot exchanged a knowing look. A long moment passed.

'He's right,' said Eliot finally.

'And you two couldn't have said any of this to Adam?'

Eliot snorted. 'Like he would've listened. But he knew the risk. That said, the choice is still yours. You're the boss.' He shrugged.

Maddie frowned. 'Why?'

'Why what?'

'Why am I the boss, in your eyes?' she exclaimed frantically. 'Adam's in danger, possibly dead. You could kill me now and take me to that bloody basement. God knows no one would find me.'

Dylan sniffed and leaned forward slightly. His eyes darted between her and Eliot as though a thought had just crossed his mind. 'Because he wants to go in there,' he said faintly.

'What. Why?'

'Because Luke's there, obviously. And probably without that much security by his standards. This is his best chance, isn't that right, big brother?'

Eliot said nothing, and yet to Maddie, he said everything.

'We still haven't confirmed that,' she protested.

Eliot put his hand on her shoulder. 'He's in there. Want my advice?'

'From a criminal?'

'From someone who's made a lot of mistakes.' He paused as Maddie opened her mouth and then thought twice.

After a long moment, a tear swelled as she gritted her teeth and gave him permission to speak with a gentle nod.

'Never ignore your instincts.'

She thought about the last few days. How she had systematically torn out the pages of her code, one by one. And now the life of her partner was in her hands. Follow the rule book and risk Adam's life. Or throw it out the window, and hand in hand with a criminal. She knew what Adam would say. The man whose moral compass twisted and turned with the wind, and yet somehow always pointed north. And deep down, she could hear her own instincts loud and clear.

She forced the decision before she could change her mind. 'I'm going in.'

'Good decision,' said Eliot. His red face bore something of the warm innkeeper he usually reserved for the café. 'Let's get moving.'

Dylan protested. 'If you're caught...'

'I know the risk, Dylan,' Eliot interjected. 'Stay here. If I'm not out, tell Tony to burn and run, then get back to the bakery to help him. There's a plan in place. He'll tell you everything.'

Dylan hesitated. He moved to protest again, but stopped himself. He knew nothing he said would change his brother's mind. The best he could do was take a deep breath and let him go.

Eliot moved into the back of the van beside Maddie. He shifted a pile of coats and blankets in the corner. Underneath was a box built into the floor of the van.

'Been keepin' these for an emergency.' He lifted the steel handle and pulled out two shotguns, two hand guns, spare ammunition for the above, and two flash grenades.

Maddie did a double take on the contents of the hidden compartment. 'Holy...'

'Yeah, sorry to add another crime to the list here. But I'm not bringin' a knife to a gun fight.'

35

Tears and Terror

Adam could see his own face reflected in the polished tile, staring back in a blurred pale pool as he came around. Pain was always conspicuously absent in the brief moment between sleep and consciousness. Now, as sleep departed and withdrew its shield, he became aware that his head weighed double. Then, right on cue, pain found him again, pounding first on his neck where the taser had pierced the skin and delivered 1,500 volts. There would be bruises, swelling, possibly a scar. Pain then introduced him to the pulsation in his nerves. Nothing compared to the searing fire of the live electrical current, but still the sharp smouldering embers of the lingering afterburn ran the length of his body. The experience had felt like a nest of blazing wasps feasting on his neurons. Now the wasps had settled into a post-lunch slumber, leaving Adam with the scars of their banquet.

It was then he noticed the cutting into his wrists. The zip tie that held them behind his back and tight against the metal backrest of the chair. Initially, he was grateful. Without them he would certainly have fallen sideways off the chair. They forced him to sit, and in those few moments, he gathered his balance and senses a little more. He could feel the opium withdrawal moving into second gear. The hammering it gave to his focus, the constant agitation that boiled his temper and lit the short fuse that lay within. Somehow his augmented glasses had stayed on his face. *Put there, more likely.* The Frenchman's handiwork. He wondered if they were still recording. Then he noticed the screen had stopped displaying the date and time as they usually did, and he doubted anyone was watching now.

He forced himself to think through the pain. They would be nearby, watching most likely. Questions poured in as though a dam had opened. *What had Maddie and the Bright brothers seen? How long it would take for the tip-off to go through? How long until the police arrive? What would that mean for him...if they were quick enough?* Deep down, he knew the answer to the last question. But Maddie, she could still get out of this, maybe see the footage into trustworthy hands.

His jacket and possessions lay on the floor before him, neatly, intentionally. Wallet, keys, badge, phone, lighter. Adam held his gaze on the poppy.

'Ah, I thought so.' The low voice behind him boomed down the corridor like someone had fired a cannon.

Adam checked he was still in the same room. It still smelled the same. From what he could make out, it was the same place, but the lights had been reduced even further to a tiny pool in a sea of darkness.

Adam craned his neck. Heavy footsteps approached, taking their time. They stopped in front of him. The figure facing him was a giant, wrapped in a fitted suit. The false Dr Dubois followed, somehow short beside this new man. He appeared to hold two ropes in his fist. He tugged at them, and from the shadows beyond a familiar face jarred forward. A man was collared and held like a dog on a leash, standing, shoulders bent, staring at the ground. It took Adam a moment, then he remembered the kid from the lighthouse, and beside him, he thought he could see the glowering eyes of a large dog.

Dr Dubois removed his lab coat and dropped it to the floor beside the giant figure. Adam had never been this close to Luke Marshall, and now here he was. It was more than he had imagined. The strange silver and gold eyes burned into him as he grinned and picked up the pill case. 'Your poison of choice,' he said quietly, the faint geordie melody diluted with travel into some unnamed cocktail of an accent. He opened it and pulled out a pill. 'Millennia since the first poppy tears were cultivated and ingested. Millennia of science and progress.' He waved to the labs around him. 'And still the oldest drug poses the best pain relief we have. That's what you want, isn't it, Detective? Relief from a pain, not physical. You can take physical pain, I can tell. No, it's the pain in here.' He held a cigar sized finger on Adam's heart, and for a moment his torso blocked out the remaining light. 'Not to mention here,' he said, tapping his temple. 'I know about your little girl. Don't blame you for wanting the pain to end. Keep the numbness coming. I'd threaten to kill you, Adam, but a bigger question in your case is, do you even want to live?' Luke turned the lighter and ran his thumb across the poppy.

Adam lifted his head and spat a mouthful of blood that was dripping through a cut inside his mouth from where he hit the floor. Whatever happened, it wasn't in him to give up. And if he was going to die, he wasn't going to let Luke Marshall smell fear.

'I'm gonna live,' he mumbled through thick dregs of blood and spit. 'And you're going to prison. Simple as that.' He dragged his head up, forcing his neck to support the weight as he stared down Luke's malicious face with a defiant, grim hatred.

'Admirable. I've had a few talk to me like that. All dead. But they were just hollow words. Most criminals in this world just speak hollow words. Talk the talk, and then bottle it when it counts. Not you, Adam. Gave my man here the best challenge he's had in years. Beat him, really. Isn't that right Jacques?'

The assassin, the man they called Jacques, stepped from side to side. In his icy glare, there was a flare of anger until Luke caught his eye, extinguishing it immediately. 'You'd have made an excellent associate, Adam. Shame really.' He seemed to be looking for the hidden mechanism within the lighter. The latch clicked. 'There it is.' Luke winked and tipped one pill into his hand. He examined it for a moment, like a jeweller scrutinising a diamond, then flicked it at Adam's face. Jacques gave a dry smile.

'A decorated soldier and a pharmacist. Nevertheless, addicted to prescription drugs. The irony. Like a firefighter who became an arsonist.' Luke laughed and flicked a few more of the pills.

Adam controlled his breathing and sat as still as possible. Conserving energy was the best he could do for now.

The laughing stopped and Luke carefully tucked the pill case back into Adam's jacket pocket.

'There's someone I want to meet, Adam. I wonder if she knows about your little addiction?'

There was a muffled scream and sobbing, interspersed by the click-clack of high heels. Finley appeared from the darkness. Beside him, two hired units of muscle threw Clara to the floor. Her eyes were sodden with tears and terror. Adam felt his spine fill with ice like it had only done once before.

'No,' he spat. 'Don't fucking touch her!'

'Ah, there it is. The short fuse, the *real* Adam Morell. Finally, at the party. Clara,' said Luke, lifting her head up by her hair. She whimpered again and struggled to pull away. She stared longingly at Adam. 'Tell me, do you know about Adam's addiction to opioids? What about his flare for breaking the rules? Probably know about those. But I wonder, do you know he's been following you?'

Clara glared at Adam. The look of longing became desperation.

A smirk crept across Luke's face. 'Ouch. Skeleton in the closet then. Not anymore.'

Adam gritted his teeth. He wouldn't let Luke break him. He was looking for another rise in his temper. Adam focused everything on keeping it hidden as he tried to reassure his wife.

'Clara...it's okay, it'll be okay.'

Luke tutted. 'The last words to your wife, Adam. A lie. That's what your husband is, Clara. A liar.'

Jacques pulled out a gun and pointed it at Clara's head. She let out a short harrowing scream, and the sonic boom of the gunshot exploded in the room.

Adam wretched forward, a primal cry sprang from his gut. The chair tipped onto the floor where the pool of blood trickled towards him. His face glowed red as his temple bulged, and another roar burst out of him as he writhed in the chair. He couldn't look. Not yet. Forcing his eyes anywhere except where Clara had knelt.

Jacques lifted the chair. Adam seized his chance, took hold of the rage and adrenaline that surged through his veins like a drug of its own, and latched his teeth into the assassin's arm. Jacques screamed and struck Adam with the butt of his gun. He pulled back and the blood poured from the bite marks in the tanned skin. Adam's face dropped, body heaving, blood cascading from his mouth and coating his chin.

Luke boomed with laughter. 'There he is again. The mad dog. I'd heard about you, Adam. But I wanted to see it. Who gives a fuck? She was cheating anyway, right?'

Adam's head snapped up. Still, he couldn't look. His mind stumbled, searching for an explanation. How could he know about that? He must have had eyes on her, but why?

'Still feel like you're in control, Adam?' asked Luke. 'Well, there's still time for one more.'

Luke approached Adam and withdrew his augmented glasses. He winced and closed his eyes, and when he opened them, his heart hammered again.

Clara's body and the seeping pool of blood had vanished from the floor. And sat in a chair before him was his wife, hands folded gently across her lap. Staring at him with cold indifference.

36

Overbaked

Eliot wore the largest of the trench coats from the van and gave another to Maddie. A holder had been sewn inside of each, so that a shotgun could hang downwards by the butt of the gun. Concealed but easily lifted into a firing position when needed. Eliot's handgun was slotted into the large side pocket. Maddie stuffed hers down the back of her jeans.

'By the way, there's nano Kevlar woven into these,' said Eliot, tugging Maddie's lapel and raising her collar. 'They're completely bullet proof. Just don't get shot in the head.'

'Yeah, let's not test it if we can,' she replied, taking a deep breath.

They climbed out of the van and Maddie slid the door closed. Eliot moved around to the driver's door and stared at Dylan through the window. Dylan nodded. The same nod he'd always given his brother. And the friendly I'll-do-my-best smile. Somewhere in the creases, there was a wish of good luck. Brothers didn't need to say it. Still, Eliot opened the door and hugged him.

'Stay alive, and make them suffer,' said Dylan.

Eliot winked. 'Don't worry about that. And remember, if we're not back in twenty, send the message to Tony and get back.'

'Will do.'

Eliot chucked him the car keys, and he and Maddie walked around the building and through the front door of AND Waterfall Ltd.

When they approached the reception desk, the plastic smile of Ashley reappeared, and Maddie matched it with one of her own. Beside her, a tall suited man stood with a friendly smile, the bulging arms poorly concealed beneath the tight stitches.

'How can I help you?' he said, interjecting before the receptionist could wrap her artificially-filled lips around another syllable.

Eliot knew the type. One of Luke's, no doubt. The newer generation of hired muscle built from protein shakes and flexing in the mirror of a gym. Well groomed, two haircuts a week and a daily skin care routine. And yet, no less dangerous. Luke's standards would never drop. This man might look like Ken stood beside his Barbie, but only the hardest, most brutal fuckers would be trusted with his security.

'One of our colleagues, DI Morell, he arrived earlier?' said Maddie sternly.

'Ah, yes.' The man's eyes flashed to Maddie's augmented glasses. She knew it was the only thing keeping him from attacking; the thought that perhaps other cops were watching the stream. Of course, in this case, they weren't.

'We're here to meet with him,' she said. 'Where is he?'

Ashley reached up to tap her augmented glasses. 'Okay, I'll just call...' Maddie reached over and gently pulled them from her face and gave them to Eliot, who pocketed them.

Ashley gasped. 'Erm, excuse me.'

'Tell us where he is and leave the building,' Maddie sneered, 'or I'll have you in cuffs for perverting the course of justice.'

The man in the suit twitched, but not fast enough. Eliot swung out the handgun concealed in the sleeve of his long coat. The flash hid most of the initial blood splatter from Maddie's view. The crack echoed around the tall room.

In the silence that followed, Ashley gawped at the body, then screamed.

Maddie moved, adrenaline surging and her own hand shaking as she grabbed Ashley's head by the hair.

'Show us the cameras now!'

Ashley fought a panic attack, fighting for each breath as she projected the camera feed onto the wall. A continuous feed of five screens, cycling through every camera in the building in sequence. Maddie dragged the woman to the corner of the long heavy table and handcuffed her to the leg. She yelled for help as Maddie checked the adjoining doors. Nothing moved.

Eliot pulled out a large roll of duct tape from another gargantuan pocket and sealed her lips.

'Always carry duct tape on me,' he said, ignoring Maddie's surprise. 'Learnt that the hard way.' He knelt down to the dead man, and examined the gun that he had failed to draw in time, before tossing it onto the corpse.

He and Maddie locked for a moment, both thinking the same thing; they were across a line now.

'They'll be coming,' said Eliot. 'Maybe not yet, though. They'll do radio checks every five minutes or so. When he doesn't answer,' he pointed to the dead guard, 'then...'

Maddie flicked through the computer, planning to deactivate the cameras in the stairwell.

'That's weird. The cameras on the stairs are already off. Same with the ones in here.'

Eliot rubbed his chin, then snorted in disbelief. 'That's Luke. He doesn't want any footage of him coming or going.

I bet there isn't one single live camera from here to wherever the hell he is. Wait, which floor was Adam on again?'

'B-six,' Maddie uttered, cycling through the feed. 'No cameras.'

Eliot mockingly tipped an imaginary hat. 'There you go. They'll have kept him there. And you can bet it'll be guarded. Most of the people workin' here probably don't know what's really going on, at least on B-six. Likely, just be a select group who know the truth, is my bet. These two here, a handful of scientists, medical staff, a few more like this feller, well paid, loose morals. So, there's not gonna be an army. Security wise we're talking maybe a handful of well-trained guys. Well, that's the hope!' His laugh carried a level of nerves.

Maddie looked around, checking no one else had come into the reception area. The lifts remained silent. 'I hope you're right...'

'I hope it's less. Anyway, I'll need to tell Dylan we're in.' He took out his burner phone and sent a text.

Maddie moved over to the revolving door and slid the manual locking bolt into the ground. They hid the body of the guard in a cleaning cupboard and tied up the receptionist beside it. Before they closed the door, Maddie shot her a fake smile and turned off the light. Then they moved through a door that led to the stairs.

'Down we go then, I guess,' said Maddie.

'You keep behind me,' Eliot ordered. 'Remember to fasten the jacket. Leave the collar up and keep your eyes peeled behind us.'

Eliot pulled out his shotgun and they descended.

* * *

Dylan's leg stopped bouncing when the phone lit up. He moved his hand, leaving a red mark on his chin from where it had rested. His eyes were wet, still adjusting to the exposure of so much daylight.

He flicked open the text from the unknown number.

'Overbaked.' And another text below it: 'Love you, mate. Proud of you.'

Dylan swallowed hard, closed the phone and stared at the looming building that was AND Waterfall Ltd. He gathered himself, took out his phone and text Tony.

37

Unknown Side Effects

Her voice had changed, that much Adam was sure of. The woman before him *was* his wife, but it was as though someone else was speaking through her like an obscene puppet. The usual gentle edge of her voice had given way to something sharper. And the accent was something entirely different. *Was that a Scottish accent?* It took him a moment to register the matter-of-fact words that fell from her mouth.

'We hacked your glasses months ago, Adam. You've had a few nasty knocks in the last ten minutes. I'll spell it out. We took your glasses when Jacques tasered you and replaced them with a nice set of our own. A very useful AI programme, deep faked to respond in horror to anything you said. So, yes, what you just saw was augmented reality with a splash of virtual reality.' She held up two sets of augmented glasses, his own broken set, and the deep fake replacement. She carefully placed them on a table between them, and a corner of Adam's mind that wasn't spinning wondered if he really was still in the corridor.

Clara lowered her voice to something intentionally softer. The calm, melodic accent would have almost seemed caring were it not for the hammer blow dealt by every word. 'I have to say, I'm a little touched by how you reacted, even though you suspected I've been having an affair. I haven't, by the way. Not really. In a sense, we've never really been together.'

Adam struggled to speak. Questions and confusion tumbled through his head with an undercurrent of paranoia. He felt his mouth move and form some sound on autopilot. He managed one word. 'How?'

Clara laughed and shared a smile with Luke, who Adam now registered beside her. Another set of figures stepped into the edge of the light. Loitering on the fringe of the nightmare. Jacques was smiling. The blunt edge returned to her voice.

'It's called deep cover, Adam. Everything about our relationship was planned from the moment I crashed into your life in a little green Mini, and poor ditsy Clara couldn't help but throw herself into your bed.' She sniggered, mockingly swooning with a hand over her brow.

Adam stared through the twisted woman who had called herself his wife. Desperately scrambling to keep his thoughts from derailing his mind. 'I don't...what the hell are you saying?'

'Oh Adam,' she mumbled, pouting her lips and rubbing his cheek. Instinctively, he reached to push her hand away but his arms wouldn't lift from his sides. 'We were *meant* to meet at those traffic lights. And what better way than to make you to think you were the big brave detective taking a damsel to hospital? As for the why. This is why.' She held her arms out to the room around them. 'It's pretty simple. I needed someone who could give me access to police records for my work. And you Adam, you were...' she searched the air and found her answer. 'Perfect.' Her eyes blazed wildly with the twisted pride of her decision. 'You really were. Single, handsome, a detective, damaged beyond hope from the death of your daughter. A thirty-something who felt he was ready for another relationship.' She exhaled and smiled contentedly.

Adam felt the knife of betrayal twist another ninety degrees in his heart. The bitter pain fuelled the fire of rage that built with every second. Anger at not seeing through the lies of the woman before him. Anger of being caught, of not calling in more support.

Before he could speak, more lights filled the room, and Adam now realised what his subconscious had only previously guessed at: they had moved him out of the corridor. *When? Had he fallen unconscious again?* It didn't matter.

He now saw himself tied to the bed in a patient room. The layout was just as the others had been; a raised hospital bed flanked by the array of medical equipment needed to conduct a clinical trial.

Now he was on the other side of the glass. The animal in the zoo.

He locked eyes with Finley as the fat man waddled into view with a fully loaded injection. The red bulbous face watched with child-like enthusiasm as he flicked the needle, gently compressing the plunger so that a spout of liquid squirted upwards. A smile curled across his drooping cheeks. 'I told you this trial only has one participant at the moment.'

Adam felt the needle enter his arm, and the burn of liquid being forced into the brachial artery at high pressure through the narrow head. After a moment, dizziness swirled the room, and a coldness bit his very soul. He lost a grip on time. It could have been seconds or minutes until he regained focus. And just as he rallied himself, another injection found its way into the same spot on his arm, then a third. The chills were replaced by a fierce heat, and the world span end over end, fading in and out. The face of Clara, if that was her name, was his only fixed point. And then, as though flicking a switch on the hellish carnival ride, the spinning slowed to a stop, and the darkness receded. Adam recovered enough to watch the manic smile of Finley as he fitted the cannula into his forearm and hooked the tube up to a bag of clear liquid.

'That's it,' said Clara. 'Procedure complete. Simple as that. This IV bag contains a lovely wee cocktail to keep you right, and it'll send you off to sleep nice and slowly. Gene therapy in a pinch, courtesy of AND Waterfall Ltd. I think you've probably figured out the broad strokes. I knew you were capable, Adam. But you know what surprised me the most?' She tilted her head and squeezed his hand with something resembling real tenderness. 'How much you cared. Oh, on the outside, no, you couldn't give a monkey's with that devil may care exterior.'

She leaned over him and stroked his face. 'But it's a mask. Inside you care fiercely, don't you? Too much probably. You cared about Charlie Lang, and the others in that file of yours — the cold cases. I'll do you a favour.' She took the pill case and tipped out the last tablet. It momentarily dropped from his view and reappeared two inches from his eyes, pinched between her manicured finger and thumb. 'Take one more of these, and you'll be another Charlie Lang or Stevie Wilks. You can finally see Poppy again.'

He suddenly became aware of the warm, thick scent of cinnamon and coffee permeating the air. As the injected serum began the next stage of its journey, the wet heat of the jungle filled the room and found its way into Adam's lungs as he inhaled the soup-like air. His skin crawled with the cold sweat that came with opioid withdrawal. Now it came for him passionately. More powerfully than ever. Perhaps it was the knowledge he could never suppress it again. Not without dying. The itch could never again be scratched.

He felt his head sag. The blurred view of the pill set before him on the table was calling out like a crisp glass of ice-cold champagne on a hot summer's day. He heard muffled voices, the hint of tension within the murmured command. Feet left the room, and when he looked back up, only Clara remained.

The smell of cinnamon found him again and struck the alarm bell in his mind. For a moment, the clear metal gong sounded above all else, freeing his thoughts for a precious second. A clouded memory filled the silence. Dylan had said something...

'Who are you?' He heard the growl in his own voice, laced with a hint of exasperation. His vision faded and the room went black, then came into focus again as the shrill laugh bounced around his head.

Clara spoke, her voice distant and echoing, like it was coming through a sheet of glass before finally melting through the pane. 'Headache, drowsiness, confusion, raised temperature. Always useful to know the side effects. Thanks darling, useful data.'

'I said...'

'I know.' The woman that called herself Clara sighed, put down her pen and notepad, tidied a crease in her dress and sat up straight. 'My name is never going to cross your ears. To you, I will always be Clara Morell. But Clara never really existed. As of this moment, her very existence is being wiped from any and every database imaginable. Her purpose has always been this.' She motioned to the labs around them and tapped the pill on the table. 'Research to change the world.'

Adam felt his hope failing. He questioned if the hope had even truly existed. At first, it had even crossed his mind that this was a sinister prank gone too far. And then the needle went in, and the realisation that this hopeful thought was nothing more than a defence mechanism. Denial of the nightmare unfolding around him. And yet, even acknowledged, he couldn't absorb that his life with Clara had been a lie.

He wet his parched and desolate mouth. 'What...what the hell are you talking about?'

Clara didn't skip a beat, relishing the accumulation of what could only have been years of work. 'Self-inflicted injury costs the economy unfathomable amounts. Drug abuse, and I include smokers and alcoholics in that. They sit at the apex of self-inflicted misery that plagues society. Governments the world over have been battling it for years. Losing the so-called war on drugs. Obviously, *you* know that better than most. This procedure is a cure.' She hung on the last word. 'Genetic manipulation tailored to each subject. You know the basics, Adam. Genes code for proteins, proteins make enzymes and receptors. Enzymes break down drugs. Change the enzymes and we can stop the drug being broken down or even have it broken down into something more...final. Add in more receptors and you can easily make someone hypersensitive to small doses.'

'You'll get caught...' The words fell feebly from his failing lips.

'Hmm, I don't think so. I mean, it helps that Waterfall bought the contract to run tox screening for the police.'

'You've murdered people,' Adam growled.

Clara frowned. 'How? It doesn't have to mean death. They have the choice. One more fix and they die. No fix, they live. Tell me that isn't fair?'

'Addiction isn't something you just turn off like a tap. You know it,' he croaked.

The cocktail of his symptoms found new ingredients. The chill returned and fell away sporadically. His vision briefly blurred, and a general swell of fatigue and nausea washed over him.

Clara laughed and took a bite of a cinnamon swirl. Crumbs dropped to the floor as she stuffed the wrapping into her handbag.

'And Charlie Lang...he was just a kid.'

'A kid on a criminal path. Another future prisoner to pay for, another leech sucking the blood of the hardworking tax payer.' She shook her head at the thought and flicked it away as though it were a mere fly. 'Besides, we needed paediatric data at some point. Why not now?'

'You don't know what would have happened to him. Or the others. He was a kid with absent parents. So was I.'

'And you're an addict,' she sneered.

'I'm also a pharmacist. A detective. I've saved lives...' Adam could see his words bouncing off deaf ears. The smirk firmly in place.

The siege on his body heightened. The lingering nerve pain from the taser and the blow to his head, the usual malaise of withdrawal from his pills, and the lucky dip of unknown side effects from the procedure advanced relentlessly, wave after wave. He pushed back against the tide of vomit threatening to breach the walls of his stomach. Now was not the time to give up.

He tried another line. Buying time, that was the goal now. 'And what about Luke? If it isn't him, how does he come into this? Who do you work for?'

Clara puffed her cheeks. 'Oh I can't tell you that, darling. It's certainly not *him*. He didn't like what was happening at first. Deaths of his loyal buyers drying up his wallet. But then he saw how much *we* would offer for patients, and I must say he became an outstandingly reliable supplier of subjects.'

'Who's we?'

Clara ignored the question, finished the last mouthful of the cinnamon roll, stood, and brushed herself down. She placed her handbag over her shoulder and lifted Adam's head. She smiled as he recoiled at the touch.

'I did love you, Adam. I've never let that happen before. I want you to know that.'

Adam heard the click-clack of her high heels leaving. They paused, lingering in the doorway for a moment. Then came the final click as the lock of the glass door slid into place.

38

One For the Scrap Book

The shotgun edged open the door to the lobby on floor B-six. The waterfall cascaded into the pool at the side of the room, frothing at the mouth. Besides this, the room was quiet, peaceful even, with the soothing overture of rushing water.

'No one here,' said Maddie, following Eliot into the room. The slate wall of crawling plants behind the reception desk, combined with the gentle mist of the giant waterfall, gave the room the faintly moist and earthy aroma of a tropical greenhouse.

'They'll be watching,' Eliot whispered.

Doors to the side clinked open. The pair faced it, guns ready.

Finley fastened his suit jacket and walked towards Maddie and Eliot with open arms. 'What's the meaning of this?' he blurted, stabbing a red finger at the guns. 'This is a research establishment. Who are you? Identify yourselves immediately.'

Eliot waited until Finley was within ten feet, then squeezed the hair trigger of his handgun. The bullet punched through the plump palm.

Finley squealed. Beads of sweat formed on his brow and ran behind his abnormally thick lenses.

'You'll be sorry,' he spat, keeping one sheepish eye on the gun. 'You have no idea what you're interrupting.'

Maddie watched Finley's eyes flick desperately at a door near the reception desk. And as he did so, a tall figure barged through, pistol outstretched.

Jacques fired twice. The shots thudded into Eliot's shoulder, glancing off the Kevlar. Another went through the chest of the man in front of him. Finley fell to the floor. He moved slowly, gasping for breath as his white shirt became red.

Maddie saw more men filing in as she dived behind a display case and fired a few blind shots over the top. Eliot followed. Another crack from Jacques clipped his side. He winced and fell to his knee beside Maddie. The glass shattered above them as another bullet tore through the air. The metal molecule statue within toppled to the floor.

Eliot responded with a shotgun blast over the top. Jacques dived behind the heavy stone reception desk. Maddie peered around the corner as Eliot sprayed out two more buck shots for cover.

PJ followed and crouched behind the stone desk, one arm bandaged and strapped to his chest, and the dog collar pressing firmly into his throat. Two more men, hired muscle, crouched low and moved with practiced steps.

Eliot couldn't see where they had landed. He fired again, missing PJ by inches, and taking another vicious bite out of the stone desk. A barrage of bullets ripped at the marble display plinth, chipping it away piece by piece.

Eliot was about to reload when he finally saw the target he'd prayed for. Luke casually strolled to cover behind the desk as though his very skin was bullet proof. Eliot knew the suit would be inlaid with a similar nano Kevlar. Probably something more advanced, knowing him. But the head, hands and feet were still exposed.

'Is that who I think it is?' came the booming voice. The guns fell silent.

Eliot grunted. 'Been a long time, lad.'

'Assuming you're not here for a job?'

'Yeah, why don't you come around here and I'll give you my fucking CV.'

Luke laughed. He pointed to PJ and Jacques to flank the display case to the left and sent the other two guards to the right. Maddie watched the reflections of the men edging closer in the smooth plane of the waterfall. She tapped Eliot and pointed at the mirror of water.

Eliot nodded. He motioned down. Maddie's eyes followed his to the flash grenade cradled in the palm of his hand. He pulled the pin, allowed it to cook for a few achingly slow seconds and launched it into across the room. A split second after it was over the display case, their ears were ringing, and a brilliant flash of light bounced off the waterfall like someone had snapped a photo with the world biggest camera. The room shook and a plume of smoke spewed from the expired grenade. Although their heads rang, Maddie and Eliot had at least covered their eyes and ears. The disconcerting rattle to the senses would be five times worse for everyone else.

Eliot stepped out and opened fire with his handgun. After a second, Maddie followed. Guns went off around them as fingers fired blindly.

Maddie aimed, and one of the hired muscle fell to his knees. Eliot put a bullet between his eyes and the body immediately crumpled. The man beside him stumbled out of cover at the sound of the body dropping. Eliot fired again, and he too fell to the floor with a grotesque chunk bitten out of his head.

Without pause, Eliot instinctively blasted another round towards Luke, who was peering over the desk. The bullet ricocheted off his chest and he disappeared from view.

Maddie turned, half expecting a hard thump into her jacket at any moment, or worse. Instead, she found the two remaining men in a tangle. Through the smoke, she couldn't make them out until one of them fell.

The knife stuck in Jacques' neck had been twisted, pulled and stabbed again. PJ withdrew the blade and locked eyes with Maddie and the barrel of her gun.

She watched as he loosened a strange collar that hung around his neck and tossed it onto the corpse at his feet. Then, without another word, he dropped the knife and ran towards the elevator.

Maddie hesitated, her finger hovered over the trigger as the sights traced the shrinking figure. And then, from nowhere, she felt her arm catch fire and her body dragged to the ground. The next thing she saw was a set of gnashing teeth inches from her eyes as she felt them searching for a way through the Kevlar. The breath of the Doberman forced its way down her throat.

Three shots were fired, and suddenly the dog's entire weight collapsed on her. She scrambled from under it, and watched the chest bleed for two or three more desperate wheezes before falling still.

Maddie turned, breathless, to the only men left standing.

Luke stared down the business end of Eliot's shotgun, somehow still smirking. Maddie watched as Eliot appeared to be savouring the moment.

Time seemed to stop. The two big men stood face to face, six feet apart.

Maddie drew her gun on Luke. Her hands shook under the gaze of his stone-like face.

Eliot could see her thinking. She wanted to, but that would make her a killer, make her cross a line that most simply could not cross, even if they wanted to. The adrenaline surged, her eyes darting in panic between the two men.

Eliot spoke without taking his eyes off Luke. 'Maddie, go. Find Adam.'

39

A Seemingly Petrified Woman

Maddie dried her eyes as she pushed through the door into a long, dark corridor. A bruise had painted her forearm with a deep purple stain where the dog had gnashed against the Kevlar. The endless room yawned towards an infinite black oblivion, edged with crystal clean lines of glass cubicles, sparsely trimmed with low lighting that reflected off the polished black floor. The imposing house of mirrors stirred the stew of disorientation simmering in her head, and stoked the sickening feeling in her gut. *How many had died by the waterfall?* Terror filled every step as unanswered questions fanned the flames of her fear. She gripped the gun, pulled back the slide, and checked the chamber for a bullet.

As she looked up, a tall, thin figure in an orange dress emerged in the distance. The click-clack of the heels were momentarily lost on Maddie as her eyes adjusted to the room. The footsteps stopped, then suddenly became rapid, trotting towards her. Maddie raised the gun and watched as the figure approached.

'Stop!' she yelled. The figure froze and trembled. The echoes of desperate whimpers rebounded from the glass walls. Maddie took careful steps, keeping the gun raised until she breathed a sigh of relief and holstered it at the sight of Adam's wife, red eyed and shivering with fear.

'Please help!' she sobbed. 'They dragged me down here... they've got my husband. They did something to him. He's locked in a room, d, down there! Please—'

'Clara! Clara. I'm Maddie, I'm Adam's partner. It's okay now. It's okay!'

Clara's mouth dropped and suddenly the tears became pearls of joy pouring from grateful eyes. 'Oh, thank God! He's, he's told me about you. I, I couldn't get him out!' She dropped to her knees before Maddie. 'I'm sorry, I tried. I was going to get help. Where are the others? They might come back.' She glanced around frantically, peering past Maddie towards the door.

Maddie took Clara's hands in her own.

'They won't. I can promise you that,' she muttered, almost to herself. The sight of the bullet ripping through the guard's head flashed through her memory. 'I'll get Adam. But you need to listen to me. Listen, get to the top floor and hide. Do *not* go through the lobby. Is there another way?'

'Erm...I think there's a set of stairs through the changing rooms.'

'Good. Take those and tell everyone to stay where they are. Do you hear me?'

Clara nodded. The tears carried her mascara into her mouth. 'Okay...but please help him. He's in room twelve.'

Maddie lifted Clara under the arm and led her towards the door into the adjoining room between the lobby and changing rooms. She pushed the fallen handbag over Clara's shoulder. 'Top floor, nowhere else.'

With a trembling hand, Clara pushed through the door which closed on a seemingly petrified woman.

Maddie turned and stopped dead. On the floor, where Clara's handbag had fallen, was a wrapper from the Bright brothers' café. She lifted it and the scent of cinnamon caught the air. A thought crossed her mind. But it was ridiculous. It couldn't be.

She forced it aside and carried on down the corridor to room twelve. The single pool of faint light in the inky glass desert. The frail figure tied to the bed stared distantly at something on a table. Maddie scrolled on the screen beside the door and turned up the lights on the lopsided man whose theory she had doubted from the start. But here he was, and everything he'd said had been right. Guilt ripped at her, and with it came a wave of determination.

She tugged at the sliding door. The thick glass clunked against the lock. Maddie aimed low and away from Adam. The trigger finger squeezed and the glass wall shattered into a thousand fragments that crashed to the floor. The light glinted off the carpet of shards, throwing specks of brilliant white against the walls.

Maddie frantically rushed over and bent down to untie him. 'Adam. Oh my god, Adam, I'm so sorry. You were right. We've got all of them. Just Luke left but Eliot has him...and Clara's safe, don't worry. She's on her way to the top floor.'

But instead of the gratitude and relief she expected to see, Adam stared at her with something closer to vacancy. A complete absence in his eyes.

'What's wrong?'

Adam said nothing.

Maddie felt panic growing inside her. Had she been too late? What had they done to him?

She cut the zip ties using her keys and rested a hand on his shoulder. Still, he said nothing.

'What Adam? What is it? You're scaring me.'

'It's her,' he said, barely louder than a whisper. 'It was always Clara.'

40

The Scarlet Veil

Eliot waited a minute after Maddie had left, never taking his eye off Luke. Six feet apart, staring down the barrel of the shotgun without moving his sights a whisker from the stone-face.

Finally, the gangster broke the silence. Eliot felt a certain satisfaction as Luke cleared his throat to speak. Apparently even he could only stare down the empty black eye of a gun for so long. But somehow, his words chilled Eliot more than any threat could have. 'Not gonna drop your gun?' he said. 'No use empty.'

Eliot snapped at the trigger. The pin fell on an empty chamber.

'Whoops.' Luke laughed quietly. 'Tut tut, Eliot.'

Eliot hid his anger. He resented his own stupidity, and with every ounce of willpower, forced it aside. For a moment the silence lingered. Eliot took a slow breath. Then suddenly, his hand snapped down and withdrew his handgun.

The gun went off as the boot came down on his wrist. Eliot lost his balance as the black metal slid somewhere across the expansive lobby. Lost in the obscurity of the dark tiles. Instinctively, he jumped back and swung the empty shotgun. 'Still looks good to me,' said Eliot, twisting the weapon so the butt was outstretched like a club in his right hand.

'Never thought you'd have the balls to come after me. Too busy making fairy cakes.' Luke was pacing now, stepping back and forth in semi-circles, readying himself.

Eliot said nothing. His stare was fixed.

Luke opened up his arms wide. 'Well, I'm here now, son.'

Inside, the cold, raw fear experienced by most in Luke's presence was nowhere to be found in Eliot Bright. He felt the tension seep from his body. Briefly, he felt a sting of pain as the fading memory of Sam flickered like a lost film reel. Happy memories. But as always, the tape ended in horror, and the final frame stoked the rage within. Eliot had made up his mind long ago. One day, he would kill Luke or die trying. There was no room for fear. He had seen red that day in the alleyway, and the scarlet veil had never truly lifted.

Eliot swung the heavy club of the gun. The metal swept through the air faster than it should. One ham sized forearm easily performing the work of two for the average man.

Luke stepped to the left. The men circled. The feet shifting as they should. Just as their boxing coach had drilled them. Eliot moved to counter each new position. The dance of the fighters.

Luke swung a ferocious fist. Eliot blocked it with the barrel of the gun, parrying the arm, and with the momentum, carried the butt towards the exposed jaw. Luke threw his weight back with another grunt. The butt glanced off the shoulder, and both men returned to the slow circling dance.

'Still got it in you,' said Luke, limbering up his arms with a fast flick of each wrist.

Eliot said nothing. He knew what came after that move.

The barrage of savage punches were as terrifying in speed as they were in power. Eliot dodged the first, the second he parried with an elbow, but the third caught his gut and the fourth his cheek. Each blow like an iron hammer square on its mark. Eliot stumbled back and swung the gun club without aiming. Anything to find some space. Luke dodged again, grinning with the confidence of a fighter on the front foot.

Eliot felt the blood drip from the cut on his cheek.

'Why the hell are you doing this, Eliot? You're a dead man and you know it.'

Luke caught the incoming club. He pummelled the arm that held it until it let go and threw the weapon across the room. Without a second pause, he rained down more blows.

Eliot threw up his guard, taking the pounding as it came, rolling with the punches in the realest sense. He had only one option. Another hit and hope. A prayer of a punch. He took a breath, ready to absorb anything that came at him when his guard was dropped, and threw a wild haymaker, feeling the bony flesh squelch at the end of the long arch.

The gangster fell back to the floor. Eliot stood, dazed, recovering from the onslaught. Luke clambered to his feet, sucked his teeth and grinned through a mouthful of blood. He spat out the red humility and wiped away the dregs from his own lip. 'First man to make me bleed in twenty years. I knew you were the only one in that sorry family with potential. Now here you are making me break you down, for what? Revenge? You think I won't find your poxy brothers after this? The smack head and the recluse.' He spat again, this time in disgust, directly on the Bright name.

Luke's chest swelled, taking in a huge breath before kicking out with every fibre of his muscle. The heel thudded into Eliot's ribs, knocking him backwards. Then the rain came again, blow after blow, and before he knew it, the hulking figure with murder in his eyes was kneeling on Eliot's arms, delivering the hammer with his right fist into the exposed face. The flesh swelled with fresh cuts and bruises left after every punch. After ten, Luke raised the arm for an eleventh and glimpsed the carnage of Eliot's face. He smiled at the unrecognisable face of a man he once called a friend, and wiped his own blood-soaked fist on Eliot's jacket.

'There's nowhere your brothers can run that I can't find them. You know that better than anyone.' He lingered, savouring the moment as he raised his fist again.

'We aren't running anywhere.' The voice was almost mouselike in comparison to the bass notes of Luke. But the gunshot that followed spoke a thousand times louder.

Eliot watched as the blood poured from Luke's neck like a tap. The mountainous man stood and reeled back, clutching at the wound. The great silver and gold eyes shone with fear. And slowly but surely, the windows to his soul held nothing of the cool confidence they were accustomed to. With each drop of blood that stained the suit, the eyes and skin faded another shade. His body reeled backwards, reaching for something to hold. Eventually, his legs gave way and Luke crashed back into the pool at the base of the waterfall.

The water gradually clouded red as Dylan stumbled and collapsed beside Eliot.

'No,' Eliot whispered. He coughed out a mouthful of blood and found some strength in his broken voice. 'How did you get here?'

'I walked,' said Dylan, trying to make light of the dark truth that dawned on his brother.

'No...' Eliot forced himself onto his front, blood dripping from his beard, and stared up at the thin pale figure wearing the same cheeky grin he had always worn best. He knew there was only one thing that would have given his brother the strength to walk that far.

Dylan pulled a small grubby bag of heroin and a needle from his pocket. 'Can't keep a junkie away from a fix. Sorry mate.' He propped himself up, sweating heavily as the first notes of a drug overdose played a symphony in his head, sapping his energy by the second. He saw the pain etched on Eliot's tormented face. But he had known that Eliot could not have beaten Luke alone. For once, *he* was the one doing the saving. For once, in his own way, he was the strong one. And a rush of pride washed through him at the thought. A feeling of worth. Something he hadn't felt for ten years as an addict. Despite screaming pain and failing lungs, he smiled.

'Suppose I won't be needing this anymore.' His arm jerked and the heroin soared into the waterfall.

They watched as it splashed in the boiling foam beside the floating body. Dylan took a deep breath and exhaled slowly.

'That feels better than you could ever know.'

Suddenly, almost as if the bag had been some kind of signal, red liquid flowed through the waterfall from the floors above. The blood of Luke Marshall recycled through the system in a scarlet veil.

Eliot Bright took no notice. For the first time in twenty years, a tear fell from his eye. He wanted to sob like he had as a child. And somehow, even though his bones ached and his muscles screamed and his own cuts bled freely, he found the strength to embrace his youngest brother like it was the last time.

And deep down, he knew it was.

41

Hidden Scars and a Saffron Sky

Official case notes of Detective Sergeant Maddie Evelyn, Northumbria Police, badge number: SC-729.
Case status: Open-ongoing.
Confidential. For internal use only, subject to legal hold.

Summary of the events of October 22nd 2040 that took place in the city of Newcastle upon Tyne following the raid of A.N.D Waterfall Ltd, herein referred to as Waterfall.

Six deceased, of note: Luke Marshall and known associate Georges Laurent (alias Jacques). All operations at Waterfall have been suspended until the investigation is concluded.

Following a distress call received from Detective Inspector Adam Morell, I investigated the premises alone and found DI Morell incapacitated within an underground clinical trial suite. Upon investigation, it was found that both his phone and augmented glasses had been wiped.

I was engaged by three assailants, and incapacitated. After approximately one hour, Dylan Bright (see appendix 1 for profile link), a known criminal, entered the building heavily armed and highly intoxicated, killing all known assailants. I was able to free myself and call-in support. DI Morell and I spent the evening in hospital before being discharged the following morning. Dylan Bright was also admitted, having suffered respiratory arrest, but passed during the night.

An extensive search of the Waterfall premises, including a full audit has since been conducted. The investigation has so far revealed legitimate clinical trials being conducted on all floors, excluding B-6. Here, significant evidence of illegal criminal trial activity including murder, kidnap, genetic manipulation and money laundering has been found. Cross references of deceased patients from both ongoing and previous clinical trials into 'addiction therapy' have so far been linked to previously closed police investigations. Reference numbers include DCE-049, DCE-050, DCE-430, DCE-489, all of which were considered 'cold' and previously under the investigation of DI Morell.

Blood and DNA testing of Dylan Bright revealed that he had also taken part in the trial (involuntarily), and hence his motive seems clear.

An interview with DI Morell cites an anonymous tip-off for the information leading to the breakthrough in the case, and as such is unable to disclose the identity of said source.

Lastly, communication between the phone of the deceased organised crime group leader Luke Marshall and police Chief Superintendent John Pearce were confirmed. John Pearce has been suspended and placed under arrest as part of the ongoing investigation.

Press releases are continuously being prepared and reviewed before release. Further case notes will follow.

Eliot Bright reached the end of the page and chuckled quietly to himself in the back of a blacked-out limousine. He and Tony faced forwards in the luxury leather seats. Adam and Maddie sat in opposing seats, facing backwards, watching their faces.

'Thank you,' said Tony. 'For keeping us out of this. You didn't have to.'

Adam flicked off the hologram displaying the case notes and nodded.

'It's good to see you...out,' he said to Tony.

Tony took a deep breath and let it out slowly, almost peacefully. 'He was willing to sacrifice himself to save Eliot. If he can do that, it's time I got some fresh air.'

Outside, men and women in black suits and dresses lingered under an oak tree by the smooth central road that ran through the graveyard.

The driver waited patiently by the car. In his experience, this was always the time for patience. When someone, a father or mother usually, needed to convince someone in pieces to take the final step out of the car to watch their loved one descend into the earth.

Eliot looked at Adam. 'Any word on...her?'

Maddie had not yet been able to fully break down Adam's wall on this topic. She jumped in before he had time to sink into that particular pit of his mind. 'Clara? Not a thing. We've searched every database, every system and Clara Morell is no more. Almost never was, from what we can find. And nothing from the scanners and cameras in the airports or the channel tunnel.'

'Gone like a ghost,' said Adam, mostly to himself as he looked out across the tinted graveyard. He returned his gaze to Eliot. 'We do know one thing, though. She was there when Dylan had his procedure. The cinnamon swirls he could smell. She was a customer at your bakery.'

Tony ran a hand through his greased back hair. 'So, who was she then?'

Adam raised a finger at Maddie's next intervention and smiled. He appreciated their questions, but this was their time to grieve, not his. 'She's history.'

Maddie and Adam stepped out the car first. Tony followed for a few metres, then stopped, waiting for Eliot. After a moment he wandered back to car and leaned in. The big man was unmoved, staring at the floor. Still the driver waited patiently.

'What is it?' asked Tony.

'It's just...Marshall was hangin' over Sam's funeral like a black cloud. Shame it couldn't have been more like this.'

Tony climbed in and sat beside him, reaching one arm over his vast shoulders.

'Marshall's gone,' he said. 'Sam can rest easy now. And so can Dylan. C'mon, let's put them both to rest.'

* * *

Adam stood among the large group of mourners. A small blotch on the otherwise green and somehow pleasant Saltwell Cemetery. He listened as the priest spoke the same solemn words that had echoed around this vast burial ground ten thousand times.

The coffin was lowered, and eventually landed on the soil six feet below.

As the priest spoke, he peered at the stone faces of Eliot and Tony. Around thirty others had come, clearly a group of addicts, probably itchy at the thought of standing shoulder to shoulder with a pair of cops from the drugs squad. But they said nothing and showed no sign of disdain. Adam was confident their funeral attire had been bought and paid for by the remaining Bright brothers. The clean formal clothing somehow seemed to take the edge off their gaunt, pale skin.

They hid the needle marks and bruises. And for now, at least, to any passer-by, they would have seemed like any normal crowd of family and friends paying their respects. In a way, it showed what they were within, just normal people — watching their friend descend and perhaps wondering how long it would be before they met him again. Not long, potentially. Not without help.

More words were spoken to bowed heads, and soil was carefully thrown in handfuls on the box in the ground.

Adam came out of his own thoughts when he saw the big shoes of Eliot Bright step forward, holding a piece of paper. His face was still bruised and far from healed, but those scars were the easiest to bear. The hidden scars always dug deepest.

'Dylan...' He cleared his throat and started again. 'No one took our mother's death well. Who does? But especially not Dylan. He was fourteen when she died, and fifteen when he first started usin'. Someone, somewhere, offered him peace from the pain through a needle. That was exactly what he'd been lookin' for. And he did find peace, for a time. But, as many know here, getting that needle out is a lot harder than gettin' it in.' A few heads nodded. 'Many people told Dylan he wasn't good enough. They saw a dirty degenerate beggar at the side of the street and nothing more. Not someone who needed help. He was told he was a waste of space and bound down by his addiction, by everyone. Our dad to start with, then his friends...' Eliot paused, his words caught in his throat, and tears formed behind a dam ready to burst. 'By me and Tony. But in the end, Dylan showed us he was braver and stronger than anyone. I like to think we patched things up, and I hope he understood that...that I'll always be proud to call him my brother. Always have been.'

The tears burst the dam. He stood back and the priest continued.

'As we bury the body of our brother, may his soul be delivered from every bond of sin. We commend to Almighty God our brother, Dylan Bright, and we commit his body to the ground: earth to earth, ashes to ashes, dust to dust. Amen.'

The mourners lingered to chat as Eliot and Tony were swarmed with heartfelt sympathy and good wishes. 'Let me know if you need anything' and 'I'm just a phone call away.'

Adam couldn't listen to it. Not again.

* * *

The sun was setting when Maddie found Adam at the other end of the graveyard. A lone figure, stood at the centre of a group of headstones awash with colour more vibrant than anywhere else. As she approached, the cuddly toys, windmills and flowers became clearer.

'Hey, wondered where you'd ran off to.'

He looked up, eyes glistening.

She read the stone as she got closer and felt her stomach twist. 'Oh...Adam I'm so sorry...'

He didn't move.

She put her arm around his waist and rested her head on his shoulder.

For a long while she held him as they stood in the cold and stared at the grave. Adam let her, feeling a genuine warmth from someone — something he hadn't known in a long time.

Eventually, he pulled away from Maddie's embrace and smiled at her. Adam took out his lighter and stoked the poppy with his thumb, before placing it down gently at the foot of the headstone. Then he kissed a few fingers on his right hand and touched the name on the grave; Poppy Morrell.

Maddie squeezed his hand and he wiped the tear from his eye.

Behind them, someone coughed. They turned to see the giant that was Eliot standing on the path at the edge of the grass.

'Sorry, I didn't mean to interrupt.'

'No,' said Adam. 'We're done here, for now.'

They joined him on the path and looked out across the sweeping panoramic cemetery, and beyond that to a golden sunset in a saffron sky.

'Just wanted to ask if you were comin' to the wake?' said Eliot. 'There's sandwiches and a load of stuff from the bakery. Cakes and the like, but er, just normal cakes, I promise.' He let out a deflated laugh.

Adam couldn't help but chuckle.

'There's a free bar as well,' said Eliot, with a raised eyebrow.

'Of course we're coming,' said Maddie.

'Great. I'll see you up there then.' Eliot walked away, and Adam watched his lumbering frame climbing the hill towards the gate.

'He must be happy Luke's gone,' said Maddie. 'Everyone here is, obviously, but he must be loving it.'

Adam was happy to see Luke Marshall dead. A grotesque weed pulled from the ground. But in the end, he knew the truth of the war on drugs better than most. While drugs were illegal, addicts would always be labelled criminals, and the demand would always be met by supply in a back alley rather than a pharmacy. Deep down, Maddie knew the truth of it too.

'There'll always be another Luke Marshall,' he said.

After a moment, they followed Eliot up the hill. Adam reached out and locked his fingers between hers. She gazed at him and hid a smile.

'So, what did you tell Chrissie Richards?' he asked.

'That was easy. Just said I wasn't coming back.'

'Yeah? And what did she say?'

'She was happy. She didn't say it. Never shows that kind of thing and she's crap at goodbyes.'

Adam nodded. 'Did she ask why you didn't want to go back to London?'

'Oh yeah, I told her I'll miss it. But it's not exactly Newcastle.'

Printed in Great Britain
by Amazon